D0761961

Funnelweb

FUNNELWEB

Russell Braddon

St. Martin's Press
New York

Library of Congress Cataloging-in-Publication Data

Braddon, Russell.
    Funnelweb / Russell Braddon.
        p.   cm.
    ISBN 0-312-05435-1
    I. Title.
    PR6052.R25F86   1991
    823'.914—dc20
                                                    90-49283
                                                    CIP

First published in Great Britain by Constable & Company Limited

First U.S. Edition: January 1991
10 9 8 7 6 5 4 3 2 1

1

According to the critics, Michael Saxon was the world's greatest dancer. According to the popular press, he was the world's most beautiful man. And according to Christopher Westbury, he should have died ten minutes ago.

Saxon, on the contrary, was dancing magnificently. Not that Westbury could see him, but he could see the faces of those sitting in the boxes and in the front row of the gods; and they were enraptured. Worse, he could feel the excitement of an audience about to erupt into rapturous applause. His intention had been that it would be struck dumb with horror.

Sir Leon Bronowski, the conductor, scowled at him, vexed by his habitual disinclination to glance at either the baton or the sheets of music in front of him: doubly vexed by his roving eye.

Westbury responded with a sour smile. He knew the music, knew the sound Sir Leon required and knew that he was too accomplished a violinist to be fired. Besides, all that mattered now was that Saxon should expire: not that the orchestra should produce twenty, perfect, final bars.

Westbury peered again at the faces in the Royal Box. Not royal, but still enraptured. Sir Leon admonished him with angry eyes: Westbury responded with a toss of the head. If anyone was at fault, it was not he but the world's greatest dancer: it was essential that Saxon's demise be punctual.

Were it not, the next four murders would lack that thread of logic he had so sportingly woven into them. And lacking logic, would offer no challenge. And offering no challenge, would transform a meticulous campaign into mindless mayhem. Even thinking about it enraged him.

He began to play with outraged passion. Sir Leon cast him a glance of approval: which changed instantly to resignation as he observed that Westbury, far from meeting his eye, had his head down and was conversing with the violinist beside him.

Actually, Westbury was talking to himself. 'Die!' he was muttering. 'Die now!'

Refusing to surrender to the onset of inexplicable exhaustion and unidentifiable pain, Saxon danced on.

'Occupational hazard,' he told himself. And later, when the pain became agony, 'Use it! Let 'em see it! You're *supposed* to be dying.' Tears poured down his face and sweat sprayed from his hair.

Naked, except for a fig leaf, he was giving a stupendous performance. 'Nearly there,' he encouraged himself. 'Stuff the pain: just feel the music.'

For some of his audience, his performance had become unbearably moving. A woman was weeping in the Royal Box: in the front row of the stalls, unheeded by her transfixed escort, a girl was sobbing: a whiff of hysteria wafted from the auditorium to the stage.

Briefly, Saxon found himself loathing his fellow dancers for the frenzy with which they seemed to be urging him on to self-destruction: then remembered that that was how he'd choreographed it, was what the music required of them, what the audience demanded of them. 'They think I'm acting,' he told himself.

He was finding it almost impossible to keep his mind on the music. As he leapt prodigiously, the words of a critic came irrelevantly to mind. 'Saxon brings to the dance the exuberance Becker brought to tennis, the balance Coe brought to athletics, and the rhythm Torville and Dean brought to skating!'

What was his name, that critic's? Wogan had quoted him. And I got shirty and told him it was the music and audience that made a performance.

And Wogan patted my knee and said, 'Such modesty becomes you, but what about all the work and the pain? The classes, the rehearsals, the injuries, the operations?'

Last interview I ever gave.

Media took umbrage.

Dad's fault.

'You want to be a what?'

'A ballet dancer.'

'Bleeding little poofter!'

Then shacked up with that prostitute from Pimlico.

Not the sort of thing one wants quoted in Who's Who.

What's happened to the music?

Hardly hear it.

Have to count.

Nearly over.

Alerted by his rasping breath, tear-drenched eyes and clenched teeth – through which he was desperately counting – those closest to him at last realized that Saxon was no longer *portraying* the death throes of a dancer, he was literally close to death.

They wanted to seize him and lead him off. But he was in full flight. It would have been easier to seize a raging bull. Anyway, they didn't dare.

'The finishing straight,' Saxon told himself: and, pivoting on the left leg, rising and falling on the left foot, counting 'One . . . two . . . three . . . four . . .', he spun around, and around, and around.

Forty, he always did. And then, just for a second, stood

stock still, facing the audience, offering himself as its sacrifice to the dance. And, finally, with consummate grace, died.

Not tonight, his colleagues willed him. Please, Mike, not tonight.

Oblivious to everything, except his duty to the music he could no longer hear, and the audience he could no longer see, Saxon continued spinning. 'Eighteen . . . nineteen . . . twenty . . . !'

But, for the first time in his life, lost his tempo.

His counting accelerated.

Conducting with all his considerable authority, Sir Leon ensured that the orchestra accelerated no less remorselessly.

The audience held its breath.

Saxon could no longer breathe.

'Thirty-eight . . . thirty-nine . . . forty!' he counted in his head.

Then stood stock still in the spotlight, his blue eyes brilliant but uncomprehending; and finally, as his knees buckled, crashed backwards on to the stage.

The curtain fell and the audience roared. And strewed the stage's apron with flowers. And clapped and laughed and shook its head in awe. And waited for the incomparable Saxon to take his bow, accept its homage.

2

Five minutes before the curtain fell, the stage manager had summoned Dame Lyndsay, the company's Artistic Director, to the wings. She had promptly assumed command.

The curtain was to be lowered as swiftly as possible the

instant Saxon fell to the stage.

An ambulance was to be called at once.

A stretcher was to be ready to carry Saxon to the foot of the stage door staircase, whence he could be transferred, with a minimum of delay, to the ambulance.

Two of the company – boys, not girls – were to stay with him until the ambulance arrived. Keep him warm. Restrain him if he protested.

Her car was to await her at the stage door.

Curtain calls were to be taken in reverse order of precedence: and were only to commence after the audience's applause had been ruthlessly milked.

She would then appear on the flower-strewn apron and explain that Saxon – having danced despite a painful injury – was unable to acknowledge this marvellous ovation because he was on his way to hospital. Nothing too serious; but she knew they would rather he took no further risks. She would send him their love, of course; and he had made her promise to send them his.

As usual when Dame Lyndsay assumed command, there were no hitches. Two minutes after the curtain fell, Saxon was on his way to the Middlesex Hospital, his two colleagues sitting opposite him, staring at his bare, dancer's feet, which protruded from the red blanket, rather than at his grey face, over which an ambulance-woman was pressing an oxygen mask.

Her announcement concluded, Dame Lyndsay – escorted by Sir Leon, pursued by a wave of sympathetic applause – hurried to her car, pausing only long enough to ask the stage door-keeper where the ambulance had taken Saxon.

'The Middlesex,' he told her.

'The Middlesex!' she instructed her chauffeur, as Sir Leon climbed in beside her. 'Like a bat out of hell!'

*

The two boys were waiting for her inside the hospital, one of them in tears, the other unnaturally calm. 'Michael's dead,' he said. 'His feet twitched. Just a little twitch. Then the ambulance lady started pounding his chest and screaming, 'Cardiac arrest, cardiac arrest.' And when we got here they rushed him away on a trolley. And then this young doctor came out and said he was sorry, they'd done everything they could, Mike was dead and did we want to see him? But we didn't.'

'Do you have any money?' she asked. They were still in their costumes – dressed like youthful balletomanes from the gods, except for their dancer's shoes.

'We didn't have time.'

She gave him a five-pound note. 'Get a taxi. Take Gary with you. He shouldn't be alone: neither should you.' She knew they often slept together, but she was a tactful lady. 'I'll see you on Monday.'

She watched them go, then turned to Sir Leon and said, 'I'll just say goodbye to Michael.'

When she rejoined him, they walked slowly out to her car. A television news crew, responding to a call from a hospital porter, was waiting for her.

'Is it true Saxon's dead?' one of them asked, thrusting a microphone into her face. She looked at him with distaste, but realized that she had to dignify the brutal question with an answer that combined the no less brutal truth with a heart-felt eulogy. The BBC had filmed the last act of tonight's performance: by tomorrow, the last minute of that film would have been sold to television companies all around the world: and whatever she was filmed saying now would be sold with it.

'Michael Saxon was the greatest dancer this country has ever produced,' she told the camera. 'Some say he was the greatest dancer the world has ever known. Tonight, although he was in appalling pain, he never even considered not completing his performance, which was as magnificent as it was heroic. Those who saw it will always

10

be grateful to him for it; but none of us should ever forget that it cost him his life.'

Having quit the Opera House as promptly as orchestra members always do at the conclusion of a performance (he was not going to draw attention to himself by hanging around), Westbury was by this time back in his Holland Park flat, watching television while he ate his supper. During a commercial break, LWT screened a news flash. Westbury watched Dame Lyndsay's tribute with mixed emotions: gratification that Saxon had died in time, irritation that no one had suggested that his death might not have been due to natural causes.

'Never mind, Chris,' he told himself. 'Come Tuesday, when the next one dies, they'll get the message.'

Rising from his chair, he poured himself another glass of wine, walked with it to the gilt-framed looking-glass (he hated people who called them mirrors) above his fireplace (in whose grate was a basket of dried flowers) and, toasting his reflection, said, 'You're a clever kid.'

Accepting the compliment with a graceful smile, the face in the looking-glass responded, 'Pity no one will ever know.'

'*Che sara sara,*' Westbury shrugged.

Raising his glass to his lips once again, he drained it; and, on a sudden impulse, hurled it into the fireplace. It shattered on the grate. The gesture pleased him. As he returned to his chair (to watch a quite appalling Australian serial about a gaggle of repulsive females in the world's most improbable prison) he decided similarly to toast the success of each of his murders.

A thought struck him. He turned back to the looking-glass and, forcing himself to utter the vulgar word, said, '*Mirror, mirror, on the wall, who now's the fairest of them all?*'

'You, of course,' the beautiful man in the looking-glass told him.

11

With a flip of the hand, Westbury dismissed the vulgar mirror and flung himself into his armchair. 'So why'd you wait till Saxon was dead to admit it?'

'Why'd *you* wait till Saxon was dead to ask it?' he heard the mirror retort. Gnawing on his thumbnail, he pretended not to have heard.

3

Saturday nights are horrific for the Casualty Department of hospitals like the Middlesex: June the sixth was no exception. Two nurses were attacked by heroin addicts; a blood-drenched teenager attempted to strangle a houseman with his own stethoscope; a maudlin alcoholic tried repeatedly, via a junior registrar's bleeper, to contact his aunty in Cork; a crashed motor cyclist and a savagely mugged blonde proved to be dead on their respective arrivals; two of the three OD cases died despite every attempt to save them; the department was understaffed; and all the junior doctors had worked for at least twenty of the last twenty-four hours.

In this context, Saxon's death was simply one of the least grisly of a long night's statistics, and the disposal of his corpse one of its least demanding chores. Usually, Casualty's corpses had to be stripped of clothing and personal effects, all of which had to be parcelled and labelled for collection by next of kin; but Saxon's body was naked except for his fig leaf.

'Rather sweet, really,' sighed the Sister, handing him over to the two orderlies who would prepare his body for the inevitable autopsy.

It was the junior of this pair who discovered that the fig leaf was part of a pouch that contained Saxon's genitalia. These had been inserted into the pouch through a metal ring, to which the mouth of the pouch was attached. The metal ring encompassed the base of the penis and the top of the scrotum tightly enough to keep the loose pouch firmly anchored, while a thin waistband of flesh-coloured elastic kept the fig leaf flat against the groin.

Having unclipped the waistband, the junior orderly began tentatively to extricate Saxon's flesh from propriety's shackles; and eventually succeeded.

'Gotcha!' he said. Then shrank backwards and squealed. 'What *are* they?'

'A cock and two balls,' his older colleague told him curtly, not bothering to look.

'In his pubes, Taff! In his pubes.'

Taff peered short-sightedly into Saxon's pubic hair.

'Now I've seen everything,' he said.

'But what are they, Taff?'

'Well, they're spiders, boyo, aren't they?'

With commendable alacrity, the Middlesex telephoned the police, anaesthetized two spiders, transferred them into a screw-top jam jar, sprayed Saxon's groin and the interior of the fig-leaf pouch with enough pesticide to exterminate a battalion of cockroaches, and surrendered both fig leaf and jam jar to an unenthusiastic CID officer.

It also patiently recited, while he laboriously transcribed, the unusual circumstances in which Saxon had collapsed, the suspicious nature of his sudden death, and the few personal details about him it had had time to elicit from the two dancers who had accompanied him in the ambulance and the Dame who had said goodbye to him before his transfer to the mortuary.

Twenty minutes later, Detective Sergeant Robinson telephoned Detective Chief Superintendent Cheadle at his home. 'Sorry to disturb you, sir,' he apologized in his bland public school manner, 'but . . .'

'I was watching the *tennis*,' Cheadle snarled.

'At this hour?'

'The semi-finals of the men's singles from Stade Roland: which Mrs Cheadle specially taped for me this afternoon so I could watch 'em in peace tonight.'

'You've got it on Pause, I trust?' Cheadle was notorious for his inability to operate anything electronic.

'Don't push your luck, laddie. Why are you calling?'

Robinson told him; and Cheadle forgot the tennis. 'Do the quacks say the spiders killed him?'

'They don't know what killed him.'

'What sort are they?'

'Not sure yet. But if it was them killed Saxon, they've got to be American, South American or Australian.'

'Who says?'

'The *Encyclopaedia Britannica*.'

'Dig us up a spider freak: get him to identify our two. And ring the Royal Ballet press officer.'

'He's not home yet.'

'Keep ringing till he is. Then ask how many there are in the company: whether Saxon's visited the States or South America lately – '

'Or Australia.'

'Or even Australia,' Cheadle conceded. 'Ask who, apart from Saxon, had access to his dressing-room; whether he was kinky for spiders; and when, before tonight, he last wore this fig-leaf contraption.'

'Yes, sir.' Robinson sounded like a grandmother being taught to suck eggs.

'Sorry. Thinking aloud. Autopsy tomorrow morning?'

'Horseferry Road, sir. Usual time.'

'Too late to interview anyone at the Opera House tonight, was it? Course it was. Media got the story?'

'A TV news flash.'

'What'd it say?'

14

'Mainly a tribute to Saxon. From Dame Lyndsay. Dame Lyndsay Wynyard. She's the company's . . .'

'I may not have a university degree like you, Sergeant, but I do know who Dame Lyndsay is. *And* I want to talk to her.'

'Thought you might, so I persuaded Telecom to give me her ex-directory number. She'll see you as soon as you're through at Horseferry Road.'

'Been busy, haven't you?'

'All part of the service, sir.'

'Has it occurred to you . . .' Cheadle stopped in mid-sentence.

'Sir?'

'Has it occurred to you that if Saxon was murdered, proving who did it is going to drive us mad?'

'Except – '

'Except it was almost certainly an inside job? I know.'

'And premeditated.' Robinson sounded sick at the thought of it. 'Deadly spiders are hardly the sort of impulse purchase one makes on the way to work and hides in a colleague's jock-strap, are they?'

'Hardly.'

'Could it have been a practical joke?'

'Don't clutch at straws, Sergeant.'

'So we're looking for an in-house executioner.'

'Who's probably a nutter.'

'Well, nutters've always been your cup of tea, sir.'

Knowing how much his sergeant enjoyed having the last word, Cheadle hung up.

Robinson collected Cheadle from his Balham home and drove him through quiet, early Sabbath streets toward the Embankment. Cheadle glanced across at him. 'You look rough. What you been up to?'

'This and that,' said Robinson, glancing back at Cheadle: who looked like he always looked – a bland, thick-waisted, middle-aged copper with thinning grey hair slicked back over a ruddy scalp.

His cheeks were ruddy too, and taut with aftershave. And Mrs Cheadle had polished his tan shoes (which he always wore with a navy blue suit) until they glittered. In short, apart from a globule of marmalade on his chin, he looked complacently mediocre. Robinson regretted that he had been brought up to eschew personal remarks. Then said, 'You've dribbled marmalade down your chin.'

Impervious to middle-class rudeness, Cheadle turned the rear vision mirror leftwards, peered at his reflection, removed the offending globule with the tip of a fastidious little finger and licked it clean.

'All right,' he said. 'I know you've had no sleep: don't sulk.' Robinson was pointedly readjusting the rear vision mirror. 'Tell me what you've got.'

Robinson grinned. It was impossible to stay angry with Cheadle: he was too crafty, and too professional. 'In any particular order?' he asked.

'As it comes, laddie. As it comes.'

'OK. First up, the spiders are funnelwebs. From Australia. Defend themselves against intruders by squirting 'em full of a neurotoxin which can be fatal.

'Second – the Royal Opera House has more than a thousand bods on its payroll; but, if you exclude front-of-house personnel, cleaners, touring companies and a touring orchestra, you can probably cut our list of suspects down to a mere two hundred.'

'Two *hundred*?' Cheadle grimaced.

'Dancers, musicians, stage hands, technicians, wardrobe: people like that.'

'Get on with it, Derek.'

'Saxon's danced all over the world. Was in Australia last January. But it's unlikely it was he who brought back the funnelwebs.'

'Why?'

'Our winter would've killed them. Mind you, the

females live for years. Males die within days of copulation.'

'Our spiders male or female?'

Robinson shrugged. 'Spider-sexers are thin on the ground in London at three on a Sunday morning.'

'Anything else?'

'According to the Ballet's press officer, Saxon's real name was Inglis. There's a Mrs Inglis, and a small daughter. An officer from the station called on Mrs Inglis, to break the news, just before midnight: found Dame Lyndsay there – and the news broken.'

Having crossed Chelsea Bridge, Robinson swung right, along the Embankment. 'There's one plus,' he comforted.

'Mrs Inglis has confessed?'

Robinson grinned but shook his head. 'The BBC filmed the whole of last night's last act.'

'The whole fig-leaf bit?'

'They'll show us a rough cut this afternoon.'

The car turned left into Horseferry Road and came to a halt outside the mortuary. Cheadle got out, hitched his trousers up on his solid paunch and ran a finger round the inside of his collar. Then, leaning through the open door, twisting the rear vision mirror sideways so that he could check that his hair was impeccably slick, he said, 'No sense both of us feeling sick: be as quick as I can.'

4

When he returned to the car, Cheadle was plainly shaken: more shaken than Robinson had ever seen him after an autopsy on an adult male. 'Bad?' he asked.

'Those spiders couldn't escape from the pouch, so they bit everything. Now why would anyone want to do a thing like that?'

'A woman might, if Saxon had raped her.'

Cheadle nodded. 'Or seduced and ditched her. Drive on. Not far, is it?'

'Behind Harrods.' They moved off smoothly. 'Could have been a militant feminist taking revenge on a notorious Casanova.'

'Could have been a jealous boyfriend.'

'Saxon was married.'

'Don't be naïve, Sergeant! As it happens, though, I meant a boy discarded by his girl in favour of the handsomer, richer, more celebrated and probably better endowed Mr Saxon.'

'Probably?'

'Priapic, when I saw it. Oedema, the quack said, caused by venom.'

'Actually, girls are turned on by bums, not willies.'

The amply haunched Cheadle glared at the trimly buttocked Robinson. 'Bollocks!' he said.

'Almost there, sir,' Robinson murmured. 'Are we hoping for anything in particular from the Dame?'

'Apart from a cup of tea and something scandalous to explain why anyone'd want to murder Saxon, nothing in particular, no.'

Dame Lyndsay surprised Cheadle, who previously had seen her only on television, and even then only as Artistic Director of the Royal Ballet Company. He had not expected her to be so small: nor so elegant in a black, sleeveless dress that could only have been worn by a woman with shapely legs, a tiny waist, a rope of pearls and a neck like Audrey Hepburn's.

And a face like Audrey Hepburn's, come to that. Heart-shaped, with huge eyes. And black hair swept backwards into a chignon like Margot Fonteyn's.

'Tea or coffee?' she asked, indicating the chair in which

each was to sit. Her gestures were minimal but fluid, graceful but imperious.

'Tea'd be very welcome if it's not too much trouble,' said Cheadle.

'No trouble,' she assured him. She sounded weary and close to tears, but her high heels clicked briskly on the parquet floor as she left them.

Cheadle clumsily mimicked the tiny gesture with which she had despatched each of them to his chair. 'It's another world,' he muttered, gazing around at photographs of Lyndsay Wynyard, the prima ballerina, being variously partnered by Nureyev, Dowell and a very youthful Saxon: of Dame Lyndsay, the Artistic Director, chatting with royal princes and princesses. 'They're a different breed.'

Again he attempted the Dame's tiny gesture. 'Got to be trained to it from birth,' he pronounced. 'Like the Queen.'

Robinson nodded. 'Never think she was born in Clapham.'

Cheadle was making a mental inventory of everything in the room.

'The Queen?' he asked, looking at a dozen or so water-colours of costume designs on the opposite wall, wishing he'd seen Miss Wynyard in them.

'Dame Lyndsay.'

Cheadle stared at him blankly.

'Was born in Clapham,' Robinson explained. Cheadle raised his eyebrows to indicate that this was not the time for tittle tattle.

Dame Lyndsay's brisk footsteps approached and she entered bearing a silver tray on which stood a silver teapot, milk jug and sugar bowl, a plateful of chocolate biscuits and three earthenware mugs.

Robinson rose swiftly to his feet, offering to take the tray.

'Stay where you are,' she ordered. 'We dancers aren't as fragile as we look.'

She set the tray down on a coffee table. 'Nor', brandishing a mug, 'as genteel. And anyway,' pouring tea, 'this isn't a social call. You're here,' sniffing, 'because darling Michael died last night and you think there was something fishy about his death.' She finished pouring. 'Help yourselves to milk and sugar: and biscuits if you want them.'

Both men rose and helped themselves.

'Georgian?' Cheadle asked, knowing perfectly well that that was what all the silver was. She nodded indifferently. 'Insured, I hope?'

'Of course.'

Kicking off her shoes, curling up in the corner of her sofa, cradling her incongruous mug in delicate hands, she stared warily at the two policemen. 'All right,' she said, 'what do you want to know?'

'Everything you can tell us about Michael Saxon.'

'Why?'

'Because something about him prompted somebody to murder him.'

'Michael *murdered*? I don't believe it.'

Cheadle told her what the doctor at Horseferry Road had told him.

Visibly appalled, she stared into her mug. 'I knew Michael for twenty-two years. Three at the Royal Ballet School, nineteen as a member of the company. Man and boy, he was beautiful: a born dancer: utterly without conceit: and we all adored him. And never, in all those years, did I hear anyone say a single bad word about him.'

'Why'd he change his name?'

'He didn't: he just called himself something different.'

'Why?'

'His father was a shit.'

'In his opinion or yours, Dame Lyndsay?'

'Michael's father was once a sergeant in the Guards; and when Michael told him he wanted to study ballet, he forbade it. Said all male dancers were queer and no son of his . . .' She raised a hand in a gesture of contempt.

'Anyway, Mum Inglis encouraged Mike, so the virtuous sergeant bashed her up and walked out on them. They moved in with Mrs Inglis's parents; and both grandparents and Mrs Inglis worked – charring, window cleaning, that sort of thing – so that Mike could become a dancer. Later, of course, he got a grant, which eased the burden on his grandparents, if not his mum; and the rest you should know.'

She smiled sadly and met Cheadle's gaze with a look of total candour. To which Cheadle ungraciously responded, 'And now tell me the real reason why Inglis changed his name to Saxon.'

'Is he always like this?' she asked Robinson.

'Afraid so,' Robinson confessed.

Replacing her mug on the tray, and avoiding the eyes of both men, she told the truth. 'Just after Michael was accepted into the company, one of the stage hands – now deceased, I'm happy to say – cornered him, told him he was the spitting image of a Guardsman Inglis he'd once known, and asked was he any relation? So Mike said, yes, that would have been his dad, was the stage hand also an ex-guardsman? And the stage hand said, no, but Guardsman Inglis had been a regular visitor backstage at the Opera House because he was a close, personal friend, nudge nudge, wink wink, of – whereupon, he named a dancer who was notoriously gay.'

'You're saying,' Cheadle challenged, 'that Saxon changed his name because his father was bisexual?'

'Certainly not!'

'A male prostitute, then?'

'He changed his name because his father was a hypocrite – which he's proved countless times since by writing to his "dear son, Michael", saying how proud he was of him, how much he missed him, and would he please send a cheque to pay for "the electric", or the rent, or whatever, signed, his loving dad.'

'Saxon told you this?'

21

'When I took over as Artistic Director, he came into my office one day, tossed a letter on to my desk and said, "What do I do about this?" It was from the loving dad: who wanted £10,000 to help buy a flat.

'Not knowing what to say, I asked could he afford it? And he said that wasn't the point. And when I said, well, what *is* the point, darling?, he told me the whole sordid story.'

'And then what'd you advise?'

'Didn't have to advise: he'd decided. He'd adopted a professional name when he first joined the company specifically so that his father couldn't cash in on the fact that Michael Inglis, the unknown dancer, was his son: fourteen years down the track, when Michael Saxon had become a star, what else but an attempt to cash in was this letter?'

'Careful with this money, your Mr Saxon, was he?'

'On the contrary, he was extremely generous with it. Ask his grandparents. Ask his mother. Ask his wife. Ask half the kids in the company – '

'Helped them out, too, did he?'

'And not just with money!'

Cheadle seemed unaware that he was provoking her. 'These kids he used to help out – and not just with money . . .' He left the sentence unfinished.

'Yes?'

'Girls? Boys?'

'Both.'

'Sounds like he inherited his father's proclivities.'

The huge eyes narrowed. And then, suddenly, she began to laugh: laughed until the tears came.

'Oh dear,' she gasped, wiping her eyes. 'I'm sorry. Really. I should have realized you were – I mean, it's all so ludicrous. And to think I've been sitting here, getting madder and madder. Trick of the trade, is it?'

'I read somewhere', Cheadle confessed, 'that, "while apparently answering every question with total candour,

22

Dame Lyndsay contrives to suppress every unpalatable truth".'

'*The Sunday Times*,' she acknowledged. 'When I was appointed Artistic Director: which the editor thought I shouldn't have been. So you decided to needle me?'

'*Would* you have suppressed every unpalatable truth?'

'Not really. Ballet companies work too hard to be hot-beds of crime. Dancers really are the most frightfully busy people. Six days a week and, often as not, fourteen hours a day. Class in the morning followed by a rehearsal from twelve till whenever, or a performance at night. I can't remember knowing any dancer who had the time, let alone the energy, to commit a murder. No, if Michael was killed by someone who worked in the Opera House, it was by a stage hand, or a musician, or the General Director, or me; but it wasn't by one of my dancers.'

'I'm inclined to agree with you,' said Cheadle, 'but I can't track down which of the stage hands, musicians or administrators was the murderer until I find out what it was that made Saxon a candidate for murder.'

'You worry me,' she told him, staring at her hands.

'Why?'

She looked up. 'I watched him dying, Chief Superintendent. Tears were pouring down his cheeks – '

'An effect of the venom,' Cheadle explained. 'Like the fluid in his lungs. And the haemorrhaging.'

'Well, he *danced* through all those tears and haemorrhages: and you can take it from me, he was in agony. You didn't see it – '

'I'm seeing a film of it this afternoon.'

'Good!' She blew her nose and inhaled deeply. 'Because Michael wasn't anyone's candidate for murder, as you put it, he was simply a quite marvellous dancer.'

'Nevertheless,' Cheadle began.

'I know!' she acknowledged. 'But he was not, as you suggested, bisexual like his father, and, if you *must* know, he wasn't frightfully interested in sex of any kind: which

23

was maddening, because he was gorgeous. And I'm not talking now about Michael Saxon, the world's greatest dancer, I'm talking about Michael Inglis, the eighteen-year-old virgin who'd just joined the company.'

'*Virgin?*'

'He *glowed* with virginity. Of which every girl and gay in the company, myself included, promptly sought to divest him! But,' she sighed, 'to no avail. Well, not so much to no avail as without it ever even occurring to him that so many of us lusted after him. Sweet boy. Cutest bum in Christendom' – Cheadle's eyes darted belligerently at Robinson, who apparently had heard nothing – 'and from that day until yesterday, he never changed.'

'He married!'

'Dear Francesca,' commented Dame Lyndsay, without a trace of affection. 'She was a student with Michael. *Technically*, very sound. And extremely pretty. But so tone deaf she couldn't tell *Swan Lake* from the national anthem and would've danced with the same exquisite lack of emotion to either. But she played her cards cleverly.'

'Played her cards?'

'Michael fell for her as a fifteen-year-old, proposed to her as a seventeen-year-old, proposed again when they were accepted into the company, and proposed regularly for the next five years of their apprenticeship as performers. She never said yes, because she wanted a *rich* husband; but gorgeous, faithful, celibate Michael made a very agreeable escort in the mean time. However, the night of his first triumph, *she* proposed to him.'

'Did it work out?'

'Francesca got herself pregnant as promptly as a newly wed Royal, just as promptly resigned from the company where she'd never have achieved success anyway, acquired a house and an au pair, *and*, as Michael's fame grew, all the trappings of the wife of an international star – not excluding a succession of well-heeled admirers.'

'Did Saxon divorce her?'

She shook her head. 'Said it was his fault: because of the unsocial hours he worked, his unsociable instincts away from work, and a libido he exhausted while he worked.'

'You make him sound – what's the word I'm looking for, Sergeant?'

'Complaisant,' said Robinson.

'Look,' she said, 'he was happy with things as they were. *He* hated parties: she adored them – and was escorted to them, with his knowledge and approval, by one or other of her admirers. *She* loved dressing up: he refused even to buy a suit. *She* wanted to show him off: all he wanted, the second he stepped off the stage, was to go unnoticed.'

'The world's most beautiful man went unnoticed?' Cheadle scoffed.

'Used to wear sneakers and baggy trousers and shapeless sweaters and a beanie. And when he walked, he loped. Even at the stage door, where the fans were waiting for him, he was seldom recognized: everywhere else, because he looked like a builder's labourer, he was ignored.'

'Mr Saxon's beginning to bore me,' Cheadle grumbled.

'Then obviously you never saw him dance,' Dame Lyndsay retorted. 'Unless,' she suggested nastily, 'what you really mean is you'd rather he'd slept around.'

'*Touché*,' Cheadle admitted.

But Dame Lyndsay was not so easily to be appeased. Turning to Robinson, who was busily making notes, she demanded, 'Do you enjoy playing Boswell to his Johnson, Sergeant, or have you a mind of your own?'

'Both, ma'am!' Robinson so tactfully responded that Cheadle beamed at him and the Dame's ill humour was quite dispelled.

'Well, we mustn't presume any further,' Cheadle announced, rising to his feet and hitching up his trousers. Robinson also rose. Dame Lyndsay, having unfolded her elegant legs and slipped on her shoes, surveyed them from the edge of her sofa. She looked close to tears.

'You'll be interviewing everyone in the company, I suppose?' – plainly hoping they wouldn't.

'Tomorrow morning.'

'At the studio?' She looked taken aback by the idea of Cheadle barging into the company's morning class. Cheadle, who had no idea what she was talking about, nodded gravely.

'Do you know where it is?'

'Boswell does!'

Rejecting the possibility that the Chief Superintendent was being sarcastic, the Royal Ballet's Artistic Director stood gracefully and extended her hand. 'When you're watching the BBC film,' she said, as he took her hand, 'remember it was only in the final five minutes that any of us realized Michael was in distress. It's a measure of his genius that when he was dying, everyone believed he was acting; and when he was only acting, everyone believed he was dying. I don't think I could bear it if all you were hoping to see today was an action replay of an assassination. Michael's last performance mustn't become like Kennedy's last motorcade.'

5

The editor of BBC2's weekly arts programme escorted the two policemen into a lift, out of the lift, down a long curved corridor, past dozens of anonymous doors and into a hospitality room.

He didn't look like an editor, Cheadle thought: more like a *Guardian* reader whose wife had just called him in from his roses to entertain her parents. He wore an open-necked shirt, gardening trousers and Hush Puppies; and without once looking at either policeman, he never stopped talking.

'Such a tragedy. Nijinsky's insanity, Solevyov's suicide, they were ghastly enough; but this . . . Such a loss. Thank God for film. Margot hated it, of course. And even Michael wouldn't *talk* to camera. Not that he needed to. One always knew exactly what he meant. Never just smiled and hoped for the best. Never just leapt about looking splendid. Marvellous communicator. Audience, soloists, principals, *corps de ballet* – involved them all. Particularly in *The Dance*, which he choreographed himself. You know it, of course?'

'Of course,' chorused Cheadle and Robinson.

But, ignoring them, the editor swept on. 'Saxon at his best. Dazzling, eloquent, honest. Who else would have acknowledged that soloists are mere athletes without the support of a company, the guidance of a choreographer, the collaboration of an audience and the motivation of music? A marvellous account of a cloistered society serving a cruel art. Do sit down. Know how to operate these things, do you?' – inserting a cassette. 'Phone there if you need me.' And offering none of the BBC's much vaunted hospitality, left them.

For a few affronted seconds Cheadle simply stared at the blank television screen, which stared blankly back: then he turned to Robinson. 'Well, get on with it, Sergeant,' he growled. 'Make it go!'

With half the film still to be seen, Cheadle had stopped looking for clues. Quite simply, he was overwhelmed. Unlike his sergeant, he had no idea that the score and theme of Act III of *The Dance* were those of Act II of *Giselle*, still less that Saxon had translated *Giselle*'s vicious wilis into adoring balletomanes. But he did know what was happening: a great soloist, in love with the dance, was being enticed to dance himself to death.

27

Totally involved, Cheadle sat rigid with awe and indignation. Awe that anyone could perform such phenomenal feats of athleticism: indignation that each marvellous feat merely elicited a challenge from the adoring balletomanes to attempt something even more taxing.

A challenge the soloist promptly accepted, even when those who encircled him, allegedly his fans and colleagues, began, one after the other, to mime a spin. And, responding to each in turn, he span: around and around and around.

'Stop it!' Cheadle muttered, like a child at the pantomime shouting, 'Behind you!' There were dozens and dozens of them, Cheadle realized. It wasn't possible.

Thirty-*eight*.

Thirty-*nine*.

Forty!

Blue eyes, tear-filled and glittering: beautiful body, naked and motionless.

Until the knees buckled, and the soloist crashed on to his back, and the curtain fell, and the audience roared.

Silent and unseeing, Cheadle and Robinson stared at the flickering screen; until Cheadle broke the silence.

'Bloody hell,' he said.

'Sir?' Robinson ventured.

'What?'

'I forgot to take notes.'

'That one was for the Dame,' Cheadle excused him. 'The *next* one'll be for us. Make it go again.'

They watched the film twice more: watched it like policemen, observing the expression on the faces of those closest to Saxon, noting the precise minute and second into the film's running time when anyone touched Saxon, charting the successive symptoms of death by neurotoxin, cursing because neither of them had thought to bring along a member of the company, or a doctor, to advise

28

them. Now they'd have to re-run it, have dancers identified, get an expert to work backwards from the moment
of Saxon's collapse to the first symptoms of his poisoning
– and thereby deduce the probable time when he was
bitten.

'For the moment,' Cheadle confessed, as they drove out
of the BBC Centre, 'we're none the wiser. When's the
company performing next?'

'Tuesday week. *La Fille Mal Gardée*. Without Saxon.'

'You do surprise me!'

'I meant, he's not billed to dance in it.'

'Get seats for it. Preferably in a box. That film' – he
shook his head in frustration – 'gives you no idea where
they go when they exit, where they've come from when
they enter, where the dressing-rooms are. Arrange for me
to go backstage as well.'

'Before the performance, or after?'

'During. What's doing about the Opera House print-
out of names and addresses?'

'We get it tomorrow morning: it'll include everyone
except singers and touring orchestras and dancers. Where
to now? Home?'

Cheadle nodded. 'There's something not right about
this case. If we're to avoid one wild-goose chase after
another, I've got to watch the French finals – and think.'

'Talking of telly, what'd you think of Saxon?'

'Unbelievable.'

Lulled into a false sense of security, Robinson foolishly
ventured further. 'Incredible elevation.'

'So'd yours be,' Cheadle retorted, 'if you had a crotchful
of spiders.'

6

DANCE MACABRE screamed the tabloid press on Monday morning, and MURDER AT THE BALLET. The story had broken too late on Saturday night for any of the Sunday papers to do it justice. This had left the field open to the four television channels, who had made a meal of it. All that could be done with the left-overs of that meal on Monday was to smother them with sensationalism. Westbury fumed as he skimmed through one tasteless piece after another.

It wasn't fair that he'd been denied a decent press simply because the first murder had had to be committed on the sixth of June – which happened to be a Saturday.

It wasn't fair that a veritable *coup de théâtre* should have been served up as mere melodrama.

And it wasn't fair that no one – least of all Scotland Yard – had had the honesty to admit that the police were utterly flummoxed.

In short, Sunday had disappointed Westbury ('Well, what'd you expect,' his looking-glass had jeered, 'a knighthood?') and Monday morning had made him impatient. Neither disappointment nor impatience weakened his resolve, however: he knew what he had to do before Tuesday morning; and, step by step, he began doing it.

Cheadle spent Monday questioning dancers, first at the studio and then at the Opera House, where, to his surprise, the company had a second rehearsal room.

As the day wore on, he became increasingly disposed to accept Dame Lyndsay's dictum that dancers had neither the time nor the energy for such extra-curricular activities as murder. As far as he could see, they worked like navvies, conformed to a code of discipline and courtesy that was downright unworldly, and indulged themselves off-stage in nothing more reprehensible than junk food and cigarettes.

On the other hand, since almost all of them had accompanied Saxon to Australia, it was feasible that one of them could, with malice aforethought, have brought back to London a couple of funnelweb spiders.

'They just don't look the type,' Robinson objected.

'Don't look the type to smoke like chimneys, either,' Cheadle countered. 'But even assuming one of 'em *is* the type, how did he – '

'Or she,' Robinson carped.

'A *she* capable of capturing, smuggling, feeding and handling spiders, Sergeant? No! No, until I'm proved wrong, our villain's male! And since we have no idea who he is – except he's almost certainly one of the hundred and fifty-odd males on this print-out – the best we can do at the moment is establish when and how he got into Saxon's dressing-room.'

'As to when,' Robinson told him, 'it must have been Saturday evening – '

'Why? I'm told Saxon performed the same role the previous Tuesday: could've been done any time after he left the Opera House on Tuesday night.'

'One of the wardrobe people collected the fig leaf after Tuesday's performance, dry cleaned it Wednesday, checked it inside and out for damage on Saturday evening – wouldn't have done if it had fallen to pieces while he was dancing – and took it to him in his dressing-room at seven fifteen. As usual, he hung it on the back of his chair so he could step straight into it after taking a shower in the interval between Acts II and III.'

'He always took a shower?'

'I'm told Act II was set in a disco. Extremely witty. Fast and furious. He used to end up in such a lather his shirt and pants had to be *peeled* off. So he used to take a quick shower, have a few minutes with his feet up, spend another minute inserting himself into the pouch and hooking up the waistband, and was always just in time to go downstairs and make a spectacular entrance.'

Cheadle took his time digesting all this. Robinson watched him intently. Experience told him that when Cheadle fell silent for the first time in a case, he had at last devised a line of attack.

'That means', Cheadle finally declared, 'that we're looking for someone – a dancer, stage hand, musician or other in-house male – who, at some time between Saxon's first entrance in Act I and the end of Act II, could have left his post without causing comment, and made his way, undetected, to and from Saxon's dressing-room.'

'Right,' said Robinson.

'You get me the names of any of the dancers not on stage at any time, excluding intervals, between Saxon's first appearance and the end of his disco thing: I'll concentrate on the stage hands.'

'What about the musicians?'

Cheadle frowned. 'Even if they're *doing* nothing, they can't leave the pit, can they?'

'Not without attracting a huge amount of attention.'

'For the moment then,' Cheadle recapitulated, 'we're looking for someone who's been to Australia sometime in the last few years; who could've got up to Saxon's dressing-room unobserved any time between Act I and the end of Act II; and who had a key to Saxon's dressing-room.'

'I'll check with the stage door chap about the key.'

'Any finger-prints on the fig leaf?'

'Wardrobe's, Saxon's and a Middlesex orderly's. But the wardrobe lady's were smudged: by someone wearing gloves.'

'Our boy's thought of everything,' Cheadle mused. 'Must be really chuffed. Well, that's how I like 'em: chuffed. How do I get out of this place?'

Robinson led the way to the street. Cheadle glared over

32

his shoulder at the building behind him. 'Place is a bloody labyrinth,' he snarled.

'Supports your theory that it's an in-house murder.'

'Not really. Mrs Inglis wouldn't have had any trouble finding her way to her complaisant husband's dressing-room. And it would've been just as easy for Mr Inglis senior to return to the scene of his youthful crimes.'

'Could either of them have got past the stage door-keeper?'

'If Saxon had authorized it.'

'I'll check that too.'

'Wait for you in the pub,' said Cheadle, dismissing him. 'Pint and a sandwich, then we'll pay our respects to the fun-loving widow and the ever-loving dad.'

In the widow's case, Cheadle's irony was undeserved. Her grief was clearly as genuine as her concern for her clinging daughter. She wore no make-up and the dozens of bouquets delivered that day lay neglected in a heap beside the staircase.

'I'm sorry to intrude,' Cheadle murmured.

'I've been expecting you,' she told him indifferently.

'Really?'

'Don't play games, Chief Superintendent. If you'd like to sit down – ' indicating a door – 'the drawing-room's through there.' She knelt in front of her daughter. 'Darling, these gentlemen are friends of Daddy's. They've come to help us. So I want you to go and talk to Karen. Ask her to make us some tea.'

The child stared inhospitably through the drawing-room doorway at Cheadle and Robinson. 'For them too?' she asked.

'Just for us,' her mother reassured her.

The child stumped off, past the heap of neglected flowers, and vanished into the nether regions of the house.

Mrs Inglis joined Cheadle and Robinson, who were still standing.

'Please!' she said, flapping an impatient hand in the general direction of two armchairs and a sofa while she moved to the fireplace where she stood looking down at them. She was as slim, trim and elegant as Dame Lyndsay, but less diplomatic.

'Well?'

'I'm sorry to bother you at a time like this, but there are a few questions we have to ask, some things about your husband we need to know.'

'And there's no way you can ask them without hurting. I'd rather you came straight to the point.'

'All right, Mrs Inglis: what can you tell us about your husband?'

'That killing him was pointless.'

'Did he have any enemies?'

'None.'

'Was he jealous of your friendships with other men?'

'No.'

'Were you jealous of his success?'

'It compensated for my lack of it. I was too tall,' she explained. 'In addition to which, as dear Lyndsay once observed, I danced with all the passion of a metronome! Michael never gave a dull performance in his . . .'

Cheadle gave her a moment to recover before continuing with his questions. 'Did you spend Saturday evening at home?'

'I went to the Royal Première of the latest Spielberg epic. My escort was Nicky Corder. And if his word for it's not good enough, why don't you ask the Princess for hers?'

George Inglis shared a council flat with the one-time prostitute who was now his common law wife. Having reached the age where not even Scottish football supporters were anxious to avail themselves of her services, Valerie worked as a cleaning lady in order to pay the rent, keep George smartly dressed and provide him with a generous allowance – to which he ungratefully referred as his 'beer money'.

When he opened the door to Cheadle and Robinson, he had obviously just returned from the pub. Having offered the *Star* exclusive rights, for a substantial fee, to the story of Michael Saxon's bereft but devoted father, he thought they were reporters.

'From the *Star*, are you?' he slurred, ignoring Cheadle's proffered identification, ushering them in. 'Well, I'm your man. Wasn't just Michael's dad, you know: I was his mate. Couldn't do enough for me, Mike couldn't. Even wanted to sub me for a decent flat. But I said, "No, Mike boy, no, you done too much already." '

They were looking at him exactly like he'd always looked at recruits. 'You are from the *Star*, aren't you?'

'Police, actually, sir,' Cheadle corrected.

Inglis's manner switched instantly from boozy conmanship to manly deference, the slurring pensioner being abruptly supplanted by a wary barrack-room lawyer. 'So what can I do for you?' he asked, as if they were his colonel and adjutant respectively.

'Just answer a few questions, sir.'

Referring frequently to God as his judge, swearing twice on his mother's grave, and thrice insisting that he spoke without a word of a lie, Inglis gave answers that were patently untrue: except for the last, when Cheadle asked where he'd been between seven thirty and ten thirty on the night of Saturday the sixth of June.

'At me local,' said Inglis, with all the defiance of the habitual liar at last resorting to the unvarnished truth. 'Till closing time. When two yobbos tried to mug me on me way through the estate. One white, now with his arm in plaster: one black, henceforth useless to his girlfriend!

35

Case comes up tomorrow. Unless they both plead guilty, I'll be giving evidence.'

'Life!' growled Cheadle as Robinson drove past the House of Commons.

'Sir?'

'Forty years ago, that bloated jerk was the 'spitting image' of the world's most beautiful man. Saturday night, he takes on two teenaged muggers and beats the living daylights out of 'em.'

The traffic lights were kind and Robinson eased his way smoothly into Whitehall. There being nothing he could add to Cheadle's soliloquy about life's little ironies, he stayed silent.

'I suppose you're going to start playing with your toys as soon as we get back,' Cheadle jeered, apparently as irked by his subordinate's silence as he would have been by any rejoinder.

Robinson suppressed a smile. Cheadle's ploys to avail himself of that computerized technology he constantly professed to despise were as unsubtle as they were inevitable.

'Just long enough to feed in all the names on the Opera House print-out,' he advised. 'And all the names of the company that toured Australia last January: dancers and technicians. The name of anyone else on the print-out who obtained a visa to enter Australia any time in the last twelve months. And the name of each of the company members who was off-stage long enough, at the relevant time, to get up to Saxon's dressing-room, plant spiders in his cod-piece and return to the wings.'

'How long'd that be?'

'At a conservative estimate, four minutes.'

'Those kids could get up the north face of the Eiger and back in four minutes!'

'It's opening and closing the door, and the business

36

with the cod-piece, that takes time,' Robinson explained. 'Took *me* three minutes. And I was using an empty glass and two *plastic* spiders. With a capped jar, and real spiders, it would've taken twice as long.'

'You telling me you went up and down those stairs in a minute?' Cheadle demanded.

'Certainly not. I asked one of the principals to do me a trial run, and he took fifty seconds.'

'What else are you going to feed into that toy of yours?'

'The names of any stage hands who were at liberty to disappear for four minutes at any of the relevant times. Then I'll ask the computer which of all those who toured or had visas to visit Australia could feasibly have snuck up to and back from Saxon's dressing-room; and *that* should greatly reduce our list of suspects!'

'To about forty!' Cheadle acknowledged. 'With no guarantee that Fred'll be one of 'em.'

'Fred, sir?'

'Well, we can't go on calling him our boy, can we? So from now on, until we nail him, he's Fred.'

7

On Tuesday the ninth of June, at 10.55 a.m. precisely, Nicky Corder parked his Rolls Royce convertible just around the corner from his Kensington health club. He had the top down because it was a fine, warm morning, and because he enjoyed people looking at him from the windows of buses, taxis, lorries, Allegros and Cortinas. Or even better, as now, from the pavement.

A tanned, blond thirty-five-year-old, the despised darling of the gossip columnists, he was dressed, as always, to catch the eye. He wore a white Lacoste shirt, white buttock-hugging shorts, white cotton socks, white tennis shoes, a pale blue head-band and a very expensive watch. Further to attract attention, he picked up his car-phone and pretended to instruct his stockbroker to buy another twenty thousand shares in recently privatized British Rail.

It then being time to move, he pressed the button that raised the top, removed the ignition key, slid out of the driver's seat, locked the door, removed the winged statuette from the radiator cap and strode to the health club.

Having signed himself in, he gave the receptionist – a plain girl who persistently pretended not to recognize him – a perfunctory smile and said, 'My secretary booked me a sun bed for eleven fifteen.'

'Name?' she demanded, opening her appointment book.

'Sir Nicholas Corder,' he sighed wearily: but distinctly enough to be heard in the snack bar beyond the foyer. Three body builders – an Egyptian, an Italian and a Cockney girl who looked like a peroxided Arnold Schwarzenegger – turned from their fruit juices to inspect him.

'Corder,' the receptionist repeated distrustfully. 'Oh yeah! You a member?'

He came twice a week, always on Tuesday and Saturday, and always at this time: and always she asked was he a member. 'Yes,' he said.

'Eight pounds,' she told him. He gave her a twenty-pound note. 'I can't change that,' she complained.

She never had change.

'Give it to me when I've finished. Which bed?'

'Number five.'

'And I'll have a towel and a locker. For this – ' showing her the statuette. 'Solid silver.'

Not bothering to look at it, or him, she handed him a key and a towel. 'One pound fifty,' she said. 'I'll take it out of your change.'

'Thank you,' he said; but her head was already buried in Barbara Cartland's five hundred and tenth romantic novel, and she gave no sign that she had heard him.

The men's changing room was empty apart from a rather pretty-looking labourer wearing torn jeans, a T-shirt, a red kerchief knotted round his throat and a dust-powdered beanie jammed low over his eyebrows – which made him look vaguely moronic. This impression was heightened by the tattoo on his right forearm. It was crude and incomplete: two thirds of a woman's profile, in blue.

Corder wondered how people like him – workmen, waiters, even some who were on the dole – could afford the membership fee: and why anyone who could afford it would leave a conspicuous tattoo unfinished.

The youth ignored him: just sat on the bench, tugging at his boot-laces. Being ignored always made Corder uncomfortable. Closing his locker door on the silver statuette and his gold watch, he sat a few feet from the youth and began to remove his tennis shoes.

'Bloody Australians!' he remarked.

The youth stared at him blankly.

'Five hundred and ninety for six,' Corder explained. The blank blue eyes went even blanker. 'The Test Match!'

The youth turned away.

An enormously tall West Indian emerged from the shower room. He needed a health club, Corder thought, like Steffi needed a forehand. Might be interested in cricket, though. But before anyone could engage him in manly conversation, the West Indian loped to the farthest corner of the dressing-room and began anointing his muscular body with Oil of Ulay.

Corder stood up in bare feet and removed his buttock-hugging shorts. The youth continued to ignore him. His determined silence, and the black man's narcissistic pre-occupation, combined to make Corder doubly determined to be noticed.

'That tattoo,' he remarked, adjusting his jock-strap. 'I'm fascinated.'

This time the youth's eyes stared at him with chilling

dislike; but Corder pressed on. 'Did you run out of money? Sober up? Change your mind? What?'

'Me prison sentence wasn't long enough!' the youth told him: and rising menacingly, stalked past Corder to a door marked TOILET, which he slammed behind him.

Feeling inexplicably threatened, Corder hastily removed his shirt and jock-strap, and, as was his wont, laid everything out on the bench so that, when he returned from the sun bed, he could shower, dry off and dress quickly enough to join the aerobics class by noon.

It was a ritual to which he had adhered for three years. It kept him tanned and sleek. It also afforded several dozen Sloane Rangers, out-of-work actresses and figure-conscious housewives an opportunity to admire him.

Wrapping his towel round his waist, and pinning his locker key to his towel, he hurried out of the changing room. He didn't want to be there when the gaolbird returned. Nor did he wish to deprive himself of a single second of his eight pounds' worth of artificial sun.

When he returned to the changing room, he was relieved to notice that both the gaolbird and the fragrantly oiled West Indian had gone. A blubbery builder (who always talked restaurants) and a foppish actor (who always talked athletics) were there, but Corder had no desire to talk to them.

Having showered, he dried himself thoroughly, stepped into his jock-strap, donned his Lacoste shirt, and strode, bare-footed and bare-assed, to the bench of hair dryers.

A minute later his damp blond hair had become an impeccable silken bob. Adjusting his pale blue head-band, he peered into the mirror and preened shamelessly, even baring his teeth to ensure that nothing marred their capped perfection. Satisfied, he strode back to the bench, sat, put on his socks and tennis shoes, stood, pulled on his buttock-hugging shorts, removed the locker key from his towel and pinned it to the waistband of his shorts, hung up his towel and headed for the gymnasium.

The taped music (*Hooked on Classics*, by the Royal Philharmonic) had already begun to pound through two large speakers, and the instructress to yelp. He took up his usual position in the middle of the second of four rows of vibrant femininity. Although he resented being yelped at by a woman it was better than being barked at by the brute who conducted the men's session. Also, he would rather be admired by girls in leotards than by men in shorts and singlets.

He glanced at the clock. Only ten past. Everyone bouncing, kicking and flinging with rhythmic frenzy.

Syncopated masochism.

Fifty minutes to go, and already he had a stitch. Should've organized his secretary to ring him. Always impressed the girls, that 'Call for Sir Nicholas Corder' over the PA system.

Except last time.

When the yelper had taken exception.

'Be quick, Nick,' she had shouted from her podium. 'It's only us girls are allowed to fake it.'

Bitch!

'Knees up, Nick,' she was yelping now. 'Higher! Higher!! That's it. One, two, three, four: five, six, seven, eight!'

He was sweating like a pig.

And exhausted.

Bloody women were tireless.

Only half-past. He daren't drop out, though.

'Too much for you, Nick?' the bitch taunted.

He made himself smile, forced himself to fling his arms faster, smack his hands louder, spring from feet together to legs astride faster and more vigorously.

The music pounded and the bitch yelped.

To hell with it; he'd walk off and explain on Saturday that he'd had the flu.

Someone watching.

The bloody gaolbird, leaning over the railing, alert and malicious.

Catching Corder's eye, he straightened and beat his chest, like Tarzan. Corder realized he wasn't any longer being ignored: he was being mocked. He hurled himself into the next sequence: the one he always described to himself as, 'Arms and legs in every *conceivable* direction, one *thousand* times, *fling!*'

Murder.

Tears ran down his cheeks.

The gaolbird pretended to cry.

'*Nick*?' he heard. The yelper sounded anxious. '*NICK*?'

Leaping from her podium, she switched off the cassette. In the sudden silence, Corder was surrounded by staring women. Unaware, he continued to fling disjointed arms and legs in every conceivable direction. And then collapsed to the floor.

The youth in the beanie leapt the railing, knelt beside him and bent to give him mouth to mouth resuscitation. The last thing Corder felt was his nostrils being pinched. The last thing he saw was the gaolbird's face, an inch from his own, apparently determined to kiss him.

He struggled; but soon succumbed.

'I'll ring for an ambulance,' the Samaritan youth said quietly: and sprinted to the members' telephone in the foyer.

Twenty-five minutes later, when no ambulance had arrived, and the club was swarming with newspersons, the manager made a second call. The ambulance service denied having been summoned earlier. The manager tried unsuccessfully to prevent the media from photographing Corder's body. Ambulance men arrived and attempted briefly to revive the stricken man: then lifted him on to a stretcher and covered him from head to foot with a blanket.

It was just after two thirty when Cheadle received a call from his opposite number at Earls Court. 'It must be presumed,' he was advised, 'that Sir Nicholas Corder was murdered at or about twelve thirty today, during an aerobics session, at the Kensington Health Club. Thought you ought to know.'

'Kensington's nothing to do with me,' Cheadle interrupted. 'I've enough on me plate already.'

'Looks like you're getting more.'

'What're you trying to tell me, Syd?'

'There were puncture marks on Corder's back, and two spiders in his shirt.'

'Any objections if I sit in while your laddies question the health club?'

'Be my guest, Charlie boy. Want to sit in on this afternoon's post-mortem?'

'Foregone conclusion, isn't it, Syd?'

'I'll let you know.'

Robinson was driving Cheadle to the health club.

'Theoretically,' Cheadle growled, 'this is either a copycat killing or a related murder.'

'Except,' Robinson demurred, 'how could anyone *else* have got hold of a couple of funnelweb spiders?'

'Which means it isn't the work of a copycat.'

'And why would anyone who hated Saxon enough to murder him have wanted to murder the man who was cuckolding him?'

'Which means,' Cheadle sighed, 'that this second murder is probably unrelated to the first. And that means . . .' He fell silent.

As usual the traffic had ground to a halt between Palace

Gate and Kensington Church Street. Both men stared glumly at the back of a stationary bus. A scarlet helicopter whipped low across the park to their right and hovered over Kensington Palace: a Royal being flown home from opening or inspecting something. Neither man even noticed it.

'Maybe,' Robinson finally, and frivolously, suggested, 'Nicky took out a contract on Saxon, refused to pay when the job was done, and the hired killer decided to teach him a lesson?'

Cheadle gave him a withering look; but Robinson – one of whose duties it was to act as whipping boy – refused to be intimidated. 'Or maybe,' he persisted, 'Corder knew who killed Saxon, and the killer knew he knew.'

'And waited sixty-odd hours to silence him?' Cheadle jeered. Nevertheless, he took Robinson's point. Almost anything was preferable to the conclusion he himself had drawn. 'No,' he decided, 'Corder had the morals of a Regency rake, but he wasn't gutless. No one who lists his hobbies as mountaineering and free-fall parachuting is gutless. If he'd known anything about Saxon's death, he'd have told us.'

'So why was he murdered?' Robinson demanded, posing the question Cheadle at last seemed ready to answer. 'Come to that, why was either of them murdered?'

'You know why, Sergeant,' Cheadle muttered; 'so I hope to God our Fred's run out of spiders.'

8

Christopher Westbury had not only not run out of spiders, he was at that very moment feeding them: or rather, tossing meal worms into the lairs of what he called his Task Force.

ITV had broken the story of Corder's death at the end of its one o'clock news programme. Westbury had arrived home just in time to hear it.

Thames News at one twenty had added an outline of Corder's life – the title and fortune he had inherited from his *émigré* grandfather, Miklos Korda; his brief but much publicized affairs with a succession of world-famous beauties; and his playboy feats of daring. As well, it included an interview with the yelping instructress. She described Corder's collapse and said he had been a member of the health club for over three years. The item ended with a shot of Corder's blanket-covered body being hoisted into an ambulance.

London Radio and Capital Radio – to which Westbury listened in turn while waiting to watch BBC2's News at Two – had repeated the story.

BBC2 told much the same story as ITV, and used much the same library film; but added an interview with the health club manager, who insisted that Sir Nicholas was the first of his thousands of clients to die on the premises, that this solitary death could in no way be attributed to the health club's aerobic programme, and that Corder probably wouldn't have died had the ambulance arrived promptly.

It was only as Corder's body was seen being removed from the club, however, that the newscaster's voice-over provided the postscript for which Westbury had been waiting. 'The police', she read, 'have issued a statement that the circumstances surrounding Sir Nicholas Corder's death must be considered suspicious. They appeal to anyone who was at the Kensington Health Club between the hours of 11 a.m. and 1 p.m. to contact them as soon as possible at the number which is now on your screen.'

Glancing at his telephone, Westbury snorted, poured himself a glass of sherry and, watching his reflection in the looking-glass as he approached the fireplace, smiled at it.

'You've done it!' The smiling face in the looking-glass congratulated him. They toasted one another.

'Didn't think I could, did you?' Westbury accused.

'Had me doubts,' the other confessed; but spoilt it by adding, 'You look tired: take a pill!'

Westbury hated these abrupt changes of mood, from admiration to solicitude. He'd just pulled off his second *coup de théâtre*, and what did Buggerlugs say? 'Take a pill!'

About to deliver a stinging rebuke, he was silenced by London Radio. The funnelweb murderer, London Radio excitedly reported, had struck again. His second victim was millionaire man about town, Sir Nicholas Corder. The question now was, would there be a third? And if so, when?

'Certainly will,' Westbury chuckled, his stinging rebuke forgotten. 'Five days from today.' He took another sip of sherry. 'And a fourth after that.' He drained his glass. 'And then the one that really matters – ' at which, he hurled his glass vindictively into the fireplace.

But his mood of elation proved short-lived as he surveyed the crystal fragments littering his hearth. Raising his eyes to the looking-glass, he sought reassurance. Staring glumly back at him, the looking-glass complained, 'Cost a bomb, those glasses did. And you've only *got* six.'

'I'll only *need* five.'

'Well, at least clear up the debris. Dead give-away.'

Westbury rejected the warning. 'Shards of glass and dried flowers? Art, that is. The Tate'd love it. Anyway, enough of this small talk . . .'

He wandered out of the drawing-room into the hall and stood there, indecisively, before entering what had once been his music room but now was his study. Ignoring the music stand, he lowered himself on to a swivel chair in front of a pinewood work bench. The bench supported his computer, disc drive, printer and half a dozen floppy disks.

He turned on the computer, inserted a disk and booted it up. Tapping authoritatively on the relevant keys, he asked an electronic device to retrieve from its plastic brain his personal account of the murder of Michael Saxon – to which he now proposed adding his personal account of the murder of Nicholas Corder.

The green words appeared, luminous and vibrant, on the black screen. Bending forward, he read them avidly.

Atrax One
Those funnelweb spiders that are found in Sydney belong to the species *robustus* of the genus *Atrax*. *Robustus* is self-explanatory: *atrax* means atrocious.

Today, or rather tonight, is Sunday, June 7. It is 2 a.m. Last night, Michael Saxon died. I killed him. And I will kill four others. No one will ever know how I contrived to kill them unless they access this disk. The title of this disk is *Atrax Series*.

I don't know how long it will take to establish that Michael died from funnelweb poison, but sooner or later the police are going to start looking for someone who brought some funnelweb spiders back from Sydney specially to kill him.

So, right from the start, they'll be on the wrong track. I didn't *bring* the spiders back: they were stowaways who came back with me! And I never had anything against Michael. In fact, if his name had been English instead of Inglis, he'd be alive this morning.

Ironically, although he was the first who had to go, he was the last I chose for that honour: and the only one of the five I've chosen that I actually knew and liked.

But that's life. Neveu got killed in an aircrash: du Pre got MS: this one gets schizophrenia: that one gets knocked down by a bus. It's all random and unfair; but that's how it goes.

Mind you, people will say there was nothing random about Michael's death. But what could have been more random than my host in Sydney giving me his old airline bag because I didn't have one of my own? It had been in his garage for years, and neither of us knew there were two female funnelwebs and scores of hatchlings inside it; at the bottom, under the canvas-covered stretcher thing which had got partially detached.

It was pure luck I decided to toss my cassettes and Walkman on top of my dirty socks, shirts and boxer shorts, because that's why I took the bag on to the plane: otherwise it would have gone into the hold, and all my stowaways would have frozen to death.

I found them when I unpacked here at home. Scared me witless. My Sydney host had shown me a colony of them he found in his tool shed. Told me all about them. So I was going to kill the stowaways until I remembered there was someone else I wanted to kill. Now I had the perfect weapon!

That was the winter before last. That's when I became a funnelweb farmer. That's when I began to plan. By March of this year, I knew there had to be five deaths in my series. By April, I knew that the first of them had to be Michael: and that the date for his death had to be June 6.

Michael was always careless with the key to his dressing-room. Always left it in the lock when he opened the door. Often forgot to take it out of the lock when he went on stage. So it was easy to pinch.

Mind you, we musicians change downstairs, so I had to invent an excuse for being upstairs. Apparent honesty seemed the best policy. I knocked on his door a few minutes after he arrived for a Saturday performance of *The Dance* in early May and asked for an autographed photograph for my non-existent niece.

48

Had a good look round while he dug one out and signed it. Saw the flesh-coloured sac thing on his fig leaf, which was hanging from the back of his chair. Thanked my lucky stars it was deep and loose enough for his goolies not to make contact with the spiders till he started leaping about. Thanked him for the photograph. And removed the key as I closed the door behind me. Michael later told the stage door-keeper he'd misplaced it. Stage door-keeper said, 'Not again!'

I had a duplicate made the following Monday and dropped the original on the staircase that night.

It was found and returned to the stage door-keeper the same evening.

Once I'd assured myself of access to his dressing-room, everything else fell into place.

The second act of *The Dance* is set in a disco. Michael had decided to use typical disco music and wanted a typical disco sound. That meant hardly any strings. So I had twenty minutes off to do what I had to do. But I'd need an alibi.

So I got our union rep to fix it that ten of us who weren't needed for the disco act could stand in the wings and watch it, because we'd never seen it. Can't see anything that happens on stage from the orchestra pit. Dead boring.

No problems on the night. All but one of my colleagues in the wings were entranced, the exception being Gavin Wilson, cellist, who was standing at the back with me. He said he hated ballet, how about a pint at the pub over the road? I said no, I loved ballet, so off he went.

No one noticed.

But first things first.

Before I left home, using a couple of salad dressing bottles and a playing card, I trapped two of the spiders in the lair I'd made for each of them. One in each bottle. In case they ate one another. Don't think they were too happy about it, but it's difficult to tell. Never look happy about anything. My father was the same.

Anyway, I locked them up in their little glass cells, popped them into my Safeway's carrier bag (along with a clean shirt and a dirty Martin Amis paperback) and took the tube to Covent Garden.

Half-way through Act II, the disco bit, I shot up to Michael's dressing-room with a bottle in each trouser pocket. Didn't have to let myself in: Michael had left the door open! Closed it behind me, put on a pair of leather gloves, took the bottle out of my right trouser pocket, uncapped it, took the fig leaf off the back of Mike's chair, pushed the mouth of the sac as far down as it would go over the neck of the upright bottle, then upturned both of them and shook the bottle.

Spider Number One plopped into the bottom of the sac.

I restored the fig leaf (sac outwards) to the back of Mike's chair. This was the tricky bit. Unless it preferred to hide in the dark at the bottom of the sac, Spider Number One could easily have escaped before I could decant Spider Number Two.

So I was watching the mouth of that sac like a hawk while I removed the bottle from my left trouser pocket, with my left hand, and my trusty playing card from the right pocket, with my right hand.

Holding the bottle upright, I uncapped it, covered its mouth with the playing card, tipped the bottle upside down, so that the spider dropped on to the playing card, and blocked the mouth of the sac with the card and the upturned bottle.

Now came the terrifying bit. Would Spider Number One react to the vibrations in her newly acquired tunnel by rushing up to attack Spider Number Two, or by cowering where she was?

Only one way to find out: whipping away the card, I shoved the neck of the bottle straight down into the sac and yanked it straight out again. As far as I could see,

50

Spider Number Two was now cohabiting with Spider Number One! All I had to do was keep them there.

I dampened a tissue, folded it and, using the recapped neck of one of my bottles, pushed it slowly into the sac. Funnelwebs like the damp, so I figured they'd stay put; but their fangs are long and strong enough to pierce a man's fingernail, so I figured they'd have no trouble biting through a pre-dampened, sweat-sodden tissue.

No more could I do: besides which, I was running out of time. So I left the dressing-room, saw no one on the stairs, and rejoined the boys in the wings.

Nobody noticed.

The cellist returned just as the disco bit was ending. Again, nobody noticed. Then came the interval and we all adjourned for a drink and everyone, including the cellist, hypocritical bastard, said how terrific it had been.

The rest is history.

On the way home, I left the duplicate key to Mike's dressing-room in the lift at Covent Garden Underground, my gloves on the train at Kensington High Street, the two salad dressing bottles in a litter bin in Holland Park, and the playing card under the windscreen wiper of an illegally parked car with a CD number plate. I may have been unnecessarily cautious, but it's not inconceivable that forensic scientists could prove that the bottles and the card had been in contact with the spiders, and that my left glove had been in contact with the surface of the plastic fig leaf.

Better safe than sorry: specially since I've got fifty-one more playing cards, and gloves and salad dressing bottles are easily come by.

If that makes me sound timid, I must add that before I left Michael's dressing-room, I borrowed his beanie: and not only have I kept it, I'll be wearing it on Tuesday.

Grunting with satisfaction at all that he had just read,

Grunting with satisfaction at all that he had just read, Westbury straightened, stretched and settled down to the more demanding task of transferring from his own memory to that of a floppy disk the story of Nick Corder's death a few hours earlier. As he tapped away at the keyboard, the green words sprang to life on the black screen.

Atrax Two: Tuesday, June 9
I borrowed Michael's beanie because I figured that if it made *him* unrecognizable it would do the same for me. Also, I knew he wouldn't be needing it.

To complete my transformation, I padded my cheeks, beetled my eyebrows, wore tinted contact lenses, drew a woman's head on my right arm, put on my oldest DIY gear and my dimmest National Front look and knotted a kerchief round my neck.

At ten to eleven on the morning of June 9 I entered the Kensington Health Club. Instead of signing in, I booked a sun bed.

The receptionist asked if I was a member and I said, yes. She asked my name and I told her Mark Gleeson. She wrote Gleeson in her book, and on the receipt.

I took my canvas tool bag (in which I had a towel, a pair of rubber gloves, nail scissors, needle and thread, some props and two bottlefuls of spiders) into the changing room. I flushed the receipt down the loo and sat on the bench to wait for Corder.

He arrived just after eleven and began his ritual of drawing attention to himself. I reacted like he was trying to proposition me. It really threw him. From then on, everything went like clockwork. In fact, if I didn't know how many months of planning and research I'd put into it, I'd say it was a piece of cake.

Suddenly overwhelmed with tiredness, he decided to

leave the rest of *Atrax Two* until the following morning. Removing the disk and switching off the computer, he went to bed. Curled up on his side, he fell instantly asleep.

9

Back at the health club, Cheadle's worst fears were soon confirmed. Listening to the instructress's account of the last fifty minutes of Corder's life was very like watching the BBC's film of the last twenty minutes of Saxon's. Both had succumbed to the combined effects of venom and exertion.

'But that's exactly what Fred was relying on,' Cheadle told Robinson. 'He knew Saxon's professionalism and Corder's vanity would prevent them from quitting. Wasn't taking any chances, though.'

'Two spiders each, you mean?'

'You can survive a bite from one, the quack told me, provided you do everything right. Like keeping still, applying a tourniquet or a crepe bandage, and getting immediate treatment with a drug called Atropine or on something called a positive pressure ventilator. But a bite from two of 'em? Even if Saxon *had* stopped dancing, and Corder *had* quit showing off, you can't apply a tourniquet to a man's willy, or round his waist, can you?'

'Seems he thought of everything.'

'He thinks he's thought of everything,' Cheadle amended. 'But already he's overlooked the one thing that'll undo him: he can't resist cocking a snook! He craves attention and admiration. Which you can't afford to if you're a multiple murderer.'

'You mean, he'll kill again?'

'If he doesn't, a week from now he'll be forgotten. And he'd hate that.'

'You could tell him so,' Robinson suggested. 'Make a statement on telly.'

'If I do, people'll say I provoked him into it when he kills again.'

'So you'll wait?' Robinson accused. Cheadle, he thought, could be as ruthless as a Field Marshal.

'Until I know more about him,' Cheadle confirmed, ignoring Robinson's rebuke. 'Which should be sometime between the third murder and the fourth: hopefully, in time to prevent the fifth.'

'We could at least *try* to prevent the third.'

'Oh, we will, laddie, we will. But it won't work. Unless, of course, when you feed the names of all the members of this health club into that ridiculous machine of yours, it comes up with one who's also on the Opera House list, who's also been to, or had a visa allowing him to visit Australia, and who also could have got into Saxon's dressing-room.'

Robinson looked chastened. 'Sorry.'

'For having ideals still? Don't be! But don't expect promotion either. Idealists can't think like villains.'

'And it takes one to catch one!'

'Don't be sarcastic, Derek: you're too intelligent for that. Besides, I need someone smooth like you to deal with that cussed cow at Reception. She and I, as Mrs Cheadle'd say, are incompostable.'

Robinson laughed. 'It's a good word.'

'She's a good woman. And you're a good sergeant. So on your bike: wheedle the truth out of Cussed Cora.'

'Surely Fred's too crafty to be a member of this place *and* the Opera House: or to have prejudiced his plan to kill Corder by being on the premises illegally?'

'So Cora let him in as a bona fide customer,' Cheadle agreed. 'But she should be able to describe any customers she admits, shouldn't she?'

'From what I saw of her, she wouldn't remember that someone who called himself Quasimodo had a French accent, was hunchbacked and looked like Charles Laughton.'

'You can but try,' Cheadle sympathized. 'She's a Cartland addict, remember. Tell her you're Scotland Yard's token lord and you want to take her away from all this to your villa in the Bahamas: only you can't unless she helps you solve this dreadful murder which was probably her fault anyway for letting in the murderer. And if that doesn't work' – plainly pleased with this flight of Cartlandish fancy – 'yank off some fingernails. That always works.'

'Couldn't I just take her to bed?'

'Before you've married her, Sergeant?' Cheadle looked shocked. 'I said a Cartland addict, not a Beatles' groupie. Anyway, ring me at home when you've got something to report.'

'More tennis?'

Cheadle ignored the irony. 'We're blind to the wood because of all the trees,' he criticized himself. 'Maybe we're even searching the wrong forest. There's something we've missed. Or misinterpreted. And it's leading us away from Fred instead of toward him. Takes one to catch one, you said: but I haven't been thinking like a villain, I've been thinking like a copper.'

Nodding, Robinson said, 'Mind if I raise something that's been bugging *me*?'

'Probably, but raise away.'

'Afraid it's hypothetical – '

'It's analogies I hate.'

'Analogous, too.'

'Get on with it.'

'OK. If you and I were on a case in Bombay' – Cheadle's eyes shot up toward his slick-backed hair-line – 'and you'd decided to kill me, and, unbeknownst to anyone else, you'd acquired a cobra, whose bite is usually fatal, would

55

you have popped it into my bed in Bombay, where my subsequent death would have seemed to be merely an unfortunate local accident, or would you have smuggled it back into England and hidden it in my locker, where my subsequent death could only have been seen as murder?'

Now it was Cheadle's turn to look chastened.

'You've just eliminated every company member who went to Australia from our list of suspects,' he congratulated his sergeant.

'There's more,' said Robinson. 'If you *hadn't* wanted to kill me in Bombay, what would you have done with the cobra?'

Cheadle glared at him with a mixture of irritation and respect. 'I'd have called Room Service and told 'em to send up a mongoose,' he snapped. 'So now you've proved that Fred didn't *bring* the spiders from Sydney: he just sort of came upon them back here in London.'

'*Funnelwebs?*'

'Back in 1988, someone in London just came upon some black widow spiders from America.'

'Oh yeah,' Robinson remembered. 'In a crate of bananas.'

'Maybe Fred found his in a carton of Castlemaine?'

Robinson looked sceptical. He also, suddenly, looked bored. And Cheadle knew that he must have strayed very far from the point to make his courteous subordinate betray anything so discourteous as boredom. The trouble was, he'd forgotten what it was he'd been trying to prove. 'Where were we before *I* began clutching at straws?' he said.

'I think we'd agreed that Fred wouldn't have *smuggled* funnelwebs into Britain, but had nevertheless come into possession of at least four of them.'

'And because he used them,' Cheadle elaborated, having got back on track, 'he's told us something about himself we might otherwise never have known. Fred's not just a psychopath, he's also an opportunist.'

56

'Not much to go on.'

'Twice what we had five minutes ago,' Cheadle countered. 'And half the number of suspects. So you pump Cora for our vital clue while I work out a more villainous strategy for our war against Fred. Give me a bell when you're through.'

When Robinson telephoned, Cheadle had finished the evening meal Mrs Cheadle had prepared for him and was helping her wash up.

He was glad to be interrupted – not because he expected to hear anything dramatic but because he'd just had a lousy thought. Mrs Cheadle wasn't a wife, he'd just thought, she was a landlady whose boarding house meals and house-proud habits he tolerated because she polished his shoes, washed his shirts, taped his favourite television programmes, shared his bed and seemed not unhappy that he was her only lodger.

As he plodded to the phone, he wondered about Fred's sex life. No need to wonder about Robinson's. Live-in girlfriend, a barrister, very cool at home, a holy terror in court. He picked up the receiver. 'Yes?'

Robinson wasted no time bemoaning the skill with which the receptionist had parried his questions, the implacable rearguard action she had fought when finally he had forced her into retreat, and her willingness to resort to any tactic, from sullenness to amnesia, to obstruct the pursuit of justice: none of this was relevant to Cheadle's enquiry, so he confined himself to the few facts that were.

It was not true, as the club had maintained, he told Cheadle, that all members signed in: a handful resented being required to do so and walked straight past the receptionist whenever she was busy.

Nevertheless, most members not only signed in but also surrendered a membership card to which an identifying photograph and signature were appended. They collected this card from Reception as they departed.

It seemed probable, moreover, that all those members who had attended the club that morning had signed in. Each signature had been checked. Every name was that of a bona fide member. Forty-two of them had been questioned. None of them remembered an unfamiliar face among those who had worked out or taken part in the aerobics class. And none of the names on the club's membership list coincided with any name on the Opera House print-out.

On the other hand, there had been some visitors to the club who were not members. These included three body builders – an Italian, an Egyptian and a formidable blonde from Hackney – who had been paid by the club to pose for publicity photographs: a West Indian hurdler who'd pulled a muscle and wanted the club's masseur to work on it: and three clients for the sun beds.

Of these, one had been a Hollywood actor whose stardom derived entirely from his perennial tan: and two were girls, friends, determined not to land in Torremolinos the following day looking pallid.

There had been two other clients for the sun bed, but they had been members. One had been the late Nicky Corder. The second was a Mark Gleeson. The latter had not signed in, but this was unnecessary for members reserving a sun bed. The receptionist not only entered their name on her booking sheet, she also wrote it on the receipt, a copy of which was handed to the client.

The receptionist could not describe Mr Gleeson, she hadn't looked at him. But he wore a beanie and had a cockney accent and a curt manner. And a rolled-up newspaper, the *Mirror*, in the back pocket of his jeans. She *had* looked at him when he headed off for the changing room, but had only seen his back. His jeans were ripped across the right buttock. He was obviously some kind of labourer.

'Couldn't any of the aerobics ladies give you a description?' Cheadle asked.

'Only of what he was wearing, really. Apart from that, heavy eyebrows and clean-cut features, but nondescript. One said he was a bit like James Dean – '

'Nothing nondescript about James Dean!'

'Her words, sir, not mine. Another said a bit like Dirk Bogarde – '

'Bogarde's twenty years older than me!'

'In his youth, sir. And the third said Sting.'

'Who's Stink?'

'A pop star.'

'I see. So all we need now is an identikit drawing that's a cross between James Dean, the youthful Dirk Bogarde and a pop star called Stink.'

'Pretty hopeless, I'm afraid.'

'As hopeless as Corder's shirt, I imagine. Earls Court tell me Fred stitched two pockets inside it to hold his spiders, but I'm not expecting the lab boys to find anything on 'em except Nicky's sweat. What time did Gleeson book his sun bed for?'

'Same as Corder. Eleven fifteen till eleven forty-five.'

'Carry on.'

After the sun bed, Robinson resumed, according to a Mr Harvey, a building contractor, Gleeson had a shower and a sauna. And after his sauna, according to the instructress, he had been watching the aerobics class when Corder collapsed.

He had at once attempted mouth to mouth resuscitation and when that failed he had offered to ring for an ambulance.

He rang from the members' coin box situated some six feet from the reception desk. The receptionist heard him make the call. He had then left the premises, saying he needed a breath of air: he'd never kissed a guy before – let alone a dead one.

According to his club file, Mr Gleeson was twenty-five years old, single and a construction worker. He had neither a private nor a business telephone number, but he resided in Courtfield Gardens, Earls Court. He had not been at his home when Robinson and another officer called.

'Going on a bit about this Gleeson, aren't you?' Cheadle growled.

'I suppose I am, rather.' Robinson fell silent.

'But?'

'The building contractor was surprised when I told him Gleeson had been on a sun bed for half an hour. Said his skin was milky white. Not even pink. So if he hadn't been on a sun bed, what *had* he been doing? Specially since both the Torremolinos girls say they saw him going into his sun bed cubicle, and heard him humming – something classical – for the whole half-hour.'

'That all?'

'No. When Corder collapsed, Gleeson vaulted the fence between the work-out area and the aerobics floor. Three witnesses have pointed out exactly where he was standing. But there aren't any prints on the railing.'

'Then why all these doubts?'

'There's a possible explanation.'

'Try me!'

'Two ladies say they *think* his towel was draped across the railing.'

'Still there?'

'Seems he took it with him to kneel on while he gave Corder the kiss of life.'

'How about the members' phone?'

'From the moment Corder's body was removed, people were queuing up to use it. And two at least of them admit they wiped it clean before and after dialling. Gym people get very sweaty; and quite a few of them dry every piece of equipment they're about to use or have finished using. There's even a tissue dispenser to encourage the habit.'

'Hmm,' said Cheadle. 'On balance, what do you think?'

'He doesn't add up. A sun bed but no tan. A copy of the *Mirror* but hums classical music. Rings for an ambulance but it doesn't come. Dresses like a labourer but is off work at eleven a.m. Is at a loose end but doesn't go home when he's done whatever it was he was doing at the club.'

'He gave Corder mouth to mouth resuscitation,' Cheadle reminded, in Gleeson's defence.

'And Fred craves attention and admiration,' Robinson reminded Cheadle.

'You taking the piss, Sergeant?'

'Certainly not, sir.'

'Wouldn't blame you if you were. What'd you say Gleeson told Cora about needing a breath of fresh air?'

Robinson referred to his notes. ' "I've never kissed a guy before: let alone a dead one." '

'Bit sick, isn't it?'

'At least half of it was true!'

'Let's stick with Mr Gleeson,' Cheadle decided. 'Leave everything else to the team. Forget all the cross-referencing: Sherlock'll sort that out.' Sherlock was Cheadle's name for the Home Office Major Enquiry System, otherwise a computer known as Holmes. 'Go back to Gleeson's place in Earls court – what number is it in Courtfield Gardens? – OK, stay there till he returns and I'll be with you as soon as I can.'

'Yes, sir.'

'Sergeant?'

'Sir?'

'I'll lay you ten to one that the Mark Gleeson who lives in Courtfield Gardens won't be the white-skinned laddie who gave Corder the kiss of life at the health club.'

'Make it a thousand to one,' Robinson told him, 'and I might just take you on.'

'Well, let's not get cock-a-hoop,' Cheadle warned. 'Mustn't forget that if the milk-skinned laddie isn't Gleeson, we've learnt nothing Fred didn't want us to learn.'

'Except he likes classical music.'
'Opera House type, he would, wouldn't he?'

10

That night, Westbury hurried home from the Opera House. He hated all of the works of Donizetti, *Lucrezia Borgia* especially; and Covent Garden's current production of *Lucrezia* was exceptionally poor. He couldn't deny, however, that it wasn't from an opera he hated that he was fleeing, it was to a lair that obsessed him. Since Saturday, in fact, he'd found himself reluctant even to leave it.

'I'm becoming a hermit,' he told his reflection in the looking-glass. 'Like my stowaways.'

'Waiting for prey, or a mate?'

'A *mate*? I've had less sex the last three years than an anorexic's had hot dinners!'

'Your choice.'

'Her choice!'

'You should eat.'

'No time.'

Pouring himself a tumblerful of red wine, he crossed the hall to his study and sat in front of his computer.

Atrax Two continued
A few minutes after Corder left the changing room, I put his shirt in my bag and followed him up to the sun beds on the next floor. He was lying on his bed with the curtain drawn. The glare from the tubes made the curtain look very white. He was in cubicle 5: I was in cubicle 1.

I took my rubber gloves from my bag, put them on,

rang Reception and told the girl to turn on bed number one. The tubes lit up. I went into the cubicle, pulled down the lid of the sun bed, put my bag on top of it and stripped down to my shorts. But I left my boots on so I didn't leave footprints on the floor.

I took Corder's shirt from my bag, turned the shirt inside out and spread it across the lid.

I took the two stowaways from my bag. Each stowaway was in an oblong packet with the top stitched up: big stitches, but enough to stop either inmate getting out. The pockets were made with material I'd cut from the back of another Lacoste shirt, or rather a fake Lacoste I bought for six dollars in Bangkok. The genuine article costs £39, and I'd spent more than enough on the baronet already.

I laid one pocket on the inside-out back of Corder's shirt, half-way up the left seam. The other one I set aside, on top of the lid, about two feet to the right of the shirt.

I took the needle I'd pre-threaded with white cotton and stitched the pocket to the left seam of the shirt: big stitches from the top to the bottom. Then I stitched across the bottom of the pocket and up the other side to the top.

I cut the thread with my nail scissors and repeated the operation with the second pocket against the right seam.

If all this sounds too easy for words, *you* try making a couple of pockets, transferring a couple of scrabbling spiders into them, and stitching up the mouth of each pocket without getting bitten. And *you* try planning every move like I did.

I admit it was sheer coincidence that the day I decided to make enquiries about joining the health club, the guy ahead of me at Reception made sure everyone for miles around knew he was Sir Nicholas Corder, and that he came to the club for a sun bed and an aerobics class at the same time every Tuesday and Saturday, and that he'd belonged to the club for three years, so why was he always being asked what his name was and was he a member?

That was six months ago; but I didn't forget. Would you have remembered? When *you* realized that it was he who had to be the subject of Atrax Two, would you have remembered what days he went to the club? And what time?

Would you have checked, on the three Tuesdays before today, that he was still going to the club, hiring the sun bed and cavorting about in the midday aerobics class?

Would you have had the nerve to go into the club snack bar at half-past ten each of those three Tuesdays, order a coffee, sneak across the foyer into the changing room when the receptionist was busy, hide in the bog till eleven, open the door to the toilets just enough to spy on Corder, get to know his ritual, and lay your plans accordingly?

Would you have left the snack bar and taken a swift gander at the members' book when you saw a young guy about your size and height signing in, so you could give his name on June 9 when you had to be sure nothing would stop you carrying out your plan?

No, you wouldn't: so don't try telling me Atrax Two was easy.

But I digress: much as I want you to know everything, it's been a busy day, what with Corder and Donizetti, and I'm too knackered to bother editorializing.

I stayed in my sun bed cubicle until eleven thirty-five, then cut the big middle stitch on the top of each pocket, repacked my needle and thread and scissors, shoved my clothes into the bag, turned Corder's shirt right-side out and carried my bag and it (by the collar) down to the changing room.

I put Corder's shirt back where he'd left it, took off my rubber gloves and stashed all my gear under the bench the other side of the room.

The clock said eleven forty-three, so I took off my shorts and hid in the sauna.

A fat *nouveau riche* type tried to engage me in pseudo

sophisticated talk about the cuisine at the Connaught. I told him I ate take-aways and went for a shower.

He followed and kept looking at my body. Obviously fancied me, so I ruined his day by getting dressed (beanie, kerchief and all) and going into the gym to watch Corder aerobicking.

All went well for about twenty minutes, until he began to flag and I realized he was about to pack it in. Mind you, he'd probably had it anyway (the venom's effect becomes traumatic after ten minutes or so, and tears were already gushing from his eyes) but I couldn't take the risk of his chucking it in and calling a doctor.

So I caught his eye and sent him up something rotten: he went berserk.

But the girl taking the class nearly ruined it by deciding all was not well. She turned off the so-called music and everyone stopped leaping about. Except, fortunately, Nicky, who carried on like a drunken sailor.

Even so, when he did finally collapse, I wasn't sure he'd had it. He wasn't as strong as Mike Saxon, but he was bloody fit.

I'm very proud of what I did then: I pulled my beanie down to my eyebrows, hopped the fence and pretended to give him the kiss of life. Having stopped him breathing through his nose, I only pretended to breathe into his mouth. Inhaled and exhaled through my nose: and didn't take my mouth from his for at least a minute. What you might call an oral *coup de grâce*.

Next, to give him plenty of time to expire, I volunteered to ring for an ambulance. Went through all the motions, said all the right things, but actually didn't dial 999 and was only talking to my brilliant self and the dim receptionist.

After I'd hung up, I told her I was going outside because I felt queasy, and promptly headed off for Kensington Gardens.

I ditched Mike's beanie in the back of an open delivery

van. Phoned ITV from a call box. Dropped the red kerchief on the steps leading down into Marks and Sparks food department. Made a present of my rubber gloves to a playful dog. Went into the Gents in Kensington Gardens and changed out of my labourer's gear into beach shorts, a floral shirt and flip flops. Left my torn jeans in the Gents. Took out the wads of cotton wool I'd stuffed into my cheeks. Pulled off the tiny clump of hairs (black toothbrush bristles, actually) I'd glued between my eyebrows. Removed my tinted contact lenses and dropped them down the plughole. Washed off my tattoo. Shaved. Wet my hair and combed it. And left.

Ditched my grubby T-shirt in a gardener's wheelbarrow. Left my boots beside a drunk who was comatose under a tree. And caught a taxi home from the restaurant beside the Serpentine.

Told the driver I'd never swim there again: like immersing oneself in a chlorinated drain. He asked was I on holiday and I said no, I worked nights: as a musician at the Opera House. He said his daughter played the violin, maybe I'd give her some tips? I said sure, and gave him my name and telephone number. If anyone asks where I was between eleven and one thirty on June 9, I'll refer him to that taxi driver!

And if you're thinking the Serpentine alibi won't work because I must have left my fingerprints on the club railing, or Corder's nose, or the telephone; or that the forensic guys will find traces of my saliva on Corder's lips, you've got another think coming. I had my towel across the rail, I held the receiver in the towel, and I very tenderly wiped Corder's face and mouth clean when I reluctantly decided it was no use trying any longer to revive him.

I admit I almost made a mistake with the needle and thread and the towel (which I nicked from a hotel in Bangkok): took them home with me. But I've rectified that. Burnt the towel, and the thread from the needle, plus the cotton reel from which I took the thread, on a

66

bonfire of dead leaves in the incinerator: and shoved the needle in a mouldy orange which is now in the garbage can awaiting collection.

In other words, there's nothing left to connect me with the chubby-cheeked, blue-eyed, beetle-browed Cockney called Gleeson who bumped off Sir Nicholas Corder.

This doesn't mean I'm hoping the police won't find out it wasn't Gleeson. Of course they will. And it would take all the excitement out of the Series if they didn't. Naturally they'll check him out. But even if he hasn't got a water-tight alibi, they'll know he couldn't have got into the Opera House to kill Mike, isn't exactly the type to be doing entrechats on stage or playing piccolo in the pit. Could be a scene shifter, or course; but they'll soon discover he isn't.

So by tomorrow they'll be back looking for the elusive Mr X. And they'll soon realize there's a pattern to what they'll start calling my serial murders.

Then they'll stop relying on clues and start concentrating on the psychological profile of me that some professor or other will draw up, like they did for the Atlanta Child Killer, the Los Angeles Night Stalker and the British Rail Rapist; but it won't identify me because I'm not like any of them. The only way they'll identify me is by cracking the code of the Atrax Series and anticipating Atrax Four or Five.

If they do that, they stand a fair chance (and I'm being scrupulously fair) of being on the scene of my proposed crime ahead of me, and nabbing me before I can carry it out.

That's what makes the rest of this series so exciting. Well, not the rest of it: the final two fifths. They haven't a hope of preventing Atrax Three, of course; but that's the one that *should* tell them they're dealing with a brilliant logician not a random killer. They'll have to be quick, though: thirty days from now it'll all be over.

Well, if I was knackered when I started this thrilling

episode in the life of Christopher Westbury, I'm shattered now. It's 4.30 a.m. and my beauty sleep's gone for a Burton. So, in future, take it as written that, money being no object, I've long since acquired all the props I need for the next three jobs; and that I'll dispose of them just as efficiently as I've disposed of those I used for the first two jobs. In future, all I'll do is give you a run-down on how I did what to whom.

And by the way, the next guest on Westbury's *This Is Your Death* is the Right Honourable The Viscount Allison. He'll die on Sunday June 14.

11

Robinson had telephoned Cheadle at his home while Westbury was still reluctantly playing Act I of *Lucrezia Borgia*. For once the Chief Superintendent sounded happy to be dragged from his beloved telly.

'Gleeson isn't Fred,' Robinson announced.

'Never!' Cheadle responded.

'He was working all day on a King's Cross construction site. I've confirmed it with his foreman.'

'Anything else?'

'The spiders were originally in sewn pockets which had been loosely stitched inside the back of Corder's shirt. Corder wouldn't have felt anything unusual when he put his shirt on because the pockets were of the same material. The spiders would've felt something, though: and there was room for them to climb out and make enquiries as soon as Corder put his shirt on.

'Once he started exercising, half the stitches pulled out and the nasties were free to roam. Bit him either side of the kidneys. There's also a suspicion he was asphyxiated – whilst *in extremis*.'

'Which explains the mouth to mouth business,' Cheadle growled. 'What a ruthless, cocky little bastard this geezer is.'

'One thing puzzles me,' said Robinson.

'Thousands puzzle me.'

'What made you so certain Gleeson wasn't Gleeson?'

'Dame Lyndsay said Saxon wore a beanie. Fred was in Saxon's dressing-room – which was sealed first thing Sunday morning. The beanie wasn't. Obviously Fred nicked it. For his next murder.'

There was a long silence before Robinson asked, 'His *next* murder?'

'Why else would he have wanted to disguise himself?'

'Would a beanie have been enough?'

'Not when he intended letting dozens of club members have a look at him.'

'Oh!'

'Thought you had a lead, did you?'

'Fred has the most amazing blue eyes. Cornflower blue, one girl said: sapphire blue, according to another. Also, he's slightly chubby-cheeked, but unshaven, has eyebrows that meet, and a tattoo on his upper right arm.'

'A *tattoo*?'

'A woman's head: very sketchy and amateurish. A West Indian athlete phoned the Incident Room and said Corder quizzed him about it.'

'Corder quizzed Fred?'

'Fred was sitting quite close while Corder was stripping.'

'Cheeky sod.'

'Corder asked why the tattoo was unfinished and Fred replied, I quote, "Me gaol sentence wasn't long enough." '

'Another red herring!'

'The tattoo or the gaol sentence?'

'Both. So what we're looking for,' Cheadle summarized, 'is a *non*-blue-eyed, clean-shaven, milky-skinned young man with a clean record and features like James Dean, the youthful Dirk Bogarde and a pop singer called Stink.'

'Sting.'

'Well, I hate to admit it, but the moment's almost upon us when we'll have to go crawling to Professor Thingummy of Wherever for one of his psychic bleeding profiles.'

'That's not like you, sir.'

'Better to do it off me own bat than wait for You Know Who to order it. Don't want him taking us off the case, do we?'

'Might the professor's psychological profile not help us?'

'Only Fred'll help us. He's the one calling all the shots, demanding all our attention.'

'But wouldn't it help if we knew *why* he's demanding our attention?'

'Don't need a professor to tell us that: he's a nutter.'

'And nutters are still your cup of tea!'

To Robinson's surprise, Cheadle did not respond. 'Still there, sir?'

'Just wondering who's next on Fred's agenda: and when he's due for the chop.'

'Haven't the foggiest, have we?' Robinson responded, instantly regretting that he'd resorted to a Cheadlesque rhetorical question.

'Someone in the public eye,' said Cheadle. 'And soon. Time's the serial murderer's worst enemy.'

'Wasn't Jack the Ripper's.'

'Maybe *he* was dying too?'

'Fred's dying?'

'Aids, probably,' Cheadle diagnosed. 'Taking as many with him as possible.'

'Wouldn't need spiders to do that.'

'Doomed, then. Like Hitler. The Gotterwhatsit thing.'

'Dammerung syndrome,' Robinson couldn't resist supplying.

Smiling, Cheadle hung up.

*

The following morning, mindful of Robinson's unsolicited vote of confidence (which he shared) in his ability to unmask murderous nutters unaided by Professors of Applied Psychology, Cheadle sought an audience of that superior to whom he invariably referred as You Know Who. The purpose of the audience was to convince his superior that a psychological profile of Fred, were it to be leaked – and they always were – would prejudice the outcome of Operation Fang.

'Why?' demanded You Know Who.

Cheadle told him: and was relieved, but not surprised, to be told that he was probably right – which was another way of saying that if, in fact, he was wrong, none of the blame for the consequent cock-up would devolve upon You Know Who.

Or so Cheadle warned Robinson.

'Great!' said Robinson.

'Appreciate your loyalty,' said Cheadle. 'Course, if there *is* a cock-up, I'll blame you.'

'It's what I'm here for,' Robinson acknowledged. 'What now?'

'For you, toy time. For me, a little walk across the road: I want to get the feel of the Opera House.'

'Haven't forgotten next Tuesday, have you?'

'La Fille Mal Gardée? No, I hadn't forgotten' – and walked out of the Incident Room like a man whose two great passions in life were French and ballet.

Watching him go, Robinson smiled at the older man's ploys and foibles: his purported inability either to remember names or to understand anything more state of the art than a pencil sharpener; his passion for rhetorical questions; his ostentatious addiction to TV; and his carefully maintained image of lower middle-class, upper middle-aged philistinism.

It had taken Robinson almost a year to understand that behind the ploys and foibles sheltered an intensely private, childless, ungregarious policeman whose instinct it

71

was to reveal nothing of himself except his ability to outwit villains.

And it was only after they had worked together on six cases that Robinson learned that Cheadle invariably signalled the turning point in an enquiry by saying something atypical. Not the beginning of the end of the enquiry, just the turning point: or, as Churchill had put it after some great victory or other during World War Two, the end of the beginning.

And, atypically, Cheadle had just said '*La Fille Mal Gardée*?' So the beginning of Fred's vicious war had ended; but Robinson shrank from the realization that victory could not be won without further casualties.

Nor could he deny, as the morning's work proceeded, that the combined efforts of police officers, forensic scientists, laboratory technicians and computers had failed to unearth anything likely to bring the war against Fred to a swift conclusion.

Admittedly, three members of the orchestra and one of the stage hands had visited Australia in the past two years; but the stage hand had spent all his time with his married brother and sister in Perth – and there were no funnelwebs in Western Australia; one of the musicians had visited Melbourne, and a second had visited Adelaide, but all four funnelwebs removed from the bodies of Saxon and Corder belonged to the species *Atrax robustus*, which is found only in Sydney; and the cellist who had visited Sydney was never unaccompanied in the Opera House the night of the sixth of June.

Admittedly, also, minute traces of dead oak leaves, nylon thread and cotton had been found on the spiders' legs, and the contents of their guts had been examined; but the nylon came from Saxon's pouch and the cotton from the pockets sewn into Corder's shirt; and the contents of each gut had been reduced to liquid by the venomous juice with which the spiders had pre-digested them.

72

In short, there was forensic evidence available to convict the murderer once apprehended, but no evidence that would lead to his arrest.

In fact, unless he blundered or confessed – neither of which was likely – it seemed to Robinson that Fred's arrest would depend more on deduction than detection, than which nothing could better suit the talents of his sedentary superior.

'Probably wrap it all up sitting on his arse watching Wimbledon,' he told himself.

The thought did not displease him. Like a good tutor, Cheadle preferred to stimulate a dialogue rather than lay down the law. Robinson would always be grateful for the way Cheadle had taught him to think for himself.

'For example,' he found himself thinking, apropos of nothing at all, 'what's Fred feeding his spiders on?' – and rushed across the road to raise the point with Cheadle, who was sitting in solitary splendour in the middle of the front row of the Grand Tier of the Opera House.

'Sir,' he said, taking the seat next to Cheadle, 'the gen from Australia is that funnelwebs have a voracious appetite. Wasps, centipedes, millipedes, things like that. So what's Fred feeding his lot on?'

Cheadle, who had been lost in thought, turned his head slowly, gave Robinson a look of terrible disdain, turned slowly away again, and said, 'You just scared off the ghost. All my life I've wanted to see a ghost. This place has one; it was just about to join me; and now it'll never come back!' He peered up into the chandelier, as if it might have taken refuge there, then down into the orchestra pit, and finally at Robinson. 'You want to know where he's getting the wasps?'

'Yep.'

'Last wasp I saw was in the summer of – what year was it we had seventeen weeks' continuous sunshine and the government declared a drought? 1949?'

'I wasn't born until 1956.'

73

'Buys 'em, I suppose. Centipedes, you say?'

'Centipedes, millipedes, lizards, insects, small frogs.'

'Have the lads question every centipede shop about pale customers who look like Dean, Bogarde and Stink and hum classical music.' Staring down into the orchestra pit, he muttered, 'He's gotta be a musician.'

'Why?'

'Corder's shirt was booby trapped between eleven fifteen and eleven forty-five yesterday morning. From nine yesterday morning, all the stage hands and technicians were rebuilding and relighting a set that disintegrated during Monday's dress rehearsal. And from ten thirty until twelve thirty yesterday morning, all the dancers were doing a class.'

'Only three possibles in the orchestra,' Robinson reminded. 'And Holmes says they're all in the clear.'

'Which three?'

'One of the trumpeters, one of the cellists and the percussionist.'

Cheadle drummed his fingers on the arm rest. 'Don't tell me Fred's an usherette!'

'Holmes also says it's no one front of house.'

'Then we've still missed something,' said Cheadle, concentrating so fiercely that Robinson stayed silent. 'It's no use,' he said finally. 'I'm not thinking: I'm just pretending to.'

Robinson knew what was expected of him then. 'Maybe you should forget it for an hour of two?' he suggested. Cheadle ignored him. 'Fancy a cappuccino?' Cheadle shook his head. 'A drive round Hyde Park?' Cheadle looked tempted. 'Watch the Household Cavalry ride home?' Cheadle remembered the carnage inflicted on the Household Cavalry by an IRA bomb in 1983.

'I'm allergic to horses,' he said.

'A boat on the Serpentine then?'

'Good idea.'

Half an hour later, relaxed in the back of their hired

rowing boat, Cheadle spoke for the first time since their embarkation. 'Saxon was murdered on the sixth and Corder was murdered on the ninth. If the next celebrity's murdered on the *twelfth*, we've got ourselves a pattern.'

'And if the twelfth passes murderless?'

'Either Fred's a random killer or,' and Cheadle chose his words carefully, 'the pattern won't emerge until the fourth murder.'

Deep in thought, Robinson dug his oars into the muddy-looking water a dozen times, then asked, 'What makes you so certain there'll be more murders? And that they won't be random?'

'The effrontery of the man. He doesn't give a stuff that eventually we'll catch him. All he cares about is winning a loony game of his own invention, played in accordance with his own rules in front of a media audience of millions. He's obsessed.'

'With what?'

'You're the expert on hypotheses!'

Robinson shipped his oars. 'Saxon and Corder had nothing in common except their looks.'

'What about status?'

'Saxon was celebrated: Corder was notorious.'

'What's that tell us about Fred's obsession?'

'Only that it's directed indiscriminately at the famous and the infamous.'

'A grudge?'

'Well, obviously.'

'Why?'

Robinson scowled: Cheadle's technique suddenly seemed less Socratic than condescending – an impression in no way diminished by the fact that he had very pointedly begun to whistle 'Frankie and Johnny Were Lovers'.

'*She did him wrong?*' Robinson asked incredulously.

'Someone did. Someone celebrated. Or notorious.'

75

'Or handsome.'

'*And* handsome, possibly,' Cheadle qualified. 'Saxon and Corder weren't enviable on account of their handsomeness: they were enviable on account of their respective skills on the stage and in the sack.'

'Don't forget,' Robinson reminded, 'Fred's good-looking, too. He could be an actor *manqué* .'

'He fancies himself, that's for sure,' Cheadle agreed. 'Master of disguise, man of a thousand voices, all that crap. Doesn't realize he only gets away with it because no one knows what he looks like *un*disguised. Not even Alec Guinness in disguise can convince you he's not Alec Guinness. Why've you stopped rowing?'

'You wanted to talk.'

'I can talk while you row! What're we doing out here anyway?' He glared around the Serpentine as if it were the Atlantic. 'We're supposed to be on a murder enquiry, not a day trip to Knightsbridge.'

12

Acknowledging that the police would certainly, by now, have seen through his health club disguise, Westbury was applying another: lying on a sun bed, he was stoically acquiring a tan.

Not at the health club, of course; and not in one session. But by Saturday, after four sessions (in four different establishments) the paleskin who had showered under the eye of a pseudo gourmet would become a golden Adonis; and would remain golden until the tenth of July, when his work would be done.

He wasn't happy, though. All his life he'd avoided the sun: now he was sandwiched between two banks of it, like batter metamorphosing into a waffle.

Also, what were the police up to? He'd played fair by them, but they seemed unwilling to play fair by him. Nothing on *Crimestopper*: no interviews with the Detective Chief Superintendent leading the enquiry: no statement from Scotland Yard: not even an identikit drawing. Loads about Mike and the Bonking Baronet; even loads about funnelweb spiders; but nothing about him.

Well, not about *him*, because no one knew who he was: about who he might be, though, and how daring he was. He was entitled to that at least.

Should he drive on Sunday, or go by train? Car'd be easier; but which car? And what if he had an accident?

'What if the train's derailed?' countered the voice in his head. 'You've made your plan: stick to it.'

He trusted his inner voice. Always positive, supportive, wise. Solomon, he called it. Unlike the voice in the looking-glass, which he'd christened the Devil's Advocate, and the voice from the TV set, which he called the Agent Provocateur. He hated the Agent Provocateur. Only way to silence him was keep the TV on. Let the screen go blank for a second and the Provocateur's voice came through loud and clear.

Don't think about him. Think about things you hate. 'I hate girls who wear sun-glasses on top of their hair; and . . . and guys who push their spectacles back with a fingertip along the bridge of the nose; and . . . grown men on skateboards; and West Indians sporting stolen Walkmans; and junk mail; and Donizetti; and, come to that, half the so-called greats since Haydn who was the daddy of them all; and ECT; and medication; and sun bed goggles, which make me feel bug-eyed like an insect; and Father, the God of Wrath. Only helpful thing the God of Wrath ever did was join British Air. But getting you discounts didn't mean he loved you. And his ex-wife . . .'
Westbury never referred to his remarried mother as anything but his father's ex-wife – except when he called her

a harlot, a Kiwi reincarnation of the Whore of Babylon: aka the Whore of Wellington.

Tears of self-pity welled out of Westbury's goggled eyes. 'None of us chose our parents, of course: but really! One a nymphomaniac, the other a bigot. And Uncle Paul a traitor. Well, thank God for Tuinal.'

Silly of him to have been conned into thinking Uncle Paul and Aunt Deborah loved him: they'd no sooner welcomed him into their Holland Park home (after the God of Wrath had despatched him from Wellington to England) than they packed him off to boarding school. Where he'd survived by becoming a manipulative little flirt and an angelic-looking tart.

Protection was all he'd wanted: protection while he played his violin, instead of sport: protection from other minders. Only twice had the price been sex; and each too-ardent protector had been expelled within hours of his night of indecent passion.

After the second expulsion, he'd been nicknamed Poison Ivy: and left alone to pursue his own indecent passion.

'*Nemo me impune lacessit*,' he assured the upper bank of flaring tubes. 'Proved it then: proving it now. Prove it to the judges of that Young Musician of the Year contest, too, if I had the time.'

With a loud clunk, as if something had broken, the sun bed switched itself off and Westbury found himself lying in a pool of sweat. Removing his goggles and raising the lid, he slid off the perspex bed, stood upright and stripped off his sweat-sodden underpants. The skin he bared was white: the rest was salmon pink.

He stared at his reflection in the looking-glass with pleasure. Not only was he well proportioned, he suddenly realized, he was a different person. Gone was the romantic aesthete: in his place stood a hunk.

'You tumescent beast!' he rebuked himself light-heartedly – and for once in his life felt clear-headed and devoid of malevolence. It was so strange an experience that he looked at his reflection a second time: and again found himself acceptable.

'So what the hell have you been playing at?' he asked himself aloud; and, not bothering to shower, dressed and hurried home. He'd kill the Task Force and its reserves; clean up the hearth; delete the Atrax Series; get rid of his remaining props; resign from the orchestra; start practising again; hire the Wigmore Hall; give his first recital; become a virtuoso, marry and have kids; and forget the past.

'Forget Saxon and Corder?' the Devil's Advocate queried as he entered his drawing-room.

For a moment he was too disconcerted to answer; but eventually Solomon did it for him. 'You think Saxon wanted to go on and on until his knees or his ankles or his back gave out and all he could dance was one of Cinderella's Ugly Sisters? You think Corder should've been allowed to go on glamorizing the dangers of promiscuity?'

'You think the Law'll accept that as an excuse for murder?' jeered the Provocateur.

Desperate to retain his new-found innocence, Westbury rushed to the TV and switched it on. Instantly, Bugs Bunny silenced the Provocateur.

'It's too late, Chris,' the Advocate murmured as their eyes met. 'If only you'd taken your medication.'

'If only, if only,' Westbury shouted, renouncing innocence. Innocence meant inertia: inertia meant condoning. A great injustice had been done: a great talent had been destroyed: a great love had been denied: and inertia was not the answer. The fourteenth Viscount Allison of Elmsmere, whose reprieve had seemed imminent, would still be executed on Sunday.

Unlike the previous thirteen Viscounts Allison, all of whom had been honourable, and most of whom had been gallant, the fourteenth was a shit. Cad, bounder, scumbag and parasite were just a few of the names fellow peers had called him; but it was the newly appointed Bishop of Southwark who had hit the nail on the head.

'I can forgive Allison for being ugly, vulgar, vicious and obscene,' he had said. 'What I can't forgive is that he's also an absolute shit.'

'Bit mealy mouthed, aren't you, Southwark?' challenged an agnostic peer recently ennobled for his services to literature. 'Why not admit that the man's a perfect cunt?'

'I don't deny it,' the Bishop had said. 'But of the two,' jabbing the agnostic's chest with a proselytizing finger, 'an absolute shit is by far the worse.'

Their Lordships debated this premise with zest and erudition; but when they realized that to oppose the Bishop was to support the hack, they voted unanimously in favour of shit.

The fourteenth Viscount had inherited the Allison title because his two cousins, the twelfth and thirteenth Viscounts respectively, had honoured the family tradition of dying for Crown and Country.

The first was killed by the French in the Low Countries, the fourth by the Americans at Yorktown, the fifth by the French at Waterloo, the sixth by the Russians at Balaclava, the seventh by the Boers on an anonymous veldt, the eighth by the Turks at Suvla Bay, the ninth by the Germans outside Tripoli, the tenth by Chinese bandits in Malaya, the twelfth by the Argentinians on the Falklands and the thirteenth (younger and only brother of the twelfth) by the IRA in Ulster.

The next in line for the title had turned out to be a

twenty-nine-year-old Canadian called Harvey Naismith – a fact that had left the British aristocracy quite unperturbed. Other Canadians had come their way, then died and been forgotten: this one would too.

The fact that this one was then tracked down to Melbourne, Australia, had worried them rather more. Melbourne they knew to be populated entirely by Irish hooligans who treated British Prime Ministers with monstrous disrespect.

Admittedly, a dissenting minority insisted that actually Melbourne was populated entirely by Greeks, and that the hubris of the Prime Minister in question had positively invited disrespect; but when it was also learnt that Naismith was the lead singer of a pop group called the Phallic Cymbals, a shudder of distaste had run through every rank of the United Kingdom's peerage.

Its only hope then was that, when he realized that his inheritance had been reduced by death duties to little more than a stately home and a massive overdraft, Harvey would prefer to remain in hooligan Melbourne entertaining its millions of Celtic-Greeks. But that hope had proved short-lived. As a patriotic Canadian (a race that has no time for British titles) Harvey hadn't been able to wait to become a viscount; and as a hugely rich purveyor of pop, he had instantly recognized his debt-ridden inheritance as an excellent investment. Not only would its park provide a splendid venue for his concerts, its debts would be tax deductible.

It was when these concerts became a fixture in England's alternative cultural calendar that the fourteenth Viscount became (in the eyes of the aristocracy, the Church, and every decent dirty-minded Briton) a shit.

Because the music he wrote was, of its genre, exceptionally good, and the lyrics were, by any standards, exceptionally wicked, he attracted vast audiences.

Because he purported to write songs that defended the rights of every conceivable minority, he commanded the support of blacks, punks, junkies, gays, flat-earthers, Social Democrats, nuclear disarmers, the disabled and the unemployed.

Because his forte was the *double entendre*, all the lyrics he wrote purportedly defending the rights of blacks, punks, junkies, gays, flat-earthers, Social Democrats, nuclear disarmers, the disabled and the unemployed could equally be interpreted as viciously attacking them, and he was adored by all those literate, élitist and malicious enough to delight in the inability of their social inferiors to understand that their supposed champion was really sending them up.

And because he combined cynicism with depravity (his publicists claimed he'd screw anything that moved – and many that didn't) his concerts also attracted coachloads of Rugby hearties, delinquent Round Tablers and smutty undergraduates.

Harvey Naismith's story was well known to Westbury, who was sitting in his study rehearsing in his mind all that he must do on Sunday. He had just returned from his third session on a sun bed. He was now lightly but unarguably tanned. Tomorrow he would go on the stronger bed – from which he would emerge, he had been assured, looking as if he'd spent a fortnight in St Tropez. Thereafter, until the tenth of July, he'd simply top it up every eight or nine days.

He felt almost sorry for the police. At this stage in the Series, they couldn't really be expected to have solved the problem he'd set them; but already the tabloid press had begun to scream about the failure of a certain Chief Superintendent Cheadle either to make an arrest or to issue the usual statement.

There was a photograph of the Chief Superintendent in the *Sun*. Peering at it, Westbury decided that he deserved a worthier opponent. A few days before or after Atrax

Four, their duel should begin: a battle of wits and words that would culminate either in his arrest or in Atrax Five: but this Cheadle looked a plodder, and plodders brought the best out of no one.

Cheadle scowled at Robinson. 'What's the little monkey up to?' he demanded.

Uncertain whether or not Cheadle meant him to regard the question as rhetorical, Robinson equivocated. 'Sixty-two and a half hours between the first and the second, sir': if the pattern had been *strictly* chronological, the third would've have happened at about three o'clock this morning.'

'If it's not strictly chronological, how can it be a pattern?'

'Maybe Fred looks at it differently. First murder, any time Saturday, two days off: second murder any time Tuesday: two days off: third murder, any time Friday.'

'You're saying his pattern is two days off between each murder?'

'Could be: which gives him – ' he looked at his watch – 'eleven hours before Friday ends and Saturday begins.'

'And if he hasn't killed by midnight?'

'There may not *be* a pattern.'

'There has to!' Cheadle shouted. 'Fred's not randomly killing prostitutes, or children, or women walking along at night: he's ritually killing well-known men who have nothing in common.'

'Assuming you're right,' and Robinson looked unconvinced, 'the pattern doesn't have to be a murder every third day: it can progress.'

'Like those find-the-next-number problems they used to set at school?'

'In pre-pocket calculator days,' Robinson agreed.

'Couldn't ever do 'em.'

Robinson refrained from comment: but Cheadle's mind

had already moved elsewhere. 'Down to us, now,' he said.

All the statements were in; all the passports issued to Opera House personnel had been inspected; every detail of Saxon's private life, and Corder's, had been scrutinized; every call to the Incident Room had been followed up; nothing that Forensic had done (and it had done everything imaginable) led anywhere; all the musicians had alibis confirmed by other musicians; and Holmes had suggested nothing that he himself hadn't considered and rejected.

'Funny expression, "down to us",' he mused. 'When I was your age, things were "up" to us. Then overnight, for "up" we had to read "down". Same with sex. Nooky was naughty and blokes bunking up together was illegal when I was a boy. Then both became compulsory. And now neither's advisable. So how come Corder's become famous by bonking?'

'With the most beautiful women in the world,' Robinson qualified.

'Why'd they pick *him*?'

'Maybe he was good at it.'

'Then why was he always a one-night stand? More to the point, why did Fred pick a victim who was famous only for bonking? He could have picked someone as legitimately famous as Saxon: an actor, or Terry Wogan, or Stink. Why'd he settle for a bonker? And if a bonker was what he wanted, why settle for someone who had it off, according to his diaries, only once every three weeks and even then failed to persuade any of his partners to come back for more?'

'Are you suggesting Fred chose Corder because he was a millionaire?'

'Two a penny, millionaires.'

'A baronet?'

'Crossed me mind. Then I remembered Saxon wasn't a

bonker, or a millionaire, or a baronet; and Corder wasn't an artist, or a complaisant husband, or a legitimate celebrity; so what *are* the criteria that make anyone eligible for Fred's favours?'

'Well, I hate to admit it,' Robinson sighed, 'but I hope we find out tonight.'

By the time midnight came, Westbury had done nothing more criminal than disregard Sir Leon's tempi three times during that evening's performance of *Lucrezia Borgia*. He hadn't planned it, and he knew that he would almost certainly be sacked because of it, but maybe that was no bad thing: it would remove him from the scene of his original crime – which must soon become the focal point of the Plodder's investigation. And even though Gavin Wilson, his cellist alibi, had gratefully accepted his suggestion that it would be unwise to admit that he'd left the wings and gone for a beer during the disco scene, so why not let him, Chris, say they'd watched it together, from beginning to end – even so, it might not be a bad idea to allow himself to be removed from the focal point of the investigation.

That very afternoon, in fact, one of Cheadle's minions had telephoned and asked him to bring his passport to the station and make a statement. Just a formality. Everyone was being asked to co-operate. Most had done so already.

Naturally, he had complied: and the detective had thanked him for being so helpful, apologized for inconveniencing him, assured him that he would be bothered no further and complimented him on his tan.

'Don't get a tan like that in this country!' he'd said. 'Where've you been?'

It had been so clumsily done that Westbury had almost laughed: instead, he had replied, 'The back garden!' And even as he said it, he had thought, 'I daren't *resign* from the orchestra; but there's no reason why I shouldn't get myself sacked!'

No sooner thought than done: thrice during that evening's performance he had drawn furious glances with Sir Leon: and after the performance, in Bronowski's dressing-room, he had deliberately made matters worse.

'You know why you're here,' Bronowski had said. 'Why'd you do it?'

Westbury was pleased with his reply, which had combined musicianship with insolence. 'Sir Leon,' he had said, 'your phrasing in two of the passages where I offended was boring; and your tempo in the third was over-indulgent. Fifty years ago, Lily Pons may have been allowed to keep the orchestra waiting half a minute while she prepared herself for her high E flats, but today's divas know better – because today's maestri don't let them get away with it! As a musician, it vexed me that you were letting Madame Ouspenskaya get away with it: and as one whom you were supposedly conducting, it irked me that you weren't getting the best out of Donizetti's admittedly banal score.'

Expecting to be fired then and there, he had been surprised when Bronowski announced that dismissal was too serious a decision to be taken in the heat of the moment. 'Come back at seven tomorrow,' he had said. And then he had leant forward and, with every appearance of concern, had asked, 'Are you all right, Christopher?'

'Fit as a fiddle,' he had answered: but the play on words had escaped Bronowski. 'Why? Don't I look it?'

'I can see how you look, Christopher,' Bronowski had replied, 'I asked how you were.'

'You're too kind,' he had answered – to prove that one didn't need a title to have class – and had left for home.

Arrived there, and avoiding even the briefest eye-contact with the Advocate, switching on the television to jam even the most determined transmission from the Provocateur, he sat in his armchair with his customary tumblerful of red wine in his right hand and the bottle on the floor beside him.

He supposed he should eat; but he wasn't hungry.

Writing up his diary, he wondered how Bronowski could avoid sacking him; not that he cared – even though he'd planned the Series on the assumption that he would be at the Opera House throughout.

'So why'd you go and gild the lily?' a voice demanded. He wasn't sure whose it was. Uncle Paul always said what he heard wasn't the voice of another party – typical lawyer: party of the third part and all that – it was simply the other half of an interior dialogue.

He'd meant well, of course. Unlike the God of Wrath, who just stated categorically there were no such things as Voices and anyone – Jesus Christ, Joan of Arc *or* Christopher Westbury – who said there were was barking mad!

'I said – ' the unidentifiable voice insisted.

'Heard you!' Westbury interrupted. 'Don't go on about it!'

In a way, though, he *had* gilded the lily. He'd Atraxed Saxon exactly as planned. Then hurled an expensive glass into the fireplace, thereby creating an unplanned precedent. He'd planned a campaign around the demands of his profession; and then, on the spur of the moment, engineered his dismissal.

'To give myself more time,' he told himself. But he didn't any longer need more time. Between Saxon and Corder, he had; but between the Viscount and Atrax Four and Atrax Five there was almost too much time. Nothing he could do about that, though: the rules demanded it.

He supposed he'd had a reason for provoking Bronowski; for the life of him he couldn't any longer justify it. Same with that business of hopping over the health club fence and faking the kiss of life. That hadn't ever been part of his plan.

Had he jeopardized the whole Atrax plan by kissing Corder and insulting Bronowski?

Gnawing at his left thumbnail, he tried to ponder the question: but was too exhausted. So, laying his diary aside, he drained his glass, and took glass and bottle to bed, promising never to gild lilies again.

13

Saturday the thirteenth of June was an uneasy day for both Westbury and Cheadle. For Cheadle because there was nothing he could do but wait: for Westbury because Sunday's plan (which was far more complex than either the preceding Tuesday's or Saturday's) seemed to him to become less foolproof by the hour.

Also there was the matter of tonight's interview with Sir Leon. If he was fired, which seemed inevitable, he feared it would draw Cheadle's attention to him.

In the event, Bronowski let him off with a warning: and Westbury, deciding that this was a favourable omen, relaxed.

Cheadle, on the other hand, grew so tense as the day progressed that he only became aware of the tennis being televised live from Queens when the BBC interrupted it to cross to Royal Ascot. He could think while tennis was on: horses he found most distracting.

During each race, therefore, he was on the phone: to the Incident Room, to Robinson, to Forensic. But Fred continued to lie low; and clues as to his identity continued to be unforthcoming. Cheadle sat up until midnight, and then rang Robinson again. The live-in girlfriend answered.

'May I speak to Derek?' Cheadle asked, deliberately not identifying himself.

'Of course, Chief Superintendent,' she said; and not even bothering to lower her voice, called, 'For you, darling.'

Cheadle could never get used to Robinson being a darling. He himself was only a dear. And everyone was a dear to Mrs Cheadle.

'*Yes*, sir?' Robinson said, so briskly that Cheadle decided he'd been asleep.

'He's had *four* days off now,' Cheadle complained. 'What I want to know is, if he kills again tomorrow – '

'You think that's likely?'

'Won't be doing anything else on a Sunday, will he? So if the third murder takes place tomorrow, four clear days after the second, which was two clear days after the first, does that mean he's planned the fourth murder for six clear days after the third?'

'Not necessarily – '

'I know,' Cheadle pre-empted him. 'Four isn't only two plus two, it's also two multiplied by two. So the interval between Murders Three and Four could be either four days plus two, which is six, or four days multiplied by two, which is eight.'

'Or,' Robinson added, 'four days *multiplied* by four, which is sixteen.'

'Why?'

'Because four isn't only two plus two, or two multiplied by two, it's also two squared!'

'You telling me that if Fred's planning five murders, the interval between the fourth and fifth could be – what's sixteen squared?'

'Two hundred and fifty-six, sir.'

There was a brief silence while Cheadle added ten sixteens, which were a hundred and sixty, to six sixteens, which were ninety-six. 'You're right,' he said. 'And that's too long. If it happens tomorrow, we'll work on the assumption that the pattern's either two, four, six, eight *ad nauseam*, or two, four, eight, sixteen *ad nauseam*.'

'Much as I hated saying it before, I'm going to say it again: I hope it *is* tomorrow.'

'You sound worried,' Cheadle prompted.

'Two, four, six, eight and so on: or two, four, eight, sixteen and so on: they're the *simple* patterns. But if the first two intervals turn out to be two and *five* days or two and six, or seven, or whatever – predicting the progression will blow our minds.'

'Blown mine already,' Cheadle grunted. '*And* they'd blow his. He's not going to risk ruining his scenario because he can't remember whether he's supposed to strike next on September the thirtieth or October the first.'

'But what if the next murder *doesn't* happen tomorrow?' Robinson persisted.

'You'll know I've been looking for a pattern that never existed.'

'At the risk of driving you mad, will you tell me again why you're so positive there's a pattern?'

'Look,' Cheadle obliged, 'the least likely place for Fred to have murdered Saxon was the stage of the Opera House; and the least likely weapon for him to have used was a couple of Aussie spiders. The whole thing was so elaborate, ingenious. Not one murder in a thousand is elaborate and ingenious. But having committed his first elaborate murder on Saturday, Fred committed his second on Tuesday.

'Why? When he could have bumped off Corder any Tuesday or Saturday between the sixth of June and doomsday, why'd he push himself to do it only *two days* after he'd bumped off Saxon?

'Seemed to me, either he must have been in a frenzy, or he must have had a schedule. But frenzied killers don't wait two days to pick off their victims, and they don't use spiders: they use sub-machine-guns and mow their victims down a dozen at a time.'

'Sounds logical,' Robinson acknowledged.

'Well, we'll soon know. But if tomorrow proves me

wrong, I'm asking You Know Who to take me off the case.'

The following morning, Westbury was awakened by his alarm clock. Like most night workers, he loathed the hours between dawn and noon, and his clock said five.

'Sparrow fart,' he groaned, quoting his uncle, whose verbal idiosyncrasies had included 'chicken foundry' for any of Colonel Sanders' establishments, 'Buggerlugs' for any of his intimates, 'Fowl's-Bowels' for any civil servant, and 'sparrow fart' for any time before breakfast.

Then he remembered that Uncle Paul was dead, and why the alarm had gone off at 5 a.m. It was Sunday the fourteenth of June: the third of his five big days.

In a way, the most significant of them – although that depended largely on Chief Superintendent Cheadle. If he continued to plod, Atrax Three would be wasted on him, Atrax Four would mean nothing to him, and Atrax Five would become a piece of cake. Which was not what he'd planned: what he'd planned was a race against time.

While he shaved (just once over, lightly: he'd have a close one late in the afternoon) he recited the day's programme. 'Drive to Hampshire: back to London to shower, shave, dress and put everything in the car: arrange lighting and sound effects: drive to Elmsmere House: bang the Phallic Cymbals: drive back to Holland Park.

'Yes,' he said, stooping to rinse his face. Straightening, he towelled himself vigorously and applied Colgate to his toothbrush.

'Just stay cool, stick to the plan, avoid any flourishes, and you'll be home and dry,' he thought – or Solomon told him. He wasn't sure which and didn't care anyway.

As he walked from the bathroom to his bedroom, he noticed how dusty the house had become. Aunty Deb'd have a fit – if she hadn't been cremated. Gliding at her age!

Uncle Paul and Aunty Deb, the only parents he'd ever had: and he, after their beastly Simon had overdosed on heroin, the only son they'd ever had. Mind you, they hadn't bought *him* a flat like they had Simon. Aunty Deb's fault. 'He's better with us,' he'd heard her tell Uncle Paul.

Pity about Uncle Paul: always so quirky and irreverent. And solicitous! He hated solicitude.

'I honestly think it's for the best,' widowed Uncle Paul had croaked, his skeletal fingers plucking at the bed-spread, his fleshless face a travesty of concern. 'A spell in hospital till you're yourself again. Then you can make a fresh start. Here – ' gesturing feebly to indicate the house beyond the bedroom that had become his world. 'Or in Simon's flat. Both be yours. Car'll be yours.' He loved his car: even kept it in a rented garage. 'Everything yours. Forgive me?'

'Of course, Uncle,' he'd said. 'Now, how about a nice cup of tea?'

'Please.'

So he'd brewed him a nice mug of tea (strong, black and sugarless, just the way he liked it: plus six Tuinal tablets, to which he'd probably not have taken exception even if he had been aware of them) and, strong arm supporting frail shoulders, he'd held the mug to his uncle's lips, sip after sip. And had made him comfortable. And watched him die.

It had only taken a few seconds to wipe the bottle, wrap Uncle's hand round it and slide it under the pillow. It had taken no longer to impress the prints of Uncle's left hand over his own on the mug.

The coroner had declared Uncle's overdose 'accidental': Uncle's executor had informed him that he was 'now a wealthy young man': the private GP who'd been treating him had sold his practice and retired to a villa in Tuscany: and nobody since had tried to section him.

But fearful lest his uncle had talked to Carmen, the Spanish daily, about the plot he'd hatched with the GP, he had sacked her immediately after the funeral.

He'd planned to find another cleaner, but hadn't – because of the stowaways. Ignoring the upstairs rooms, he'd hoovered and dusted only the drawing-room, the bathroom, the study and his bedroom. And had polished nothing. The house smelt musty, and looked drab.

Not that it mattered. No one ever came into it: not even the old biddy in the basement. Let her get so much as a toe in the door, she'd be dropping in day and night.

Maybe he should Tuinal her.

Plenty of it around. Small brown bottles of it in Uncle's sock drawer, the upstairs medicine cabinet, the back of the fridge and the desk, behind a packet of Aunty Deb's yellowing love letters to Uncle Paul.

Obviously the old boy'd been determined never to return to Bed Pan Alley. Nice to have been able to lend him a hand.

'Lend A Friend A Hand' had been one of Harvey's chart-topping singles at the height of the Aids epidemic. Ostensibly composed to extol the virtues of platonic love, it was actually a brilliantly crafted piece of musical and lyrical porn – as was its follow-up, 'Two Heads Are Better Than One'.

'Well, enjoy it while you can,' Westbury urged the absent Harvey Naismith, 'cos by the time I'm through with you tonight, you're gonna wish you'd been born anyone but heir to the thirteenth Viscount Allison.'

15

Dusk had fallen, the sky was clear, a capacity audience packed the grassy arena and the Phallic Cymbals were in captivating form.

In addition to Harvey, there was a group of four, each recruited for his looks as much as his musicianship. They were unusually costumed, theatrically groomed and erotically choreographed.

The marble stage was devoid of the usual pop concert clutter; and the set, which combined ambiguous Corinthian pillars with explicit Greek statuary, was so lit as to make it a classically decadent folly and a gateway to Elmsmere Park.

Because he lacked the splendid physique of each of his supporting Cymbals, Harvey's costume was designed to conceal rather than reveal, flatter rather than enhance. Where they projected virility, he exuded satyriasis. While each of them wore a white Cossack blouse and white linen breeches with a black Cossack belt and black Cossack boots, his blouse and breeches were of pale blue chiffon, and his pale blue belt and boots were both of the softest leather.

The thin blouse, tightly cinched at the waist, hung loosely from his broad chest, disguising the flab on his rib cage; the gauzy breeches, tightly gartered below the knee, and clinging to his buttocks, hung loosely around his unmuscular thighs and transformed each pelvic thrust into a pendulous caress. The soft boots made his sloppy calves look sculpted, and their soft soles enabled him to pirouette in a way that made the gauzy fabric cling and set the female fans shrieking.

His audience had deployed itself in sectors, like the strata in a rock, the punks closest to the stage, behind them the blacks, behind them the gays, and behind them the gloaters – débutantes, undergraduates, Sloane Rangers, Hooray Henries, racists and sexists.

Each group stood where it stood because that was where it preferred to stand, making its way there as soon as it climbed out of its coaches or cars, or off its motor cycles.

Harvey had observed the phenomenon at every concert: and had long since rationalized it. Because they wanted to grope him (a practice he did not discourage) the punk girls dragged their boyfriends to the foot of the stage. Because they wanted to distance themselves from white performers, but not be relegated to the rear of the auditorium, the blacks chose the second stratum. Because they wanted the best view of the Cymbals, the gays chose the higher ground of the third stratum. And because they wanted to look down on those he maligned, the gloaters stood at the back.

As to the latter, however, his rationalization did him less than justice. Certainly the gloaters wanted to look down upon those he derided; but what made that possible was the clarity of his North American enunciation of lyrics that combined the complex rhymes of an Irving Berlin with the staccato tongue-twisters of a W. S. Gilbert. To miss a syllable of a Naismith lyric was probably to misconstrue a sentence: to miss a word was almost certainly to misunderstand the song: and no one but Harvey had ever been able to do justice to his lyrics.

Tonight he was enjoying himself. The gays and the gloaters were quick to take each point; the blacks were responding to the music and choreography with a fervour that galvanized the Cymbals; and the punks, shedding their customary air of lethargic anarchy, had joined him in a journey to a sexual Wonderland.

Fantasy, however, was not really what he had in mind. Fantastic though his audience was, the talent was tardy and abysmal. Only three offers so far: and the best of them like something by the Elephant Man out of Dracula's Daughter.

But there was still time: he still hadn't given them the song that never failed.

More fun to pull one first, though.

Then keep her on a string; sing 'Two Heads' and make her fight her way through a cordon of shrieking harridans to get what she wanted.

One like her'd do!

In a way, she was grotesque. Purple lips etched in black. Scarlet eyelids etched in black. An inverted green triangle suspended from each cheekbone. The rest of the face, beige. Each eyebrow a disdainful circumflex half an inch higher than eyebrows ever grew. Jet black hair cut short at the back and sides: cerise on top, where it had been swept upwards into a feathery comb.

But the eyes were clear, the bones good, the small teeth white behind the purple lips, and her expression self-assured.

Not even her black uniform of leather jacket, woollen T-shirt, short skirt, unflattering tights, flat-heeled boots and mittens denied her individuality. Not even her chains, studded dog collar and wristband convinced him that bondage was her scene. A punk with class, he thought. Now that could really be something.

At last her eyes met his, and he sang for her: sang dirty lines to which she responded with a small smile and a mocking circumflex.

Reaching inside her jacket, she drew out a half-bottle of whisky. As he thrust his pelvis at her, she raised the bottle to him: and drank from it. Pirouetting, he allowed his head to jerk, signalling her to join him.

When he faced her again, she was looking at him thoughtfully, still undecided. He smiled at her, and jerked his head a second time.

Shrugging, she picked her way through four rows of punks until she stood immediately in front of the stage.

Making no effort to climb on to it, she raised a black-mittened hand.

Stooping, he seized her by the hand and wrist and hoisted her on to the stage. As her body swung against his, she thrust one leg between his legs, tight black wool between loose blue chiffon; and evading his attempt to kiss her, whispered, 'Two heads are better than one.'

'Where?' he whispered back, swirling her round as if they were Astaire and Rogers.

'Behind that pillar!' she dared him.

'Baby, this is England,' he protested. 'How about my dressing-room? End of this set?'

'I'll follow you. And I'll join you when you're stripped.'

'You're on.'

'I know.' And, prising his hands from her buttocks, jumped off the stage.

He swung instantly into 'Two Heads Are Better Than One' and almost at once the stage was swarming with clamorous, amorous, groping, groupie punks.

It was not difficult to incorporate them into his act: he had done it a hundred times in a dozen countries. Making two of them kneel before him, he grabbed a head in each hand and thrust his pelvis into them, singing the words that matched the deed, dismissing rival supplicants for his simulated favours, inviting his audience to share whatever it was they thought he was purveying.

At the end of the number he walked slowly between the pillars, past the statues of ancient fertility gods, through a cloud of dry ice and out of sight. Taking the steps down from the stage two at a time, he ran towards a caravan parked between two ancient oaks.

The security man assigned to guard the caravan stepped from the shadows. 'Evening, my lord. Fabulous show.'

'Watch it from the front, then,' Harvey told him.

'Thank you, my lord.'

He headed off smartly. His lordship got very pissed off if you embarrassed the incoming crumpet.

And if you frightened it off, he fired you.

Harvey watched him go, then turned to look for the girl with the purple lips. She was strolling languidly toward him, but halted when she saw him waiting: and stared at him. Obediently, he let himself into his caravan, left the door ajar and tore off his clothes – first his soft leather boots, then the garters, then the belt, then the blouse and finally the breeches.

'Lie on the bunk,' she whispered through the doorway, 'and turn off the light.'

He lay naked in darkness.

Her silhouette filled the doorway.

'Don't touch me yet,' she whispered, sitting on the bunk beside him. 'I'll tell you when.'

She took the bottle from her jacket and unscrewed the cap. 'Drink?'

'Couple of those and I'm anyone's.'

'You're mine already' – running her fingers down his belly. He groaned and gulped the Scotch.

'I want to kiss your back,' she announced.

He turned on to his front and she kissed the small of his back.

He groaned again and finished the whisky. 'Do what you want with me,' he sighed. 'I'm all yours.'

'Then lie just like that so I can look at you while I get my gear off,' she ordered. 'Know what I'm gonna do then?'

'Tell me!'

She bent down and whispered in his ear. 'Oh, Gard!' he shouted.

He heard her unzipping her jacket: heard the clinking of her chains: heard her humming: heard her moving around, taking her time, making herself at home: and finally, shockingly, heard her say, 'Sorry, Harvey, I've changed my mind: you're not my type.'

Rearing up, he was just in time to see the door close behind her. Rushing to the window, he watched her stroll languidly back the way she had come. Snapping on the light, he dragged his blouse over his head, his breeches up his legs, a garter up to each knee and his boots on to his feet. Cinching his blouse tightly under his flabby abdomen, he stamped back to the stage.

As he reappeared between the pillars, his drummer, who loathed him, gave him a friendly smile and mouthed, 'How was it?'

'Fan-tastic,' Harvey mouthed back.

The Cymbals brought their own composition to an abrupt conclusion and struck up a Naismith perennial. The crowd roared: and Harvey resumed his performance.

Striding the stage, gyrating, thrusting and pirouetting, he worked his audience into a state of hysteria. He knew they wouldn't let him go until he'd given them all their favourites: that he wouldn't stop until he'd pulled another bird.

The sweat poured from him. His costume clung so tightly it looked like peeling skin. Tears began to gush from his eyes.

16

Cheadle barely managed to conceal his delight when a Sussex Chief Superintendent telephoned to tell him there had been a third funnelweb murder.

The victim, thirty-one-year-old Viscount Allison, also known as Harvey Naismith, lead singer of the Phallic Cymbals, had died in the caravan which was his dressing-room only minutes after giving a concert in the grounds of Elmsmere House.

A girl who had been in the caravan with him at the time of his death had raised the alarm. She was still being questioned.

A second girl had visited him in the caravan half an hour earlier: for sex, according to the Phallic Cymbals' drummer. Witnesses had given a detailed description of her, but she had not, as yet, been located.

Four other girls had been in close proximity to the deceased while he was performing. Arrangements had been made to intercept them when the coaches on which they were believed to be travelling reached their various destinations – London, Bristol, Birmingham, Oxford.

All six girls were punks.

Two spiders had been discovered in the deceased's calf-length boots.

The Sussex Constabulary and CID would collaborate with Cheadle's team in London: link up their computers, pass on anything from Forensic, and track down as many as possible of the estimated three thousand fans who had attended the concert.

'I'll be down in an hour and a half,' Cheadle promised; and ten minutes later, with Robinson at the wheel, was on his way. 'Right,' he said. 'Now we know! We've got eight days to stop him doing it again.'

'If what the Sussex boys tell us is true, it's not just him we've got to stop, it's her as well.'

Cheadle fumed, but said nothing. Staring ahead, he fought to control his temper, telling himself that Robinson was only doing his job; and reminding himself that his worst failing was a reluctance to accept even the most trifling amendments to his own convictions.

'You're right,' he conceded.

'But you don't think so.'

Cheadle shook his head. 'If Fred's a transvestite, he'd have turned up looking like Joan Collins, not a punk.'

'Whichever,' Robinson murmured, 'seems he always turns up dressed to kill.'

Cheadle grunted. Robinson had a point. Black tie for Saxon. A beanie for Corder. Punk for Allison. Unless they could stop him, what the fuck'd the little wanker be wearing next?

17

Atrax Three: Sunday, June 14
Actually, it's now Monday. Last night I was too knackered to do anything but toast my success, clean my teeth and crash into my pit. But today's another day, and I'm on the front page of every paper, so I feel myself again.

As per my plan, yesterday morning I drove down to Clanville, via Andover, and inspected the cottage I'm supposed to be buying. Nice couple, pretty garden, grotty cottage.

Told them I was a violinist and needed a place where I could practise without driving the neighbours mad. Admitted I had four other houses to view, but said I really liked their cottage, so please could I photograph it and ring them early next week?

Same boring patter at a nearby Georgian farmhouse. Took photographs, told the dinosaur colonel and his ancient memsahib I was sure none of the next three houses I had to inspect would be half as good at theirs, and promised to keep in touch.

Didn't go near the other three, having photographed each of them from the outside last month. I now have a full reel of snaps to prove that on Sunday, June 14, I was driving all round Hampshire, from Andover almost to Salisbury, from nine in the morning until at least three fifteen in the afternoon. Must get them developed tomorrow.

Actually, I was back here by two thirty, to complete my preparations for Elmsmere.

Stashed three plastic cans full of water in the back of

101

the car. Also a plastic washing-up bowl, a bottle of shampoo, a cake of soap, a roll of cotton wool, a large jar of Pond's Cleansing Cream, a bottle of petrol, two towels, and a change of clothing.

Checked the times on the four automatic switches that normally turn on lights and radios et cetera, thereby convincing burglars one's house is full of fearless teenagers and rabid Dobermann Pinschers.

As soon as she got home from her Sunday lunch with her thick son Reg and his even thicker wife Josie, I knocked on Mrs Green's door: she's the old biddy Uncle Paul let have the basement flat for a tenner a week when she could have afforded forty and it was worth a hundred and fifty. Told her I'd just got back from house-hunting in Hampshire, but she wasn't to worry, I'd make sure her tenancy was protected when I sold this place.

She was properly grateful and pretended to be concerned that living in Hampshire would mean a lot of travelling for me, to and from the Opera House, six days a week.

I said I was going to chuck the Opera House and concentrate on recitals. 'Which I'm afraid means hours and hours of practice,' I told her. 'Starting today!'

'Oh dear,' she said (she hates the violin). 'Couldn't you have practised while I was visiting?'

Reminded her I'd been in *Hampshire* that afternoon, looking for a *house!* 'Oh, yes,' she said, 'I forgot.' She'll remember now.

Shaved next, then punked my hair (black back and sides: cerise on top, where I also used about half a pound of sugar and a couple of cans of hair spray to create a spiky confection that gave me the look of an outraged parrot) and finally made up my face. The Whore of Wellington herself wouldn't have recognized me; and one glimpse of me would have killed the God of Wrath.

Spent the following half-hour practising one of the more difficult passages in the Haydn sonata just to let Ma Green know I wasn't kidding and give her a taste of pleasures to come when the anti-burglar device switched on first Uncle's antique tape recorder, then my cassette, then my music centre and finally my ghetto blaster, all of which were loaded with tapes of Chris rehearsing the Haydn piece that got him to the final of the BBC's Young Musician of the Year.

Dressed then and, even if I say it myself, looked rather fetching. Fetching enough to catch Harvey's eye anyway. In Australia, he was notorious for dragging groupies off to his dressing-room. I saw him do the same thing at Elmsmere Park at the two concerts I attended in April and May. So I was confident I'd be invited to his caravan last night.

I snuck out of the house at six thirty, which is when Ma Green, a creature of habit, is in her kitchen cooking what she calls her tea. Drove to Elmsmere. A few odd looks *en route*, but no problems. None in the car-park either. Took the half-bottle of Scotch (two thirds emptied and the remainder liberally laced with Tuinal) out of the glove box and slipped it into my jacket. Joined the punks in front of the stage.

Caught Harvey's eye, pretended to drink his health, accepted his invitation to join him on stage, made him an offer he couldn't refuse, and was told to follow him to his Shaggin' Wagon as it's known to the *cognoscenti*.

He was waiting for me in the dark and the altogether, as per my instructions, and if you don't mind I'll draw a veil over most of what followed. Suffice to say, he lay on his front, guzzling my mickey-finned whisky, while I (he thought) was getting out of my gear preparatory (he thought) to joining him in sexual congress.

All I was really doing, of course, was shaking a couple of stowaways out of two small Pond's jars into his pretty blue boots. And having done so, I told him he wasn't my type and left him.

Strolled very casually (but sexily) round the back of the

stage, past the restless multitude (who were impatient for another dirty ditty) and up past the Portaloos to the carpark. No one on duty at the exit. Drove quietly away.

Calculated I had twenty minutes before Harvey collapsed, and forty minutes before patrol cars were alerted and started flagging drivers down on the motorway.

So once I was clear of the car-park, I drove like the clappers for thirty minutes before turning off the motorway on to a minor road. A couple of miles down that there's a track leading into a wood. Pulled up out of sight, filled my plastic bowl with water and shampooed my hair. Took two shampoos and rinses to get the dye out.

It also took three handfuls of Pond's cream and about ten wads of cotton wool to get the make-up off my face: and then a couple of washes to get the shine off my skin.

But it didn't take long to do it all. Or to strip and change into my Yuppie-in-the-Shires gear: brogues, cavalry twill slacks, checked shirt, silk cravat and tweed cap. By which time I looked so different I could hardly believe it was me had just terminated the fourteenth Viscount Allison.

Certainly no patrol car policeman would have believed it, specially after I'd shed one mitten here, the other there, the black tights in a ditch, one boot and all the Pond's jars in a stream, the second boot on a grass verge and the plastic dish and cans in a builder's skip in Swiss Cottage.

And don't bother looking for the cotton wool: I doused it in petrol and set it alight between the tracks of a railway crossing in the wilds of God knows where because I don't, not after the dozens of detours I made.

Getting excited now, aren't you? Think I've made a couple of boo-boos. Think I left fingerprints on the whisky bottle. Wrong! Mittens! Didn't!

But ah hah, you're thinking, he's still forgotten his leather jacket!

Wrong again! London in the wee small hours is full of dossers, runaway kids and bag ladies; and one of them's got my jacket. And I don't like your chances of persuading whichever of them it is (at Euston Station, or King's Cross, or on an Embankment bench, or in a doorway, or under the arches) to admit it.

No, this is the only evidence you've got against me. And who's to say I didn't make it up?

Using all the details provided by the media, and a vivid imagination, it wouldn't have been difficult. And whereas you won't be able to produce a single witness to say I killed anyone, I can produce dozens to prove I couldn't have.

In addition to which, I didn't have any motive to kill Saxon, Corder and Allison. I liked Saxon: I had no feelings at all about Corder: and Naismith was a musician I admired who wrote great lyrics. So why would I go to so much trouble to kill any of them, let alone all of them – and most of all, poor Bunty Reading, who's next?

He's a dear, kindly, sweet old man, is Bunty; but he's got to go. Not my fault. Nor his. Just a logical imperative. So eight days hence he'll be dead.

I'll tell you about it in Atrax Four.

18

Cheadle and Robinson were sitting in the typically small, cramped office which is apparently all that can be afforded for some of Britain's most skilled and senior policemen. They were reviewing Operation Fang in the light of the evidence provided by their colleagues in Sussex.

'Doesn't tell us much about him we didn't already know, does it?' Cheadle complained. 'He's thorough: he's got bottle: and he leaves nothing to chance. Stopped Corder breathing with a phoney kiss of life: tricked his Lordship into swallowing the equivalent of three double Scotches mixed with Tuinal: and wasn't in any of the coaches that left after the concert, so probably cleared off in a car or on a motor bike well before it ended.'

'Be a bit conspicuous on a motor bike,' Robinson objected.

'Under a crash helmet and a pair of leathers? Anyway, how long'd it take to wash out the hair dye?'

'Boots stock two lines: the stronger of them takes three shampoos, the other comes out in one.'

'Guess which line Fred used! But I'll still want field glasses at the Opera House tomorrow. If I spot a single scarlet hair on the head of anyone in that orchestra, I'll put him under immediate surveillance and keep him under it for at least eight days.'

'And if you don't?'

'I'll out-think the little sod.'

'And if you can't?'

'I'll emigrate.'

He shoved a sheet of paper across his desk to Robinson. 'This tell you anything?'

Robinson studied what Cheadle had typed.

June 6, Michael Saxon, English dancer, Inglis.
June 9, Sir N. Corder, Hungarian bonker, Korda.
June 14, Lord Allison, Canadian singer, Naismith.
June 20, X ? ?

'It tells me there's a timetable, which you always suspected: all the victims are public figures, which you always said they would be: each of them is a different nationality – '

'Was! Corder and Naismith are now British.'

'And all of them have changed their name.'

'So who's X? What was his nationality before he became British? What sphere of public life does he perform in? And what was his name before he changed it?'

'Answer in no more than one line and less than a week,' Robinson summarized glumly.

'*Who's Who* must have computerized all their entries,' Cheadle encouraged him. 'Run their thingummies through our whatsit and extrapolate everyone who's a naturalized British subject or the son of a naturalized British subject.'

'Saxon wasn't either,' Robinson pointed out.

'Shit!'

'How about extrapolating all those who are titled?'

'Saxon wasn't titled.'

'All right,' said Robinson, convinced that Cheadle's list must be trying to tell them something. 'All those who've changed their names.'

'Be thousands of 'em, including almost every show business personality in the land and every peer in the realm. Still, try it. It's not right – Fred's an amateur mathematician, not a nuclear sodding physicist – but it's better than nothing.'

'The answer's here, though, isn't it?'

'Wood for the trees, laddie,' Cheadle nodded. 'Forget it for today, though. Go home, put your feet up, watch telly, ask Diana how she got on in court, sleep on it, and come in tomorrow with a name and a pair of binoculars.'

'You going home, too?'

'I'm making a statement for ITN and the BBC. Just a little something to wind Fred up until *Crimewatch* on Thursday – when I plan to enrage him by quoting everything that's least flattering about him in Professor Whosit's profile.'

'It's in already?'

Cheadle shook his head. 'Not till Friday. But I rang the Prof and he gave me the gist of it. Fred'll hate it!'

Cheadle confronted the news cameras with composure. He was what producers call a natural: also he knew exactly what he wanted to say.

'Before I start,' he warned the two crews, 'you'd better

know, in the immortal words of *'Allo, 'Allo,* that you must listen very carefully because I shall say this only once.'

'Right,' they acknowledged: and gave him the signal to start saying it.

'This is a difficult enquiry', he admitted forthrightly, 'because it concerns a series of motiveless murders committed in accordance with a preconceived plan by a rational but ruthless psychopath.

'Like all multiple killers, the Spider Maniac, as you people call him – or Fred the Nutter as we refer to him – is an egocentric loner. He doesn't kill for gain, or revenge, he kills to attract attention: and he will go on killing until we catch him, which we will because – and listen to this, Fred: I know you're watching – because *you* crave publicity and *we* now know so much about you and your plan that you're running out of time.

'Meanwhile, there's nothing the public can do to assist us in our enquiry – that's being handled by a team of several hundred police officers and a battery of computers – but I can assure the public that the ordinary man or woman in the street is in no danger. As to the two or three individuals who *will* be at risk during the next three weeks, we are confident that we will soon be able to predict who they are and therefore to protect them. At some time within that three-week period, I expect to make an arrest. Thank you.'

Ignoring the ensuing flurry of questions, he walked past the cameras, away from the Royal Opera House (in front of which he had insisted that his statement be recorded and photographed) and strode across the road into Bow Street Police Station.

Westbury watched Cheadle's performance in a state of open-mouthed fury. Until then, he had found that day's reaction to Atrax Three gratifying in the extreme. SPIDER MANIAC STRIKES AGAIN, the press had raged: and FUN-

NELWEB VICTIM NUMBER THREE: and PHANTOM OF OPERA SLAYS POP PORN PEER. He couldn't have asked for more.

Even better, from all over Britain came reports that anything that had eight legs was being squashed flat with brooms, fish slices and copies of *Woman's Own*.

In a mere nine days, six funnelweb spiders had so besmirched Australia's image that *Crocodile Dundee*, on BBC2, had attracted fewer viewers than a debate on the need for a fourth London airport on ITV; the Australian High Commissioner had been forced to admit that no one had applied for a visa for almost a week; Australia's cricketers were booed as they took the field for the second Test; and the President of the British Federation of Women's Institutes had implored the Queen to cancel her imminent Australian tour lest she fell victim to one or other of its innumerable arachnidae, serpents, sharks and saurians. Westbury was delighted.

No less delightful were the editorials damning the police for their failure to identify the most daring killer in the annals of British crime, and requiring the Home Secretary to bestir both himself and Scotland Yard before the Spider Maniac became a folk hero in whom the worst traits of Dick Turpin, Jack the Ripper, Sid Vicious and the late fourteenth Viscount Allison of Elmsmere were combined.

But here, now, incredibly, was the Plodder, slandering him as Fred the Nutter, dismissing him as an egocentric loner, and denigrating his sporting challenge as ruthless slaughter.

It was too much. He took a long swig from his bottle of Bordeaux. He had a good mind to Atrax Cheadle. First, make a fool of him (by knocking off Bunty), then execute him (as a curtain raiser to his grand finale).

'Do it!' urged the Provocateur, despite the fact that he'd switched the TV on as soon as he got home from the car-wash.

'Don't vary the plan!' ordered Solomon.

Gnawing at his thumbnail, he rose from his chair and crossed to the fireplace. He needed to reassure himself that he was not the monster Cheadle had described. The looking-glass told him that he was unchanged. A bit drawn, perhaps, a bit darker under the eyes, but still charismatic. To hell with the Plodder.

'He's on to you, Chris,' the Advocate warned. 'You can't undo what's done, but don't make it worse. I know it's not your fault; but it wasn't theirs either. Isn't even Bunty's – '

Rushing to his linen cupboard, he took out a sheet and returned with it to the drawing-room. Standing on a chair, he draped the sheet over the looking-glass. 'That's settled your hash,' he said. 'You may mean well, but I've had you.'

He returned to his armchair, took another swig of Bordeaux, and tried to review Cheadle's statement objectively.

So they've worked out the timetable, he told himself; but that's why I set myself one – to give them a chance, then beat them at their own game.

The thing is, have they worked out the rest? 'Two or three' are still at risk, the Plodder'd said. But logically it *couldn't* be three. So did that mean they hadn't cracked all of his code?

Or were they only pretending they hadn't?

Obviously they hadn't worked out who he was or early this morning they'd have battered down his door, hauled him out of bed and lugged him off to a cell for what they laughingly called verbals.

So would they be lying in ambush when he went to meet Bunty on the twenty-third?

What had the Plodder said? Something about being confident they could *soon* predict and protect the next two *or three* victims?

After all the hassle he'd had from the media, surely, if the predictions had *already* been made, the Plodder would

110

have said, 'We *know* the names of the remaining victims; and we're going to *prevent* them from being killed.'

More than likely, then, all they knew was the dates of Atrax Four and Atrax Five. Which'd make it impossible for them to stop him getting to Bunty. But once he'd killed Bunty, they'd certainly be able to predict that handful of people of whom the final victim was one.

Well, he was prepared for that. Had been since the sixth of June. And as long as they hadn't picked him as a suspect *before* he killed Bunty, he should still be able to pull off the Series.

But what if they *had*, by then, picked him as a suspect? They'd question him, of course; but he was looking forward to that. They'd search the house; but they'd find nothing. They'd hand his car over to their forensic experts; but the car-wash had removed all traces of Elmsmere. And they'd put him under surveillance; but he'd worked out a way of circumventing that.

'So what're you worrying about?' he asked himself. 'The game's the thing; and the game plan's working. And once the game's over, all they'll have for their pains will be *my* verbals – on a floppy disk!'

19

Cheadle and Robinson were the sole occupants of the Royal Box for Tuesday night's performance of *La Fille Mal Gardée*. Bolt upright, and shamelessly ensconced on one of the two chairs made especially for Queen Victoria and Prince Albert, Cheadle was aiming his binoculars at each member of the orchestra in turn. The orchestra was tuning up.

'Couldn't they do that somewhere else?' he complained. Robinson, having declined his superior's suggestion that he park his cute little commoner's bum on Prince Albert's royal throne, sat silently on a commoner's chair and tried to avoid the curious glances of those in the stalls and the opposite boxes.

Either oblivious or indifferent to the attention he was attracting, Cheadle continued ostentatiously to scrutinize one musician after the other. As he had intended, they had become aware of his inspection; but, contrary to his expectations, they found it more provocative than unnerving.

Staring back at him, they exchanged what were clearly ribald observations.

The third violinist scrawled something on a sheet of his music, ripped it off and passed it to the first violinist: who looked up at the Royal Box and laughed.

The drummer tore off a whole page, drew something on it and brazenly held it up for Cheadle's inspection.

Cheadle observed a cartoon of himself dressed as a portly Queen Victoria, complete with little crown, peering down from her box through a telescope. Sergeant Robinson, dressed as her Consort, cowered behind her. And the bubble floating from her mouth said, 'Albert, why are my musicians not amused?'

'Bloody anarchists,' Cheadle growled. 'All look like Fred to me.' He swung his binoculars back to the violinist whose note had precipitated their hostility. Leaning back in his chair, Westbury stared insolently into the binoculars.

'Third violinist's giving me the evil eye.'

'Second violinist's giving you the evil finger.'

Cheadle swung his glasses indignantly leftwards. The second violinist repeated his lewd gesture; and mouthed a legibly obscene instruction.

'Don't they want us to stop these killings?' Cheadle grumbled.

'They've all been interviewed twice already,' Robinson

reminded. 'Maybe they're beginning to think, "Why us?" '

'Because one of them's a murderer,' Cheadle raged as Bronowski entered the pit.

'I don't think anyone's told them that,' Robinson said mildly.

'Well, what do they think I'm telling them now?' asked Cheadle.

That night's performance of *La Fille Mal Gardée* was the worst the company had ever danced, or the orchestra ever played, and the fault was entirely Cheadle's. As Michael Saxon always used to insist, not even the greatest dancer or musician can turn in a good performance without the support of an audience. Cheadle's binoculars, unwaveringly trained on the pit rather than the stage, as menacing as a periscope scanning a convoy, distracted both dancers and musicians, and virtually destroyed the audience.

The sickly began to cough, the weary to shift from buttock to buttock. Husbands who hadn't wanted to come anyway dozed off: wives made invidious comparisons between the lithe young men on the stage and the middle-aged oafs in the seats beside them. A group of French tourists hissed like cobras: and Robinson cringed at his superior's insensitivity.

As the house lights came on, Cheadle looked at him with something close to contempt. 'Embarrassed you, have I?'

'Did you achieve anything?'

Rising stiffly from his royal chair, handing Robinson the binoculars, Cheadle said, 'Get me backstage.'

'They'll lynch you.'

'I want a word with the conductor.'

'He'll shoot you!'

Cheadle waved him out of the box. 'Backstage, Sergeant. Chop chop.'

Bronowski made no attempt to conceal his fury as Cheadle entered his dressing-room. 'I trust you've come to apologize,' he challenged.

'*I* don't tell you how to conduct an orchestra,' Cheadle retorted. 'I suggest you don't tell me how to conduct an enquiry. In case you don't know it, I'm looking for a killer.'

'In my orchestra? You can't be serious.'

'I'm always serious.'

'And I'm your chief suspect, I suppose?'

'Not since Sunday. You could hardly have dined with Dame Lyndsay *and* murdered Lord Allison, could you?'

'Then whom do you suspect, for God's sake? My harpist?'

Cheadle dismissed the suggestion. 'The punk drag queen who killed Allison has been described as being about five foot eight: your lady harpist's about five foot three. Tell me, those millions of notes on each page of your score: do you read all of them while you're conducting?'

Bronowski glanced quickly at the closed score on the table beside him. 'When did you look at my score?'

Peering through imaginary binoculars, Cheadle replied, 'While you were conducting.'

'Looking for clues, were you?'

'Just curious.'

'Chief Superintendent, did you come here just to ask whether I read all the notes on my score?'

'Good grief, no, Sir Leon: I came to ask had any of your musicians been behaving oddly since Mr Saxon was murdered: and, more particularly, did any musician behave oddly while Mr Saxon was actually dancing and dying on the stage above him?'

'Musicians constantly behave oddly,' Bronowski snapped. 'Tonight, for example, their union representative advised me that if ever he saw *you* in this house during a performance again, he'd call a strike.'

114

'Who's your union rep?'

'The percussionist.'

'The laddie who draws offensive cartoons?'

'If obscenity offends you, yes.'

Cheadle reverted to his original tack. 'The night of June the sixth,' he prompted, 'while Mr Saxon was dancing?'

'A splendid performance!'

'Your orchestra's? Or Mr Saxon's?'

'Mr Saxon's was superb: ours was merely splendid.'

'No exceptions?'

'Discipline within the orchestra isn't your concern, Chief Superintendent,' Bronowski equivocated.

'Since June the sixth, it has been,' Cheadle contradicted. 'Who was the culprit? And before you tell me to mind my own business, let me remind you that it's an offence to obstruct me in the execution of my duty.'

'One of my violinists,' Bronowski answered curtly. 'Christopher Westbury.'

'Sits third in line?'

'How did you know that?'

'How'd he offend?' Cheadle countered.

Visibly reluctant, Bronowski said, 'Westbury's an excellent musician with a phenomenal memory. Half-way through rehearsals, he's note perfect; and from that moment on never looks at his music. For a conductor, that can be rather distracting. When he never looks at your baton either, because he's also memorized your tempi and phrasing, it's doubly distracting. But when his eyes are constantly roving round the audience behind and above you, it's maddening. On the night of June the sixth, I was obliged to admonish him.'

'How?'

'Just a look. It's usually enough.'

'When?'

'I'll show you.' Bronowski reached for a score.

'No point. Just *tell* me. Was it during the Whirling Dervish bit?'

'A few minutes earlier.'

'Ever had to admonish him before?'

'Frequently.'

'Then you've lost me!'

'The point I'm making isn't that I had to admonish him,' Bronowski explained, 'it's that he smirked at me when I did.'

Remembering the way Westbury had stared back into his binoculars, Cheadle knew what Bronowski meant. 'That it?' he asked.

'Not quite. He then passed an obviously mutinous remark to his neighbour. That done, though, he got down to it with a will.'

'During the Whirling Dervish bit?'

'Correct.'

'So you forgave him?' Cheadle suggested with a disarming smile.

'It must be maddening to be a mere musician when you aspire to be a virtuoso,' said Bronowski.

'Bit of a soloist *manqué*, is he?' Cheadle avoided Robinson's eye. 'Anything else you want to tell us?'

Relieved that he had escaped having to reveal Westbury's misdemeanours during *Lucrezia*, Bronowski said, 'No, nothing else.'

'No cheeky cellist or schizophrenic saxophonist?'

'I'm a conductor, Chief Superintendent, not a psychiatrist.'

'Well, be careful, anyway,' Cheadle warned, 'because we've reason to believe that one of the gentlemen you conduct is a homicidal maniac.'

'You really think Bronowski's next for the chop?' Robinson asked as they left the Opera House.

'Course I don't. Apart from opera-goers and balletomanes, who ever heard of Sir Leon Bronowski? And even if you say, "Everyone but you, you wally," Bronowski's

116

the name he was born with – which, for some reason I can't fathom, seems cause enough for Fred to reject him as a potential victim.'

'Then why scare the poor bastard shitless?' Robinson shouted, halting in the middle of Bow Street and glaring at the man whose occasional falls from grace never failed to enrage him.

Cheadle confronted him without flinching. A taxi swerved to miss them. They ignored it. Then Cheadle put his arm round Robinson's shoulder and said, 'Because he was lying, laddie. *Suppressio veri*, as the legal fraternity so eloquently put it. And if I have to scare the shit out of him to make him unsuppress the truth, so be it.'

'I still don't like it,' Robinson grumbled, the rage gone from his voice.

'Me neither,' Cheadle admitted, squeezing his subordinate's shoulder before taking him by the elbow and leading him to the pavement. 'But somewhere out there' – halting and gesturing at the city around them – 'is someone Fred's going to kill unless you and I can stop him; and we don't like that much, either, do we?'

'No, sir.'

'Take notes of all that stuff about Westbury?'

'Yes, sir.'

'Make anything of it?'

'Not much.'

'Worth asking him where he was on Sunday, though. *And* that bolshie percussionist.'

'Anyone else?'

'Those two'll do for the moment.'

'Tomorrow morning?'

'While they're still half asleep. Westbury first. Pick me up at seven. I'll ask Mrs Cheadle to make you some breakfast.'

'I'll type up my notes so you can read them on the way to Holland Park,' Robinson promised. Cheadle, he noticed, looked suddenly exhausted. 'Home now?'

'Suppose so.'

'You wait here. I'll get the car.'

Watching him stride away, Cheadle shed his air of exhaustion and smiled. Always a good ploy to make the young 'un feel protective.

'There you are, dear,' said Mrs Cheadle, placing a plateful of vulcanized eggs and barely warmed bacon in front of Robinson. 'Tea or coffee?'

'Coffee, please.' Robinson had tasted Mrs Cheadle's tea on a previous visit. It had been lukewarm and so strong it had furred his teeth with tannin. Apparently her husband liked it that way.

While he hacked at the least rubbery of the three eggs, she made him a cup of coffee. Sipping at it, he made a note in future to ask for a glass of water.

Noticing that Cheadle had retreated behind his *Express*, and that Mrs Cheadle was cleaning her immaculate stove, he wrapped his four rashers of pink bacon in his handkerchief and stuffed them into his pocket. Then, thinking, Oh well, in for a penny, he wrapped two of the eggs in Mrs Cheadle's paper napkin and stuffed them in on top of the bacon.

'Delicious,' he pronounced, laying his knife and fork neatly together to indicate that he had finished and could eat no more. 'Thank you, Mrs Cheadle.'

'Lovely to see you, dear. You should come more often. Bring Diana.'

Folding his newspaper and placing it precisely on the corner of the table, Cheadle said, 'Time we left.'

Teatowel in hand, she watched them drive away. Robinson honked a farewell: Mrs Cheadle waved: Cheadle read Robinson's typed notes until they turned a corner: then said, 'Now ditch the nosh.'

Shamefaced, Robinson emptied his pocket. 'Sorry, sir. Very rude of me.'

'Bollocks,' said Cheadle. 'Mrs Cheadle is God's gift to Weight Watchers.'

Westbury opened his front door to them wearing only a dressing-gown. Despite his tan, he looked sunken-eyed and in need of sleep; but he had his wits about him and seemed unconcerned by their arrival.

'Not that it matters,' he said as he showed them into his drawing-room, 'but is it sparrow fart or crack of dawn?'

His breath stank of wine and the house smelt musty. 'It's quite early,' Cheadle admitted, 'but we didn't want to miss you.'

'Must clean my teeth. You'll excuse me?'

'Of course.'

Switching on the TV, Westbury left them. Each promptly began to survey the room. They heard a tap running and water splashing: then Westbury padding into his bedroom, opening and closing drawers.

It was five minutes before he rejoined them. Hair combed, neat in T-shirt, pressed jeans and jogging shoes, he was a different person.

'I'll get us some coffee,' he said.

'Not for us, thank you, sir,' Cheadle told him. 'We've just had breakfast – ' But Westbury was already in his kitchen. Totally self-possessed, he was also, Cheadle realized, so much in charge of the situation that it was they who were feeling ill at ease.

When he returned, he gave each of them a small but amiable smile, sat on a straight-backed chair, crossed his legs, sipped his coffee, uttered a long sigh of satisfaction and said, 'Well now, what can I tell you?'

'Mind if I turn off the telly?' Cheadle asked.

'I do, actually,' Westbury replied. 'Some people do cocaine: I do telly. Ridiculous, isn't it?'

'Not at all, sir,' said ·the similarly addicted Cheadle. 'Well, it's just a formality, but we're asking everyone – '

'Of course, you are. And there's no need for formality.'

'Very kind of you, sir.' Leaving it at that, Cheadle attempted to bluff Westbury into doing the talking: but Westbury simply stared back over the cup from which he was sipping, and it was Cheadle who was forced to break the silence. 'I'd like you to cast your mind back to Sunday, June the fourteenth,' he said, 'and tell us how you spent it.'

'Which year?'

'This year, sir.'

'Last Sunday?' – glancing at his diary.

'That's correct, sir.'

'You're still being very formal. Can't we just talk?'

'Nothing I'd like better,' Cheadle assured him. 'My sergeant'll disapprove, but that's why he's still a sergeant.'

They glanced at Robinson, who scowled at the notebook on his knee. Amused, they looked back at one another. 'How'd you spend last Sunday?' Cheadle repeated.

'House-hunting in Hampshire', offering the diary.

'A house in Hampshire wouldn't be very convenient, would it? For your work?'

'Well,' shrugging, 'I don't have to work: and I'm sick of the repertoire at the Garden.'

'Independent means, have we, sir?'

'Isn't that getting a touch *too* informal, Inspector?'

'Chief Superintendent, sir.'

'Did you ask all the others whether they had independent means?'

'I was only *talking*, sir.'

'Ah! Well, that's all right then, isn't it? Yes, I'm well off. My father left everything to my uncle, in trust for me. My aunt left all she had to my uncle. And my uncle left everything to me: this house, his car, his life assurance, shares, everything.'

He stared round the room and his eyes filled with tears.

'Didn't mean to distress you, sir.'

'No one left now.' Knuckling his eyes, he stumbled into

the kitchen to wash his face. Cheadle opened the diary at
June 6.

*Got a rocket from Bronowski for not watching him with sufficient
respect. Actually, a couple of fleeting glances! Seems he'll never
learn. All the same, he got a great performance out of us.*

*ITN has just announced that Mike died on the way to hospital.
Can't believe it. Coronary, I suppose, but he looked as strong
as an ox.*

Westbury returned and dumped a yellow Kodak envel-
ope in Cheadle's lap. 'Photographs of the houses I saw,'
he said. 'All hopeless.'

Cheadle perused the photographs: compared with the
houses Westbury found hopeless, his was grotty. The
village clock in one of the photographs said three fifteen.
'What time did you get home?' he asked.

'Home?' Westbury looked perplexed. 'I don't know.
You could ask the old biddy downstairs. We arrived at
the same time and I had a word with her: about her
tenancy if I sold this place.'

'What does "practised" mean, sir?'

Westbury looked even more perplexed. 'Skilled?' he
suggested. 'Accomplished?'

Cheadle laughed. 'You misunderstand me. I meant' –
glancing down and reading from the entry for June 14 –
' "To Ma Green's fury, practised"?'

'Oh, that! Means I practised a Haydn violin sonata, and
Mrs Green hates Haydn, the violin *and* sonatas. Another
reason for moving: so I won't disturb people.'

'Do your stint every day, do you, sir?'

'Only since I decided I'd have to quit the orchestra and
give some recitals. I'm bored witless in that pit. And I
can't stand Donizetti! Had a row with Bronowski about
that.'

Rising from his chair, he took the diary from Cheadle

and turned it back to June the twelfth. 'There you are,' he said.

Several times during Madame Ouspenskaya's appalling performance, I played as per the composer's intentions. Sir Leon displeased. Am to be carpeted tomorrow.

'What happened?' Cheadle asked.

'He let me off with a warning.'

'How long did you practise? Last Sunday?'

'Oh, three and a half, four hours: the usual.'

'From whenever it was you got home?'

'No, I hoovered and made myself a bite to eat first, then practised: and finished in time to watch the umpteenth repeat of *Bringing up Baby*. I'm a Katie Hepburn freak.'

'You've been very helpful, Mr Westbury. You won't mind, will you' – heaving himself out of his armchair and handing Robinson the diary – 'if my sergeant makes a note of your itinerary last Sunday?'

'Of course not,' said Westbury, following Cheadle into the hall.

Halting outside the study, Cheadle looked over his shoulder for Robinson. 'Come on, Sergeant,' he shouted, knowing perfectly well that Robinson would be examining the drawing-room: then, turning back to Westbury, nodding toward the study, said, 'Your den?'

'My music room.'

As if it were the most natural thing in the world to inspect a private householder's music room without either an invitation or a warrant, Cheadle walked into it and gazed around it like an excited child.

'This where you do all your practising?'

Westbury nodded, half impatient, half amused.

Cheadle moved to the work bench and stared reverently at the violin that lay inside an open case. 'Yours?' he asked, and not waiting for an answer, shouted, 'Sergeant, come and look at Mr Westbury's music room.'

Robinson appeared in the doorway and surveyed the small room. 'Word processor useful for your work, is it, sir?'

'Don't be a plonker, Sergeant,' said Cheadle. 'How could a word processor help Mr Westbury play his fiddle?'

'I use it to write letters,' Westbury told Robinson in a quiet aside that dissociated him from the Chief Superintendent's bullying. 'And anyway, no one nowadays should be computer illiterate, should they?'

'No,' mouthed Robinson, with a meaningful glance at his superior's computer illiterate back.

Cheadle turned from the work bench, stepped to the music stand and glanced at the closed cupboard affixed at shoulder height to the wall behind it. 'A place for everything and everything in its place,' he approved.

Determined to prevent him from opening it (and discovering therein the tape recorder, music deck, cassette player and ghetto blaster that had successively been activated by time switches to madden Mrs Green on the evening of June the fourteenth) Westbury withdrew into the hall and waited there with such visible forbearance that Cheadle was obliged to announce, 'We've outstayed our welcome, Sergeant.'

'Not at all!' said Westbury; but nevertheless led them to the door and closed it promptly behind them.

20

A little later that day, at Cheadle's behest, a detective constable called on Mrs Green. She confirmed that on Sunday, June the fourteenth, Westbury had hoovered between the hours of five p.m. and five thirty, and driven her mad with his violin between the hours of six and nine thirty. The hoover, she explained, was clapped out and rather noisy; and the violin was clapped out and unbearably noisy.

At more or less the same time, at Cheadle's request, a Hampshire detective constable visited Westbury's estate agent in Andover. He confirmed that he had arranged for Westbury to view a thatched cottage and a Georgian farmhouse in Clanville, and three more desirable or bijou residences in various other villages between 9 a.m. and 4 p.m. on Sunday, June the fourteenth.

Both Clanville householders confirmed that Westbury had called on them: the three other householders confirmed that Westbury had telephoned them and been authorized at least to photograph their homes and gardens, and peer through their windows, should two of the couples not have returned from Sunday lunch with friends and should the third have left for afternoon tea with the grandchildren.

All five householders volunteered the information that Westbury had telephoned them yesterday, Tuesday, June the sixteenth, to advise that he would not, after all, be buying: he hoped he hadn't caused trouble or disappointment.

Four of them considered this an act of unprecedented courtesy: the fifth, the ancient Clanville colonel, stated categorically that Westbury had never intended buying, had visited his home only to case it, and was a cat burglar by profession, not a violinist.

'Too good-looking,' he explained. 'Had a subaltern like him. Rubber cheques everywhere! Told him, twenty-four hours to do the decent thing. That night, shot himself. This feller, same type.'

'Thought Blimps like that were extinct,' Robinson commented after reading the Hampshire report.

He and Cheadle had had a frustrating morning. Westbury had treated them with blithe unconcern, and

Maguire, the bolshie percussionist, had been charmingly co-operative. In consequence, Cheadle was feeling irritable, and Robinson was feeling uncharitable.

'Ninety-three years old: two world wars: decorated in both: the man's entitled to his views,' Cheadle snapped. 'And the least you should do before judging him is translate his Edwardian jargon into modern English.'

Surprised to realize that Cheadle was serious, Robinson skimmed through the telex a second time. The Hants constable had quite an ear for dialogue. He could almost hear the colonel's crisp voice carping: *Too good-looking . . . subaltern like him . . . told him . . . shot himself.*

'Still sounds like the genuine hang 'em, shoot 'em, flog 'em voice of the Raj,' he insisted.

'Never agree about that, will we?'

'Capital punishment?'

'What'd you make of that room?'

'Wondered at first about the mirror with the sheet over it, and the fireplace full of broken glass, and the smell of dust and mildew. But when he started to weep – can last years, grief.'

'Checked the uncle's will?'

'Eight hundred thousand. Net. Be more now, with property and interest rates and stock markets the way they are.'

'So why hasn't he got a char?'

'Maybe he values his privacy; maybe he's keeping everything as it was when his folks were alive; maybe he just likes dirt.'

'And maybe he's only seven notes to the octave!'

'He's the right height.'

'Does he look like Stink?'

'No.'

'Nor Dean. Nor Bogarde. Bit like Terence Stamp, though. In *The Collector*.'

'I thought he looked a bit like Brando in *Street Car*.'

125

'Seems Master Westbury looks different to each beholder. Like Master Gleeson.'

'Who had white skin!'

'Not difficult to acquire a tan, is it?'

'As easy as getting rid of a Mohican hair-do.'

'Neither of which Master Westbury may have done,' Cheadle pointed out. 'Logically, *couldn't* have done – because he was in the wings with colleagues while Saxon's jock-strap was being sabotaged, in the Serpentine while Corder was being murdered, and tormenting Mrs Green while Allison was being murdered.'

'Quite apart from the fact that he's never been closer to Australia than Bangkok,' Robinson reminded.

'So why's he stick in my craw? The drummer doesn't.'

'The drummer has five children under the age of seven, his wife is pregnant with a sixth, and the entire family spent all of last Sunday not reaching Brighton on account of the awful traffic jams, and half the night not getting back to London on account of the even worse traffic jams; and all the time the kids were being car sick, which only Irish kids can do in stationary cars. Also, he gave you that cartoon he did of you, and you were dead chuffed. That's why the percussionist doesn't stick in your craw.'

Both men fell silent, Robinson wondering why he remained so suspicious of Westbury, whose passport proved he'd never been to Australia, Cheadle wondering what it was he'd seen in Westbury's home that had given the lie to one of his alibis.

'Before we call on Bronowski,' he said, 'make me a list of every item you saw in Westbury's house that appeared to corroborate – or refute – any of his alibis.'

Robinson returned half an hour later. 'A small thing,' he said, handing over the single sheet of paper to which Cheadle required him to confine all his reports, 'but mine own.'

126

Cheadle cast his eyes down the list:

diary
hoover marks on the rug
open music on music stand
violin in open case
word processor and floppy disks
sheeted mirror
fragments of three wine glasses
empty bottle by armchair
empty bottle by bed
dusty house
immaculate jeans
car had just been washed
spider webs

'The word processor could have been his uncle's,' Cheadle said.

'Sure, but there's no dust on the VDU. I think he uses it more than he said: isn't as disorganized as he'd like us to think.'

'Hm,' said Cheadle. Then, '*Three* wine glasses?'

'I counted the bases.'

'And empty bottles everywhere. What do you think? Goes home each night, gets a bit Brahms and Liszt, breaks the occasional glass and kicks the bits into the fireplace?'

'I think it's odd.'

'Why mention "immaculate jeans"?'

'Nothing else was immaculate.'

'Could've been his Sunday best. You sure his motor'd just been washed?'

'The only spotless car in the street. In spite of the fact that he'd just driven to Hampshire and back.'

'*Or* Elmsmere and back.' Cheadle tapped Robinson's last item with his pencil. 'Spider webs?'

'A bit Conan Doylish, that one, sir.'

'Meaning you didn't see any?'

127

Robinson nodded.

'Need a warrant, really, don't we, Derek? Can't apply for one on the basis of this lot, though.' He tossed the sheet of paper on to his desk.

'Not what you wanted?'

'Exactly what I wanted. Proves that whatever it was I saw, you saw it too. Except for the jeans, the VDU screen, the clean motor and the non-existent spider web, our lists are identical. But it's not one of them. Didn't even notice them. It's something I *noticed*: something that rang a bell.'

Robinson stepped up to the desk and read his upside-down list. 'So it's something to do with the diary, the hoover, the music stand, the violin, the mirror, the broken wine glasses – '

'Not the bits of glass. Nor the empty bottle. I remember thinking they were interesting but didn't prove anything. What we've got to recall is something I've forgotten I decided about something we both saw.'

'Now?'

Cheadle shook his head. 'The more we try now, the deeper we'll bury it. Anyway, Sir Leon's expecting us. Don't forget your notes.'

If Cheadle was expecting to meet a contrite, and therefore amenable, Bronowski, he was doomed to disappointment. It was Sir Leon's handsome daughter, Rachel, who met him and Robinson at the front door of the conductor's St John's Wood home, and she escorted them into the presence of her mother, not her father.

'Lady Bronowski,' Cheadle greeted her; but she made no attempt even to approach him, let alone offer her hand. 'May I introduce – ?'

'My husband told me you were coming,' she interrupted. 'But I'm afraid – glancing at her watch – 'you're early. If you'll take a seat . . .'

Thicker set than her daughter, but no less handsome,

she was perfectly groomed, expensively dressed, unassailably matriarchal and formidably distant. Hands loosely crossed over her stomach, she watched indifferently while they sat, and then, with the slightest of nods, left them.

Bronowski, elegantly informal, entered exactly on time; strode into his ornate drawing-room exactly as Cheadle had seen him stride across the orchestra pit to his dais; and acknowledged them with a 'Gentlemen' and a vague smile, as if they were musicians he was about to rehearse.

To his dismay, Cheadle found himself standing, murmuring, 'Sir Leon,' and awaiting permission to resume his seat. Noticing his discomfiture, Robinson also remained standing.

'Please,' Bronowski urged them offhandedly.

'Seems we're intruding,' Cheadle began.

Bronowski laughed. 'My wife's very protective,' he explained. 'Reporters, television crews, radio interviewers – '

'Policemen!'

'Policemen took her whole family away in '44. Only she survived the war. So I forgive her her protectiveness. Besides, I adore women.'

Desperately seeking a link between Bronowski's adoration of women and *suppressio veri*, Cheadle said, 'Do you have a son?'

'Only daughters, praise God. Four women in the house is exactly right. When Rachel marries, I've told Lady Bronowski either she presents me with another daughter or we adopt one.'

'And I thought conductors were tyrants,' mused Cheadle. 'Mind you, I should've known: Chris told us otherwise.'

Bronowski was amused by the laborious transition. 'Told you von Karajan and Solti were sweeties, did he?'

'Actually,' Robinson intervened, referring to his notebook, 'he told us you should have sacked him for a much more serious breach of discipline than the one you said he committed the night Mr Saxon died. Chief Superintendent Cheadle has been wondering why you chose not to advise him of that later incident; and why, despite its seriousness, you decided not to dismiss Mr Westbury?'

The young 'un's protecting me again, thought Cheadle.

The scribe's ticking me off, thought Bronowski. 'I didn't tell you because you didn't ask,' he answered.

'We didn't ask,' Cheadle retorted, 'because we didn't know. You did. And suppressed it.'

'Not at all. I merely omitted to mention it.'

'Sir Leon,' Cheadle warned, 'the law takes a dim view of those who withhold evidence.'.

Refusing to be intimidated, Bronowski insisted, 'I withheld nothing about which I was competent to bear witness. I told you at the time that I was a conductor, not a psychiatrist. I also told you that Westbury was frequently guilty of acts of indiscipline.'

'Of not looking at his music, not looking at your baton and not controlling his roving eye.'

'Precisely.'

'Where used it to rove?'

'Usually up into the boxes opposite. Where you sat on Tuesday. With your binoculars.'

'Women?'

'Meaningless flirtations: though rumour hath it it led to one liaison.'

'With whom?'

'A blonde, I'm told. You may recall that I not only have millions of notes to read while I conduct, I also, as is customary in my profession, stand with my back to the audience. So who Christopher's blonde was, I've no idea.'

'But that's not what you omitted to tell us, is it?'

'I omitted only what I believed was the inexpert opinion of an incompetent witness.' He turned calmly to Robinson. 'Have you got those dozen words, Sergeant?'

'Yes, sir.'

'Kindly read them back to me.'

' "What I believed was the inexpert opinion of an incompetent witness," ' Robinson dutifully recited.

'You wish that sort of evidence, Chief Superintendent?'

'I wish any sort of evidence, Sir Leon: and I'm still waiting to hear what it was you omitted to tell us last time when we talked about discipline in your orchestra.'

'If you insist,' Bronowski acceded. 'I decided not to dismiss Westbury because I sincerely believed he might not have known what he was doing.'

'Not known? You mean epilepsy? A black-out?' Bronowski refused to be drawn. Cheadle pressed on. 'Temporary insanity? Schizophrenia?'

'Probably none of them. Probably I should have sacked him. And that's all I can tell you.'

'Very helpful, nevertheless.'

'Then perhaps you'll explain why you sought such help from the boy's conductor rather than his general practitioner?'

'We can't find the boy's GP. The National Health one he was assigned has never even seen him. None of London's hospitals, public or private, has ever heard of him. And no one but you has ever even hinted there might be something wrong with him.'

'Then before you go,' said Bronowski, rising to indicate that the interview was at an end, 'let me remind you that I also hinted that there may be nothing wrong with him.'

21

Neither a roving eye nor an aversion to the works of Donizetti being proof of murderous intent, and a Musical Director's reluctance to fire an unruly subordinate being no proof of that subordinate's insanity, Cheadle spent the rest of Wednesday, and most of Thursday, searching for some other suspect – indeed, any other suspect – than Christopher Westbury.

But the violinist continued to stick in the Chief Superintendent's craw: and the damning but forgotten significance of something he'd observed in Westbury's home continued to defy his every effort to recall it.

Five years ago, such a lapse would never have happened: nowadays it happened half a dozen times a day. Names eluded him and words escaped him: so he feigned an eccentric indifference to both, referring, whenever necessary, to whosit, whatsit and thingummy.

The terminology pertaining to computers – whose labour-saving abilities he hugely admired – had proved so alien to his ear that he had been unable to acquire a word of it: so he also feigned a distaste for all things electronic.

He hadn't minded when his eyesight began to deteriorate and his left ear to go deaf: he hadn't even minded when he discovered that he could no longer run upstairs two at a time or watch news flashes of bomb outrages without premonitions of violent death: all those changes were inevitable. But an increasingly impaired memory . . .

When first he had noticed it, he had thought it would pass, and had joked about it. 'It's me Alzheimers,' he used to tell his colleagues. But when it persisted, and slowly worsened, he had used all his guile to conceal it. Nevertheless, he was convinced he would end up, like his mother, gaga and incontinent.

In the mean time, however, his ability to concentrate on a case, to correlate, winnow and sift the evidence, was undiminished, and his sergeant – who had never known him in his heyday – was an ideal partner.

When they whipped him off to a ward for the prematurely senile, would Derek visit him? he wondered. Or call on Mrs Cheadle?

Probably. He'd always been chivalrous: always made

sure interviewees were so placed as to address his good ear, supplied the words and names he was pretending he hadn't forgotten, protected him from the arrogance of Sir Leon and his ilk, treated him as an intellectual equal despite the disparity of their academic backgrounds, and driven him home when he was knackered.

Yep, Derek'd visit him in the Funny Farm: when the time came: if it came. He might only go half gaga; might only have to take early retirement because he couldn't any longer concentrate, correlate, winnow or sift, had begun jumping to wrong conclusions.

When the time came, he'd know. Or Derek'd tip him the wink. Never let you get away with anything, Derek didn't. Still wasn't convinced they weren't putting all their eggs in the one basket. Which they were. Or rather, he was. If Westbury turned out *not* to be Fred, he was going to look a real wally.

'We'll protect those two or three who are at risk,' he'd promised; but even if Westbury *was* Fred, he'd be lucky to protect those unknowns who were still at risk.

'I expect to make an arrest within three weeks,' he'd said; but if Westbury wasn't Fred, he'd be lucky if it was less than three months.

'I said it to rattle Fred,' he'd explained to You Know Who; but whether Westbury was Fred or not, he'd be lucky if Tuesday passed without a fourth murder.

'Time is the serial murderer's enemy,' he'd told Derek. Who had replied, 'It wasn't Jack the Ripper's.' Tuesday was now only four and half days away: time had become his enemy, not Fred's.

Well, he still had two cards to play, and tonight he intended playing both: *Crimewatch* and surveillance.

Not only had the BBC spent a lot of money on that Thursday's monthly edition of *Crimewatch*, it had been plugging it hard for days; and when it went on air, few British viewers were watching anything else.

It opened with a catalogue of murders. 'On June the sixth,' the first presenter intoned, 'at the Royal Opera House, Covent Garden, Michael Saxon, the greatest dancer of his time, was murdered. The cause of death was the venom of two funnelweb spiders.'

'On June the ninth, after an interval of two days,' the second presenter intoned, 'at the Kensington Health Club, Sir Nicholas Corder, millionaire baronet and playboy, was murdered. The cause of death was the venom of two funnelweb spiders.'

'On June the fourteenth, after an interval of four days,' intoned the first presenter, 'at Elmsmere Park, Viscount Allison, also known as Harvey Naismith, lead singer of the controversial Phallic Cymbals, was murdered. The cause of death was the venom of two funnelweb spiders.'

'The police have good reason to believe,' the second presenter concluded, 'that the man who has killed three times already will shortly strike again. So let us return to the night of June the sixth: to the Royal Opera House and the murder of Michael Saxon.'

Westbury sped home from Covent Garden. He had taped *Crimewatch* and he was both exhilarated and intimidated by the prospect of watching it.

The presenters' introduction, so succinct and dispassionate, was not to his liking. The way they harped on the spiders, but referred to him only once, was palpably provocative. And the presence of the Plodder, who sat between them, was curiously unnerving. He looked self-possessed and delphic. 'But of course he does,' Westbury told himself as Saxon started dancing. 'Every word the presenters utter is his.'

The film clip upset him. It had been re-edited so that both genius and agony were brilliantly portrayed. He had no desire to be known as the man who destroyed Saxon's genius and caused him agony. Which made it more essential than ever that he complete the Series. Only after they'd acknowledged the legitimacy of Atrax Five would people understand the necessity of Atrax One.

The Plodder – looking dangerously confident, sounding alarmingly precise – was addressing any viewers who might, on the night of June the sixth, have been waiting outside the Opera House stage door immediately after the performance ended.

'Can you describe the first two or three men to come through it before the ambulance arrived?' he asked. 'Did any of them seem anxious – if only to escape your scrutiny? You were waiting for autographs: you almost certainly saw a murderer. You may even have seen an item of headwear like this' – holding up a beanie – 'protruding from one of his pockets. These may seem trivial matters to you: to us they are vital links between suspecting a man of murder and being in a position to charge him with it.'

The presenter gave telephone numbers viewers could dial, fed Cheadle a few pertinent questions and introduced the programme's second film – a re-enactment of the Kensington Health Club murder, with members and staff playing themselves and actors playing Nicky Corder and the so-called Mark Gleeson.

Westbury was amazed by the accuracy of the BBC's reconstruction. He recognized half a dozen of the women members: the Royal Philharmonic belted out the classics: the aerobics class leapt and cavorted: the instructress yelped: Nicky battled: Gleeson mocked: Nicky lurched: the instructress called out to him and switched off the tape: the class came to an uneasy standstill, all eyes on Nicky: Nicky fought on . . . and fell.

But it was the mass of detail in the remainder of the film that Westbury found chilling: a close-up of Gleeson's right hand as he vaulted the railing, all of the hand, except the little finger, resting on his draped towel, the little finger resting on varnished wood: a close-up as he pinched Corder's nostrils and put his lips over Corder's mouth: close-ups of the crude tattoo on his right arm, the strip of buttock exposed by his ripped jeans, his boots, his head. And finally, a tracking shot as he walked along Kensington High Street toward the station.

'Were you in Kensington High Street between 12.55 and 1.15 p.m. on Tuesday, June the ninth?' Cheadle asked. 'Did you see this man' – a *Crimewatch* Video-Fit appeared on the screen – 'with the beetling eyebrows, the vivid blue eyes, the pale clear skin . . .' But Westbury had stopped listening.

Had they really found a print from his little finger on the railing? Had they compared it with the same print on the passport he'd taken to the station? How much more did they know than he'd thought they knew? And what was he worrying about, for Christ's sake, if *that* – as a police Photo-Fit flashed on to the screen – was what they thought the alleged Mark Gleeson would look like *without* his beanie, sapphire eyes, beetling brows and pudgy cheeks?

Crimewatch's third film consisted of a library clip from a *Panorama* programme intercut with shots of a punk girl with a scarlet Mohican *coiffure*.

The library clip was of the Phallic Cymbals' first concert at Elmsmere Park, and the actor who played the punk girl was the young man who had earlier played the alleged Mark Gleeson. His make-up (from black circumflex eyebrows to green triangular cheekbones and black-edged purple lips) exactly matched that worn by Westbury. As he watched, Westbury was almost convinced that the film was a video of the concert he had himself attended, with close-ups of himself in the audience.

He knew it wasn't, but the illusion was so disturbing that he retired into the kitchen to make his supper: a large packet of crisps, a small tub of taramasalata and a cheap bottle of wine.

While he was opening the bottle, he heard Cheadle asking last Sunday's drivers had they seen this girl on the motorway in the early evening, or on any of the roads that led back to London, between 10 p.m. and midnight? And had any of those who attended the concert seen her leaving, because the police were extremely anxious to locate her car?

'Well, of course you are, you silly old fart,' retorted Westbury as he returned to his armchair. Ignoring the presenter lady, with her cool looks and crisp accent, he opened his cellophane packet, extracted half a dozen crisps, dipped them one after the other into the taramasalata and stuffed them in swift succession into his mouth. Munching noisily, he couldn't hear a word she was saying: but when Cheadle reappeared, he took an urgent swig of wine, gulped down the lot and listened intently.

'To answer your question,' Cheadle told the cool, crisp lady, 'we're looking for a psychopath who's so arrogant he actually *signalled* his intention to become a multiple killer by choosing a great dancer, who hadn't an enemy in the world, for his first victim.

'We're looking for a man' – and his eyes peered contemptuously into Westbury's – 'who's profoundly inadequate. Sexually inadequate, emotionally inadequate, socially inadequate, and, more than probably, professionally inadequate.'

By now Westbury was standing rigidly at attention, except that his clenched fists were drumming at his thighs and his head was swinging from side to side. He was no longer listening to Cheadle, still less meeting his contemptuous eyes, but there was no escaping the policeman's spiteful litany of lies.

'A life of frustration,' he heard. 'Isolation . . . parental separation . . . never learns from his mistakes . . . an under-achiever . . . self-destructive.'

'Shut up!' he shrieked. 'Shut up!' – his fists still drumming, his head still denying, tears blurring his vision of the hateful Plodder: who ignored him.

'It's not fair,' Westbury moaned, now circling his drawing-room, flapping his arms like a wounded bird, maddened by Cheadle's implacable, pointed, probing, unexpected questions.

'Have any pet shop proprietors in London sold anyone resembling this young man' – again the Photo-Fit – 'the sort of insects spiders might feed on?' he asked. 'Stick insects, wasps, moths, grubs?'

'Sadist!' Westbury hissed.

'Does any assistant in any London chemist's shop remember this young man buying several cans of hair spray and dye – probably Flamingo Peach and Fire Red – any time in the last three months? Remember, this is a killer who planned everything well in advance. He may even have bought his make-up' – the punk girl's Photo-Fit reappeared – 'at the same time. Is there anyone watching this programme who remembers a young *man* buying make-up in *these* colours – ?'

'*Dentist!*' Westbury snarled, clamping his hands over his ears, almost tempted to switch off the set, only refraining because that would instantly ungag the Provocateur.

Fortunately, Solomon broke the silence with the sort of soft, comforting noises a mother uses to soothe a child. 'Shush,' Solomon said, 'shush': and, when his rage and terror had subsided, 'Don't panic. You're cleverer than them. They're only reacting. You act: they only react. So act!'

Galvanized, he stuffed his mouth full of crisps and taramasalata and sped into the kitchen in search of furniture polish, dusters and gloves. If they'd lifted his little fingerprint from the health club railing, he must remove every fingerprint from every surface in the house.

They mustn't be able to come into his house and find

a print they could match with the one they'd lifted at the health club.

And having removed every last one of them from everything in the house, he must never again leave fresh ones. Every second he spent at home, he must wear gloves.

But shouldn't he hoover before he polished?

Running to the hall cupboard, snapping on his rubber gloves before he opened the door, he took out the vacuum cleaner and, beginning at the front door, hoovered every inch of the ground floor. Not just the fitted carpet, but the walls as well.

And the bed, chairs, bookcases and curtains.

The telephone rang.

Running to it, snatching up the receiver, he snapped, 'Yes?'

'Do you know what time it is?' screamed Mrs Green.

'Yes!'

'I'm going to ring the police.'

'You do and I'll bung your rent up two hundred quid a week.'

'Christopher!'

'Sod off!' and, hanging up, he rushed back to hoover the first flight of stairs.

Then the first floor.

Then the second staircase.

And finally the second floor.

That done, he ran downstairs and started polishing. Started at the front door, spraying Pledge and polishing everything: doors, handles, lintels, switches, taps, fittings, fixtures, windows, the telephone, the TV, the looking-glass, each page of his music, every horizontal surface, every empty bottle, his toothbrush handles, his razor, the toothpaste tube, his shoes, everything in every cabinet, on every shelf, in every drawer.

Suspecting that prints could be lifted from textiles, he put load after load of clothes into the washing machine; and between loads, because it was already after nine in the morning, took his suits and sports jacket to the dry cleaner.

Back then to wash and dry each fragment of glass from the fireplace, his three surviving wine glasses, all his tumblers and every piece of crockery and cutlery. He even washed his jogging shoes.

Next he removed the last four Task Force funnelwebs (each in its own lair – a florist's cellophane box lined with damp, dead leaves) from the upstairs bathroom (where he turned off the heater that had kept the spiders comfortably alive) and hid them behind the brick incinerator, under a pile of grass cuttings, in the back garden.

And finally he remade his bed with clean linen, hung clean towels in the bathroom, draped a clean sheet over the looking-glass, changed into clean clothes and shoes, threw the dirty, sweat-drenched clothes he had been wearing into the washing machine, put on a new pair of rubber gloves and surveyed his handiwork.

The house gleamed, smelt fragrant. Aunty Deb would have been ecstatic. Chuckling to himself, he let himself out of the house and set off briskly for Marks and Spencers.

'Target now out of the house and heading toward Kensington High Street,' a CID officer radioed from the surveillance van parked twenty yards up the street.

'Target now entering Marks and Spencers,' reported a second surveillance officer who was trailing him. And ten minutes later, 'Target leaving Marks and Spencers with purchases of clothing and food. Heading back the way he came.'

'Target re-entering house,' the officer in the van reported.

'Stupid bastards!' Westbury muttered as he closed the front door behind him. Did they really think he wouldn't notice a battered blue florist's van parked in a short street where every resident's car was as familiar to him as his own? A plumber's van, maybe. But a florist's? When every

140

house had its own garden which, in this most splendid of summers since whenever – as the weather forecasters never ceased reminding everyone – was in full bloom?

'Really, Mr Plodder,' he chided his adversary, feeling quite excited nevertheless because all this new development meant was that the police had no hard evidence against him, only suspicions.

Still, just as well he'd anticipated it: left the house with his gloved hands in his pockets: kept them there – the handle of his carrier bag hooked over his wrist – while he walked to and from Marks and Spencers: had the cunning to buy T-shirts, socks, handkerchiefs and food as well as half a dozen pairs of cotton gloves.

Marching into the drawing-room, he switched on the TV, drank thirstily from his bottle of wine and yawned happily. 'Poor Chris,' he told himself, 'you're shattered.' So he stripped off his rubber gloves, pulled on a pair of cotton gloves (grey, not white: didn't want to look like a Korean traffic cop): reminded himself to dispose of both pairs of rubber gloves: set the alarm for five thirty: kicked off his shoes: and fell backwards on his bed.

'Do your damnedest,' he mumbled at the absent Cheadle: and fell instantly asleep.

22

Cheadle's damnedest, that Friday, June the nineteenth, consisted mainly of sitting in his office staring at two lists.

> June 6 Michael Saxon born Inglis
> June 9 Sir Nicholas Corder born Korda
> June 14 Lord Allison born Naismith

Hoover
Word processor
Diary
Music stand
Mirror

More than ever he was convinced that the answers he sought lay in those two lists; but no answers came.

In fact, he thought, all they're doing is ask me two more questions! Denying himself the luxury of exasperation, he appended the new questions to his first list:

June 23 WHO? born WHAT?
July 10 WHO? born WHAT?

He was not particularly surprised that the *Crimewatch* programme had failed to elicit any hard evidence against anyone. Nor was he particularly disappointed. His intention had been not so much to elicit information as to demoralize Fred – which was why he had told the BBC not to bother reshooting the close-up of the actor's hand when its little finger mistakenly overlapped the towel and touched the railing.

The trouble with that, though, was that Fred had a plan from which no amount of demoralization was likely to budge him. The best he could hope for – in the absence of a flash of inspiration generated by his two lists – was that a demoralized Fred would betray himself on the twenty-third of June.

He grimaced at the realization that he had accepted the inevitability of a fourth murder: and for the twentieth time accused himself of stubbornness because he had refused seriously to consider anyone other than Westbury as a suspect.

Certainly his surveillance team had reported nothing to justify his stubbornness. 'Target is spring cleaning,' one of them from the van had reported shortly after eleven thirty the previous night. And all through the night the same report had come in. 'Target still spring cleaning.'

One of them had even peered through a window, which could easily have alerted Westbury and rendered the whole costly exercise futile: so he'd put an end to that!

Besides, why wouldn't Westbury spring clean? House was knee-deep in dust: and he and Derek must have shamed him when they called. In those circumstances, anyone would spring clean.

On the other hand, the psychiatrist had said Fred was almost certainly schizophrenic, and that lots of schizos had a thing about washing their hands. Cleansing themselves of guilt. If Westbury was Fred (whose burden of guilt must by now be almost insupportable) a house'd be the least he'd feel compelled to clean.

But nothing he'd done this morning was suspect. If buying knickers and crisps and taramasalata was proof of homicidal mania, half of London'd be locked up.

'But!' said Cheadle: and refraining from asking himself, 'But what?' (because the purchase of six pairs of gloves confirmed the psychiatrist's theory about the schizophrenic's obsession with clean hands) ordered a research team to be set up on Monday to investigate Westbury's background.

Monday: the first day of Wimbledon. Must remember to tell the missus to tape it. When he switched on the video, maybe those lists would come up with some answers.

His telephone rang. 'Target's arrived at the Opera House,' the Incident Room advised. He looked at his watch. Fifteen minutes till curtain-up. Derek, who didn't need binoculars, would be in his seat by now. Front row of the gods, right-hand end, looking down into the orchestra pit.

For the next half-hour he attended to paper work, until Robinson knocked on his open door. 'Well?' he asked.

Robinson shrugged. 'Like Bronowski said, his eyes are

everywhere. Wagner tonight – *Rheingold* – but ten minutes into the first act he spotted me.'

'Give you the evil eye?'

'Smiled, actually.'

'Look at you often?'

'Just the once. Didn't seem bothered.'

Cheadle shoved his revised lists across the desk. 'Copy those. Take 'em home with you. If you have any thoughts, give me a bell.'

'Where?'

'Here. I'm going over everything we've got. Again!'

'Sir . . .' Robinson began to protest; but Cheadle cut him short.

'Don't worry, laddie. We senior coppers, to quote Dame Audrey, are tougher than we look.' He frowned and rubbed his eyes. 'I mean, Dame Whosit. Looks like Audrey Thing.'

'Does, too,' Robinson agreed, as if so brilliant a comparison would never have occurred to him.

'Haven't the faintest idea who I'm talking about, have you?' Cheadle accused.

'Course I have,' Robinson bluffed: and then it came to him. 'Dame Lyndsay Wynyard. Who, now that you mention it, is a dead ringer for Audrey Hepburn.'

For once, Cheadle decided, young Robinson was not going to have the last word. 'Copy these,' he ordered, jabbing at his two lists, 'and piss off home before I report you for patronizing a superior.'

The weekend was busy for all concerned.

To give the surveillance team something to think about, Westbury left his house three times on both Saturday and Sunday.

To ease his conscience, Cheadle ordered Robinson to sit opposite him in his cramped office and review with him all the evidence he had himself reviewed on Friday night.

On the Saturday night, armed only with inconspicuous opera glasses, Cheadle watched Westbury playing Massenet's *Manon*. He sat in the gods, where Robinson had sat the night before; and Westbury's roving eye found him almost immediately.

The look he gave Cheadle was sardonic; but Cheadle was less surprised by that than by the composure with which he was playing his violin. It amazed him that anyone could simultaneously look so inattentive and perform so precisely. Which proved nothing: except, if he was honest, that Westbury was behaving no differently now than he had done during hundreds of performances prior to Saxon's murder.

Common sense suggested he should call off the nightly chore of watching Westbury at work: perversity argued that he should persist. As he left the Opera House, he checked its offerings for the following week. Ballet again: to music composed by Stravinsky, Tchaikovsky, Prokofiev . . . The man with the roving eye must have a memory like an elephant so effortlessly to recall such a repertoire.

The thought bothered him; but was irrefutable. So it was something else that was bothering him. If his life had depended on it, though, he couldn't have said what.

Back in his office, he put the question to Robinson. Robinson was unable to say what either. They worked doggedly. 'Target has left Opera House,' they were told. 'Target has caught tube from Covent Garden.' And, 'Target has returned home.'

But no member of the surveillance team reported, 'Target wearing gloves,' even though Westbury was obliged to remove his right hand from his pocket twice to show his season ticket, and once to open his front door.

Westbury smiled as he closed the door behind him. He

felt, he imagined, exactly like soldiers must when they return from a night patrol into no man's land.

He was pleased with the sight and smell of his immaculate house: so pleased that he removed his street-soiled shoes even before he switched on the TV. And later, when he went into the kitchen for a packet of crisps, he tucked a clean tea towel into his belt so that, wherever he moved in the house, he could dust as he walked.

To prove his point, he gave the top of the TV a rub *en route* to his armchair, his armchair a couple of swipes before he sat in it, and his wine bottle a brisk wipe after he'd drunk from it.

He found this exercise so satisfying that he was unable to resist repeating it. Looking like a naughty boy, he sneaked out of the drawing-room and into his bathroom, pressing the tea towel against the wall all the way – except when he jabbed swiftly at spotless light switches – and repolishing the cistern while he stood in front of the bowl.

On the way back to his armchair he spread both arms wide and shuffled, so that the tea towel dusted a swathe along the right wall, his gloved palm a swathe along the left wall and his stockinged feet a double swathe along the carpet.

On Monday, he decided, he would ring an agency and hire a cleaner: for an hour every Monday, Wednesday and Friday: until July the tenth. Not only would this keep the house absolutely glittering, it would also adorn it with fingerprints. A complete absence of fingerprints would be almost as damning as the existence of prints matching those on the health club fence. Westbury couldn't wait to watch one of Cheadle's minions painstakingly lifting the cleaner's prints and taking them away in the hope of matching them with Gleeson's.

Nor could he wait, on Sunday, to lead the surveillance team a merry dance as he strolled to Notting Hill Gate, descended the steps into the Underground, sprinted to the steps that led up to the street from the other side of the station, ascended as his tail descended the far staircase, bought some newspapers and strolled home.

'Target disappeared. Presumably catching train from Notting Hill Gate. Not sure which line or in which direction,' his crestfallen tail reported.

Cheadle was more irritated than dismayed by the news that his surveillance team had lost Westbury. Tuesday was the next day of reckoning; and even if Westbury had planned his third murder for one minute after midnight on Monday, he was unlikely to have set out to commit it on Sunday morning.

Taking no risks, however, Cheadle was in the process of ordering that henceforth Notting Hill Gate station be covered as well as Kensington High Street when a further report came in that Westbury had returned home. Apparently he had gone out for no more sinister purpose than to buy the Sunday papers. At the moment, he was playing his violin.

In fact, having switched on one of his tapes and slipped into his jogging shoes, he was in his back garden, behind the incinerator, feeding his Task Force. With gloved fingers he dropped meal worms into each clear, plastic box, replaced each perforated lid and watched each spider emerge from her cover of dead, damp leaves: watched her rear up on her four hind legs, strike and begin to devour her prey.

'And that's your lot till Wednesday!' he told them severely as he closed the tobacco tin in which he kept the seething worms. By Tuesday afternoon, all four spiders would be strong but hungry. He would use the most active pair on Bunty, and feed the surviving pair the following morning – and every morning thereafter – until July the tenth.

Carefully removing his joggers before he re-entered the house, he stepped across the threshold of the French

147

windows and padded across the drawing-room to his armchair.

Cheadle, he decided, as he settled down to read what the Sunday papers said about him, must by now be resigned to the inevitability of Atrax Four. He hadn't cracked enough of the code to protect Tuesday's victim. He hadn't unearthed sufficient evidence to entitle him to require his chief suspect to spend all of Tuesday helping the police with their enquiry. And he was relying on his surveillance team (which he must now know to be fallible) to do its job so skilfully that not once in twenty-four hours on Tuesday would a brilliant and daring suspect be able to elude it.

None of which, Westbury acknowledged, meant that Atrax Four would be a doddle. He wouldn't be able just to walk out of his house, shake off his tail, walk up to Bunty, drop a couple of spiders down his neck and walk away again. Barring acts of God, and sheer misfortune, however, he should be able to do what he'd planned: and God had told him that He regarded the Atrax Series as His work, and that fortune (always the enemy of misfortune) favoured the brave.

Unpardonably, none of the papers mentioned his Series; and he had no interest in the press's obsession with the balance of payments crisis, inflation and an early general election.

Hated politics, actually. *And* politicians. And middle-aged guys with greying, rubber-banded pony tails. And women at check-out points extracting small coins from only slightly larger purses. And tripe, junkies and schizo-phrenics.

Schizophrenics, he thought, should be put down.

He looked at the telephone which never rang. He felt like company; was even tempted to invite the occupants of the battered blue van in for a cup of tea: but knew it was only a whim. He hated company.

'Twenty-six,' he told himself, 'and my life's over.'

148

So would hers be soon.

That'd teach her.

He started laughing.

And then began to cry.

Cheadle telephoned Robinson. 'Sorry to ruin your Sunday,' he said, 'but I need you here.'

'Of course, sir. Problems?'

'Solutions, if I'm right. Seems to me, Fred's got to have dual nationality and two passports. British and Australian, or British and New Zealand. That way, he could have left here for Singapore, say, on his British passport, stopped over a few days, flown to Australia on his second passport – either as a returning Australian or a visiting New Zealander – Kiwis don't need a visa to enter Australia – stayed as long as he liked, flown back to Singapore – '

'Or Bangkok!'

'Exactly! Entered as an Aussie or a Kiwi: and flown back here as a Brit.'

'If you're right, Master Westbury's got some explaining to do.'

'If I'm right, all it proves is that Master Westbury did, after all, have an opportunity to acquire funnelwebs. But so would anyone else on the Opera House print-out who has the right pair of passports. We'll have to check the lot.'

'Big job.'

'Use your toys. Pity it's Sunday.'

'By midnight it'll be Monday morning in Sydney and Auckland. Their Passport and Immigration people should be able to feed all the data – passport numbers and dates of entry and exit – back to us by what Westbury calls sparrow fart. Tomorrow morning we can cross-check all exits from the UK to anywhere abroad on British passports. Tomorrow afternoon we can start asking awkward questions.'

'Go for your life then, laddie. Set it up.'

23

In Auckland, a vital computer went down: in Australia, half the Commonwealth Civil Service was on strike: and in London, Robinson and Cheadle waited vainly through Sunday night for the information that would enable them to ask awkward questions on Monday afternoon when, in fact, Westbury was tapping away at his word processor.

Atrax Four, Monday, June 22
Am writing this now for two reasons. First, tomorrow will be too action-packed to do it then, what with a session on a sun bed at nine; supervising Anton who's coming a day early, because he's got an audition on Wednesday, and then putting on tapes and inserting cassettes etc by one thirty; crossing to Simon's flat and becoming poor Gareth Williams; meeting Bunty at three thirty; returning to Simon's flat; changing back into Christopher, The Fairest Of Them All; and leaving here for the Garden at six.

Secondly, there's a slight risk the Plodder might at last have worked out that, thanks to the fact that the Whore of Wellington and the God of Wrath were once joined in unholy wedlock, I've got a New Zealand as well as a British passport, and therefore didn't need a visa to enter Australia. If so, he'll be inviting me to assist him with his enquiries the moment he hears about Bunty: and that could tie me up for days.

If I were him, the moment I heard about Bunty I'd ring me to find out if I was in: so I've buggered the phone.

150

When he gets an out-of-order whine, I imagine he'll contact his little blue van and they'll tell him I've not left the house all afternoon and am playing my violin. Unusual to have an alibi from people who haven't even seen their suspect, but it should work. Except, I *must* be home by five thirty, in case the Plodder carves up the peak-hour traffic (*bee baw bee baw bee baw*) and gets here in less than fifteen minutes.

So it's going to be a close-run thing. But I've always known that: and I've planned accordingly.

I suppose you're wondering how a semi-colonial, pacifist pleb like me managed to get himself invited to meet a blue-blooded officer and gentleman like Bunty who was blinded at Arnhem and awarded a Military Cross? Simple! I rang him three months ago, told him I was an undecorated ex-private who was blinded in the Falklands, said I was coming to London from Newcastle on June 23 and asked could he spare me a few moments before I caught the train back. Said I needed his advice about raising money to buy guide dogs in Northumbria.

He called me his dear chap, said of course he could, and congratulated me on asking his advice on the only two things (raising money and helping the blind) about which he knew anything.

Didn't tell him I knew that because I'd looked him up in *Who's Who*: nor that, if *Who's Who* had listed his special interests as needlework and dairy farming, I'd be seeking his advice about using acupuncture on cows to increase their milk yield.

I'm telling you all this because I want you to understand how difficult it is to arrange the death of a specific stranger on a specific date using a specific weapon.

Would have been dead simple if all I'd had to do was knock off any old stranger on any old day using any old weapon, but that would have been psychopathic and unsporting. And once I'd realized that it would be too easy just to knock off the subject of Atrax Five (and she's the only one I've always wanted to knock off) I knew I had to attempt something more spectacular and challenging.

For reasons that will become obvious, the only day I can kill her is Friday, July 10. So, starting from there, I worked backwards, reducing each of the three components in each equation in accordance with three different scales of retrogression.

And that's how I got back to June 6 and Mr Michael Saxon, who changed his name from Inglis.

I hope you'll believe me when I say I tried really hard to find another celebrity who satisfied the second two parts of my formula, but I couldn't. So, much as I liked him, I decided he'd have to be Atrax One, even though that would immediately point the finger of suspicion at someone who worked in the Opera House, which wouldn't have been the case had I pleaded illness, taken the night off from work and knocked off someone else.

Anyway, Mike it was, and Atrax One became the first of a series that is progressing in terms of date, rank and alphabet, which will make it much simpler for you to predict than one that retrogresses.

It's now pretty obvious, though, that you're unpardonably slow on the uptake. Mind you, you could know more than you've let on: you just might have worked out that the subject of Atrax Four can only be Bunty. Well, we'll soon know.

To be completed tomorrow night: I hope!

24

Otherwise known as the Most Honourable the Marquess of Uppingham, Bunty Reading was waiting to receive his guest. Blind himself for two thirds of his life, he was acutely aware of the stress young Williams would suffer as he attempted to cope with the unfamiliar terrain and atmosphere of a gentlemen's club.

Apparently extrovert to the point of eccentricity, he was, in fact, an intelligent, conscientious member of the House of Lords who dreaded the probability that his fellow working peers found his face repellent and his debating skills ill-informed.

'Am I disfigured?' was the first thing he asked when he regained consciousness at Arnhem: not because he was vain but because he thought how unfair it would be to expect his fiancée to marry a hideous man.

'Handsome as ever,' a brother officer quite truthfully assured him. But that was what he himself would have said had their positions been reversed; and the fact remained that, as soon as she decently could, after his repatriation, his fiancée had broken off their engagement: since when he had been convinced that he had the sort of face that frightened horses.

'People with chronic halitosis must feel the same,' he once confessed to the woman he eventually married. 'They know they offend, but there's nothing they can do about it.'

'So why do you think I married you?' she retorted. 'To become a bloody marchioness?'

Mindful of the fact that she had twice refused his proposal of marriage precisely because she was unwilling to become a marchioness, he had laughed; but she had never been able to cure him of the habit, when he thought he was unobserved, of trying to read, with his fingertips, the extent of his disfigurement.

Nor had his noble friends in the House been able to convince him that they treasured his contributions to their debates for their brevity, logic and wit. Ever conscious of his lack of expertise in anything but blindness, and the shortage, in the Lords' otherwise excellent library, of up-to-date material printed in braille, he was obliged to debate in the purest sense of the word, refuting the non-

153

sensical, debunking the partisan and clarifying the obscure. Having spoken, he would resume his seat, help himself to some jellybeans and take up his knitting.

Now, however, he stood by the porter's desk – tall, erect, white-haired, sightless but steady-eyed – awaiting the arrival of his guest. He recognized the sound of his car as it approached, and stepped forward into the entrance.

'Mr Williams, my lord,' his chauffeur said, so positioning the dark-spectacled younger man that his employer's hand would find his guest's elbow.

'My dear chap,' said Lord Uppingham, 'how good of you to come. Thank you, Dean. I'll be ready at five.'

'I'll be here, my lord.'

'It would be best, I think, if I steered you,' he said, guiding Williams inside and marching him briskly through the lobby.

'Staircase,' he advised. They mounted it steadily, turned left at the top, and then left again.

'Doorway,' he said. 'I'll take you to my table – they keep it for me so that I don't wreck the place looking for one that's unoccupied – and then I'll get us a cup of what they laughingly describe as coffee. Comes from a machine specially designed to scald the unwary. There you are. Seat's by your left hand. Be with you in a minute.'

Williams sat cautiously, carefully placed a gift-wrapped jar on the left-hand side of the table and explored the rest of the table-top with his gloved right hand while Lord Uppingham collected their coffee. Several members watched him briefly, then averted their eyes.

'Didn't know whether you took sugar so I brought you two lumps,' said Uppingham, setting both cups carefully down. 'In the saucer, directly in front of you, six inches from the edge of the table.'

'You're very helpful, sir.'

'Know what it's like. Nothing worse than capsizing one's coffee in someone else's club. Dean on time, was he?'

'I'm the one that's usually unpunctual, sir. A bit early or a bit late. Afraid I can't read our kind of watch. Hands were burnt.'

'Falklands?'

'Yes.'

'Rotten luck. Means no books either. I'd be lost without me books. Music?'

'Top of the pops: stuff like that.'

'Chap in the Lords composed pop. The one that spider loony did in. Inherited young Allison's title. Absolute shit. Still, so was Wagner. You don't take sugar, I gather?' – stirring his own cup vigorously.

'Sweeteners, actually.' Williams took a small brown bottle from his jacket pocket. 'And you do, I gather?'

'Three!'

'The consultant made me give up sugar, alcohol and cigarettes.'

'Gareth Williams,' Lord Uppingham reflected. 'Obviously Welsh, but your accent . . . ?'

'I've lived most of my life in Geordieland, sir: apart from four years in the army.'

'Of course. Now stir in your filthy sweeteners' – stirring again himself – 'and drink up. Then I'll fetch us another cup and we can get down to business. Mustn't make you miss your train.'

Williams sipped at his cup: Uppingham drained his. 'Finished?' he asked.

'I'm a bit slower than you, I'm afraid, sir.'

'Take your time. Who else have you seen about your project?'

'Only my MP.'

'Burnside, would that be? Or Walters?'

'Mr Burnside.'

'Nice chap. Got a very good Military Cross in '56 in Malaya.'

'He told me you got a very good Military Cross at Arnhem in '44.

'Kind of him, but quite untrue. Would've run away only I couldn't see. Asked the fellow next to me to guide me, but he was so full of Gerry lead he couldn't move, so we stayed put. Now people say how frightfully brave we were. Awful thing is, I've forgotten his name. Alexander, was it? Jenkins? Something like that. His father played the fiddle, I remember; and his mother, poor darling, always used to get frightfully tight at balls, but what his name was . . . It's me synapses, my quack tells me. Sort of cerebral short circuit. Harley Street's euphemism for going gaga. Tell me about your guide dog thing.'

Williams told him about his project to raise enough money to provide every sightless Northumbrian with a guide dog, and then noisily gulped down the rest of his coffee.

Uppingham left the table and brought back two more coffees. 'You'll need a lot of money,' he warned. 'I'll have my secretary type a letter to Tyne Tees Television, get you an interview. And there are a couple of Japanese firms who'll chip in if I twist their arm. And I'll have a word with Burnside. He's got a Private Member's Bill going through the other place: I'll threaten to obstruct it in the Lords if he doesn't play ball . . .'

Williams loudly stirred and sipped his coffee, which prompted Uppingham to do the same.

'Ring me at the House this day week,' Uppingham concluded. 'I'll give more thought to the problem of contacts. Editors and so on. Tell you what I've come up with then.'

'I hadn't meant to be any trouble, sir,' Williams protested.

'Least I can do, dear boy.' He rubbed his face as if suddenly tired, and absent-mindedly fingered the scar across his forehead.

'Well, I'm very grateful to you,' Williams assured him. 'And I hope I won't seem presumptuous if I offer you this small token of gratitude from me and my committee,' and slid the gift-wrapped jar across the table. 'It's beside your cup,' he said.

'Too kind,' Uppingham murmured, his hands examining the unexpected gift, his face registering sudden amusement. 'This what I think it is?' He held the parcel to his ear and shook it.

'Probably,' Williams admitted shyly.

'My dear chap, how absolutely splendid. And how original. The last gift a committee gave me was a quite ghastly cigarette lighter in the form of a plastic antique pistol. Tell your friends I'm most grateful – the more so since my own jar is almost empty. Can't thank you enough' – and setting the gift aside, flipped open his wrist-watch and put his finger to the dial. 'Three forty-five,' he pronounced. 'What time must you leave?'

'About four fifteen. Give me time to find my way up to the tube at Piccadilly.'

'Dear God,' Uppingham reproached himself. 'What must you think of me? Never gave a thought to how you'd get back. Here' – reaching for his wallet – 'let me give you the money for a cab.'

'No!' said Williams. 'Really, sir, no. You've done too much already.'

'Quite sure?'

'Yes, sir.'

Neither, then, seemed to know what to say next. Uppingham rubbed his face again. Williams rummaged through every pocket in his jacket. 'Bugger it!' he muttered.

'Something wrong?' Uppingham asked him.

'Not really. Except I'm dying for a cigarette and I've forgotten to bring any gum.'

Uppingham pushed the jar of jellybeans across the table. 'Help yourself,' he said.

'No, sir. They're yours.'

'And you're my guest.'

'Well, I will if you will.'

'After you.'

Williams removed the cellophane wrapping and the glass stopper, prodded at the jellybeans on either side of two agitated spiders and pushed the jar across the table to Uppingham.

Uppingham picked up the jar with his left hand and inserted his right hand. One of the spiders scuttled up his hand and sleeve, across his shoulder and on to his neck: the other reared up on its four hind legs and bit his finger. Frowning, Uppingham put three jellybeans in his mouth and slapped at his neck. The spider on his hand fell to the floor. The spider on his neck sidled swiftly around to his throat, reared up and struck. Uppingham brushed irritably at his throat, and the second spider fell to the floor.

'Hope they're OK,' Williams said. 'My wife asked for the best.'

'First class,' Uppingham assured him. 'But I think this place must have become infested with fleas.' His voice was suddenly slurred.

'You all right, sir?'

'Bit woozy actually.'

'I've kept you too long . . .'

'Not at all. Anno domini.'

'I'll leave you to rest until your driver comes.'

'Might be best. I'll see you out.'

Much less steadily than when he had escorted Williams into the club, Uppingham led him down to the entrance. Williams raised his face to the afternoon sun and tapped at the top step with his white stick.

'Thank you for everything,' he said.

'Know the way, do you?'

'Right to Lower Regent Street and then left to Piccadilly Circus.'

'And I'll hear from you this day week?'

'Yes, sir. At the House of Lords.'

Uppingham patted him on the back. 'Four stairs to the pavement,' he warned. 'Safe trip home.'

'You too, sir,' said Williams – and not attempting to shake hands, to which he knew English gentlemen were averse, he tapped his way down to the pavement and along Pall Mall toward Lower Regent Street.

Steadying himself, Uppingham took a deep breath and forced himself to stride past the porter and into the Reading Room, where he sank heavily into a deep leather armchair, leaned back, closed his eyes and fell profoundly asleep.

25

Less than a mile from Pall Mall, Cheadle, who was sitting at his desk, apparently day-dreaming, suddenly shouted, 'Sergeant!'

Robinson appeared at his door within seconds. 'We've been idiots,' Cheadle told him.

'I know,' said Robinson. 'Saxon was a mister, the next step up is a knight, then come baronets – '

'Sir Nicholas Corder.'

'After baronets come barons, then viscounts – '

'Allison.'

'And after viscounts – '

'Earls followed by marquesses. Sometime today, Fred's going to murder a marquess whose family name begins with R.'

'R?'

'Saxon was born Inglis: begins with I. Skip a letter and you get to K. Corder was born Korda. Skip *two* letters from K, you get to N. Allison was born Naismith. Skip *three* letters from N, you get to R. I want a list of all our marquesses. Ring the editor of Debrett's.'

Robinson passed him a sheet of paper. 'I'd just done it when you called,' he said.

Cheadle merely glanced at the list before handing it back and pushing his telephone across the desk. 'Ring 'em again and get each one's *family* name. Correction: get each one whose family name begins with R.'

Debrett's editor proved as knowledgeable as he was co-operative. 'There's only one,' he said. 'Uppingham. Family name Reading, nickname Bunty, blinded in World War Two – '

'The one who knits?'

'Probably sitting in the House doing just that at this very moment.'

'I'm obliged to you,' Robinson thanked him, and hung up. 'It's Uppingham,' he told Cheadle. 'He's probably at the House of Lords right now.'

Cheadle grabbed the telephone and tapped out 219 3000. 'Detective Chief Superintendent Cheadle here,' he announced. 'If he's in the House, it's imperative I speak to Lord Uppingham.'

'He may be in the Chamber,' the girl on the switchboard protested.

'If he is, lassie, get him out. You may just save his life.'

'I'll call the desk at the Peers' entrance. If Lord Uppingham's in attendance, I'll have a messenger check the Chamber.'

Cheadle waited impatiently until she returned to him.

'Lord Uppingham's at his club,' she told him. 'He had an appointment there at three thirty.'

'With whom?'

'I've no idea.'

'Look,' snarled Cheadle, 'he's been in great danger for an hour and twenty minutes already. He's blind and he's defenceless. What's his club?'

She told him: then added, 'I'll ring and warn him.'

'I'll do that,' he snapped. 'Just gimme the number.'

*

Lord Uppingham's head had fallen to one side. At the far end of the Reading Room, a fellow member put down his newspaper, rose from his chair and headed for the bar. As he passed Uppingham, he glanced down, smiling affectionately: and noticed the sleeping man's swollen throat and wet, livid face.

'You all right, Bunty?' he asked. *'Bunty?'*

A distinguished surgeon, the only other occupant of the room, disturbed by the unprecedented sound of a raised voice, looked up from his crossword puzzle: then swiftly crossed the floor, took up Uppingham's wrist, felt for a pulse and, lowering the wrist, said, 'Poor old boy.'

The porter hurried in, looking agitated. 'Excuse me, gentlemen,' he apologized, 'but has either of you seen Lord Uppingham?'

The surgeon stood aside and gestured soberly at the late Marquess of Uppingham.

'Oh, my God,' the porter moaned. 'The police have just rung to say they're on their way; a member's just killed two spiders in the Coffee Room; and his Lordship's dead in the Reading Room. This is supposed to be gentlemen's club, gentlemen. What will people say?'

'You sure you don't want to call in at the club before you question Westbury?' Robinson queried as he drove Cheadle through Trafalgar Square.

'What's the point? Uppingham's dead: Fred left the premises fifty minutes ago: there's nothing we can do that the two lads I sent there won't do equally well: Forensic'll find nothing but two squashed spiders: I've got the surveillance boys on red alert – '

'The pair stationed near Westbury's home did say he'd been heard playing his violin on and off all afternoon,' Robinson warned.

'Nevertheless,' muttered Cheadle.

'You're sure it's him?'

'No.'

In brooding silence, they drove up Constitution Hill and *bee bawed* their way through the snarl of traffic at Hyde Park Corner.

'Gloves, white cane, surgical collar, black glasses, burn scar on his right cheek; he'll stick out like a male stripper in a nunnery,' said Robinson.

'Until he sheds 'em.'

'Using the Underground, do you reckon?'

'Unless he's got a helicopter: which I wouldn't put past him.'

'Tapes for the violin playing?'

'Has to be, doesn't it? When we find *them*, we've got him. He's good; but he can't have thought of everything. The spiders could be anywhere: Opera House, in the park, up in his rafters, anywhere. But those tapes . . . By the way, the thing we saw that I knew would give the lie to his violin alibi if only I could remember it: it's the open music on his music stand.'

'Why?'

'Once he knows a piece, he *never* looks at his music. He put that there to make an already credible alibi even more credible. It's his one weakness: unnecessary detail.'

'Wouldn't exactly hold up in a court of law.'

'Tapes won't either.'

'So?'

'Unless we catch a blind man wearing a surgical collar tapping his way up to Westbury's front door, we've got sixteen days to prepare the ambush that'll capture him red-handed as he attempts to murder his next victim.'

'But, sir!'

'I know. After marquesses come dukes, and after dukes come Royals. And skipping four letters after R, for Reading, takes us to W, for Windsor. Could be Prince Charles, who's become Wales: or the Princess Royal, who became Mrs Phillips, or Princess Margaret, who became Countess Snowdon.'

'Or the Duchess of Kent, who *was* a Worsley,' Robinson added, to Cheadle's obvious displeasure. 'The Queen's not going to like it.'

'Don't suppose the Waleses, Phillipses, Snowdons and Kents'll be overjoyed,' Cheadle told him sourly. 'Still, this time we'll have the Security Services and the Royal Protection Squad on our side. I wonder if Fred's thought of that?'

26

They stood a moment on the front door step, listening to the sound of a violin. The same phrase was repeated three times. Cheadle rang the door bell and the playing ceased. Westbury opened the door to them.

Carrying his violin in one hand, his bow in the other, he was dressed in a T-shirt, running shorts and a pair of white socks. 'Good heavens,' he said. 'Didn't expect to see you again. Come in.'

'Evening, Mr Williams,' said Cheadle, not moving, looking him up and down.

'Westbury,' the violinist corrected him with a smile.

'Of course. Sorry about that.'

'Sorry I'm improperly dressed. If I'd known you were coming – '

'I did try to ring – '

Westbury nodded. 'Telecom told me there'd been a complaint.'

'Oh? When was that?'

'Not sure exactly. An hour ago? Tempus fugits when I'm practising. Is that why you came? To tell me my phone has been out of order?'

'Not really, sir, no.'

163

'Then come in, for God's sake. Or would you rather hover?'

As he stood aside, Cheadle and Robinson stepped into the hall and waited for him to close the door. 'You know the way,' he said, gesturing with his bow.

'After you, sir.'

Apparently bemused by their formality, Westbury led them down the hall, past his bedroom on the right and the dining-room opposite it, and past the staircase on the left.

'Bathroom if either of you needs it,' he said, nodding leftwards. 'Otherwise, sit yourselves down in the drawing-room and I'll be with you as soon as I've put this away' – brandishing the violin.

He padded into his music room, opposite the bathroom, and, taking a polishing cloth from his violin case, applied it with unhurried care to both his fiddle and bow before laying them in the case and closing its lid. When he turned to leave the room, to rejoin the two policemen, he found them standing in the doorway, watching him intently.

'Always do that, do you?' Cheadle enquired, moving to the music stand, glancing at the music.

'All violinists do.' He led the way out, halting in the doorway beside Robinson; but Cheadle stood his ground.

'Same piece, I see.'

'You're getting absent-minded in your old age, Chief Superintendent,' Westbury rebuked him good-humouredly. 'Forgetting my name, forgetting the recital I'm practising for. Come on' – and marched off into the drawing-room, where he sat in front of the TV. A first-round singles was in progress on the Centre Court of Wimbledon.

Cheadle and Robinson took their seats, their eyes scanning the room, slowly. Seemingly unaware, Westbury watched a long rally between a young Chinese American and a deceptively indolent Czech. When the Czech won the rally with a delicate drop shot, he applauded.

Cheadle, seeking to regain the initiative, observed, 'You *have* cleaned the place up, haven't you?'

Westbury glanced at him coldly. 'You been spying on me, Chief Superintendent?'

'Beg pardon, sir?'

' "You *have* cleaned the place up, haven't you?" you said,' Westbury accused. 'Which could only have meant that someone had told you about it, and what you now see confirms his report.'

'Expressed myself badly, sir.'

'Badly but accurately,' Westbury amended. 'Only a half-wit would say, "You *have* cleaned the place up, haven't you?" when what he meant was, "You've cleaned the place up!" You're not a half-wit, are you?'

'I doubt any successful policemen are, sir.'

'Nor are any gifted violinists.'

Their eyes met, Cheadle's thoughtful, Westbury's mocking. Cheadle decided to change his tactics. 'Seem to have got off to a bad start, don't we, Chris?'

'Depends where we're going, doesn't it, Charlie?'

Despite himself, Cheadle scowled. All innocence, Westbury said, 'Not Charlie? You look like a Charlie to me! Maybe we should avoid familiarity. Or were you being . . . avuncular?'

'Avuncular is not how I feel,' Cheadle assured him. 'Look, can we start again?' He glanced at the cup on the small table by Westbury's chair. 'Have some coffee and a chat?'

Westbury glanced at his watch. 'No time. Unless, of course, you've brought a warrant for my arrest?'

'Nothing like that, Mr Westbury. Just a few questions.'

'Short questions, I trust?'

'Well, try this for size. Why didn't you tell us you had a New Zealand passport?'

'Never occurred to me you'd be interested.'

'Why do you think we asked to see everyone's passport?'

165

'Ours not to reason why, Chief Superintendent. Having watched you destroy an entire performance of *La Fille*, we all realized there are more strange things in Scotland Yard than are dreamt of in our philosophy.'

'Why did you use your New Zealand passport to enter Australia?'

'If one's flying from Auckland, surely that's the logical thing to do?'

'What took you to Auckland?'

'I was holidaying in Bangkok. Nothing but pimps, pox and prostitutes. My mother'd just died. Never felt lonelier in my life . . .' Tears welled out of his eyes. 'Decided I wanted to visit her grave in Wellington, say goodbye.' He wiped the tears away and stared blindly at the television screen, where a jubilant Chinese American was shaking the hand of a subdued but expressionless Czech. 'Sorry,' he mumbled. 'We were very close.'

'Didn't mean to upset you, sir. And after you'd said goodbye to your mother, you went –?'

'To Sydney. No sense hanging round Wellington, being morbid. Last thing Mum would've wanted. And living in England, I'd really missed lying on a beach in the sun.'

'I can see you're a sun worshipper.'

'Not the same on the back lawn, though, is it?' Suddenly dry-eyed and cruel, he said, 'You obviously hate it: you're as pale as the belly of a dead fish. And he's no better' – turning on Robinson.

'We work anti-social hours, sir,' Robinson explained. 'Like twenty a day, seven days a week. Psychopaths aren't the most considerate of clients, you see.'

'And conductors aren't the most considerate of masters,' quibbled Westbury, who hated conceding even the smallest of points, 'but I don't whinge, I do something about it.'

'Like preparing for your recital?' asked Cheadle, sounding innocuous, but looking, Westbury thought, too offhand to be anything but dangerous. For some incompre-

166

hensible reason, Mr Cheadle kept reverting to the subject of his preparations for his recital.

'You could resign from the police, study law, become as famous as Judge Jeffreys,' he said, thinking, 'Preparations . . . practice . . . alibi . . . tapes . . . burnt 'em.'

'Afraid neither of us has such an aptitude for the law as you have for music,' said Cheadle. Westbury said nothing. 'Nor do we have your phenomenal memory.' Westbury waited for Cheadle to come to the point. 'Every night, a different opera, another ballet. Verdi, Tchaikovsky, Stravinsky, Prokofiev.' He tapped his temple. 'They're all in there, you know them all: right?' Westbury nodded: and Cheadle pounced. 'But Haydn you *don't* know, eh?'

'I not only know Haydn,' Westbury calmly contradicted, 'I adore him.'

'Adore him so much his is the only stuff you can't play by memory?'

'Adore him so much,' retorted Westbury, rising furiously to his feet, 'his is the only "stuff" I wouldn't *dream* of playing by memory! As a successful policeman, Mr Cheadle, you may be better than a half-wit: but as an amateur musicologist, you're worse than a moron. Now, I've got to get dressed, go to the Garden and play Donizetti, whose "stuff" I detest, even if it did influence Verdi. But since my passion for Haydn seems to have been your only excuse for gate-crashing me, let me just add this before you go: in future, when you and your minions are discussing great instrumental composers, as doubtless you often do, you'll be well advised never to forget that Franz Josef Haydn was the daddy of them all. OK?'

'OK.'

'Time you left then.'

'There are a few more questions, sir.'

'After the show,' said Westbury firmly. 'I'll be back here about eleven fifteen. Or do I have to go to your station?

Because, if so, kindly have dinner waiting. Nothing chee-sey. I hate cheese.'

'No need for you to come to the station, Mr Westbury,' said Cheadle, heading for the front door. 'We'll probably drop in later, as you suggested.'

'Ring me if you change your mind,' said Westbury, letting them out. 'The phone's fixed, thanks to your com-plaint to Telecom.'

'You've been most co-operative,' Cheadle told him. 'So why don't we return the compliment by driving you to the Opera House? And after the show, we'll drive you home again. Least we can do.'

'Be with you in five minutes,' Westbury agreed: and closed the door.

As they walked to their car, Cheadle told Robinson, 'Give him a minute, knock on the door and ask can you use his bathroom. Don't pry: just make sure he doesn't erase those tapes. The search warrant'll be waiting for us when we get back to the station: we'll use it tonight.'

Cheadle looked less than pleased when three of West-bury's colleagues escorted him to the car outside Bow Street Police Station. Led by the red-headed Kevin Maguire, they made it plain that they didn't trust the police to respect Westbury's rights. They even offered to follow him home and protect him from harassment and brutality.

'Now why did you do that?' Cheadle demanded, as they drove down Bow Street. 'All we're asking is for you to help us with our enquiries.'

'Told them that.'

'Why tell 'em anything?'

'It amused me.'

'Well, it didn't amuse me.'

'It was you suggested driving me here and back. You telling me now you didn't expect anyone to notice?'

'Never thought of that,' Cheadle confessed, having in fact relied on it to embarrass his suspect and provoke a contretemps. 'Anyway, water under the bridge, least said soonest mended.'

'What a way you have with words.' But Cheadle seemed impervious to sarcasm, and Robinson deaf to it, so they drove the rest of the way in silence.

Westbury unlocked his front door, pushed it open with his knee, entered the hall, nudged the light switch down with his elbow, motioned the two policemen inside, removed his key from the lock, slipped it into his trouser pocket, pushed the door shut with his rump, took a folded handkerchief from his pocket as he led the way into his dark drawing-room, pressed the handkerchief against both the TV remote control button and the light switch and dropped into his chair.

'Make yourselves at home,' he said, stuffing his hands into his pockets, leaning back, stretching his legs, displaying no apprehension about his visitors' intentions – nor any interest in them.

'You're probably feeling like a cup of something before we start, sir: and a bite to eat,' Cheadle suggested.

'How solicitous you are.' But Westbury remained in his chair, almost recumbent, head backflung. He was neither thirsty nor hungry because Kevin – on being apprised of Cheadle's intention to resume his questioning after the performance – had bought him a meat pie, a sausage roll, two ham sandwiches and a bottle of beer during the interval. Allowing his head to roll indolently rightwards, he glanced in turn at Cheadle and Robinson, looking hopefully for symptoms in them of malnutrition and dehydration.

'I see you've broken another glass,' Cheadle remarked.

'Careless of me, wasn't it?'

Robinson's eyes flickered round the immaculate room. 'You don't seem the careless sort,' he smiled. 'Did you break the mirror too?' – surveying the sheeted looking-glass.

'Kept telling me I was the fairest of them all,' Westbury wisecracked, staring up at the ceiling. 'I got sick of it.'

'Now that's *most* unusual,' commented Cheadle.

Head lolling in his direction, Westbury asked, 'What is?'

'A mirror that *volunteers* flattery. Usually they have to be asked. "Mirror, mirror, on the wall, who's the fairest of them all?" one asks, if I remember rightly.'

Westbury resumed his inspection of the ceiling, cursing himself for his levity, for departing from the script: which said that the looking-glass was dirty but too tall to clean without a step ladder and he didn't have a step ladder. 'Don't explain,' Solomon whispered. 'Attack.'

'That memory of yours,' he sneered.

Stung by this gratuitous rudeness, Robinson was about to spring to his superior's defence when Cheadle silenced him with a warning hand. Certainly the insult had struck home; but it had delighted him as well. Cruelly piercing insights into others' weaknesses were the prerogative, in his experience, of scorned women and cornered madmen.

Inadmissible in court, of course; but at long last he felt confident that his stubborn suspicions were well founded. If Westbury ran true to form, having first attacked the Achilles heel, he would next go for the balls.

'All one's faculties are impaired by age,' he tempted equably. 'One can't hear as well, run as fast, see as far – '

'Get it up as often!'

Unseen by Westbury, Cheadle glanced at Robinson and gave him a thumbs-up. Robinson acknowledged the old boy's success – the nature of which eluded him – with a nod.

Cheadle turned back to the recumbent Westbury, whose psychological profile had described him as sexually inadequate. 'Bit of a Don Juan yourself, are you?'

170

Westbury stiffened: then, sitting slowly upright, said furiously, 'I think it's time you left.'

'Ah,' Cheadle remonstrated, 'don't be like that, Chris. I mean, it was you raised the subject: and your generation's so much more open about sex than mine, isn't it?'

'Has so much more to be open about,' Westbury retorted, wondering by what possible means he could side-track the hateful Cheadle from this hateful subject. 'And we're only open about it with our contemporaries.'

'Several of whom', Robinson advised him, 'have told us you once had quite a thing going with a certain blonde in a certain box.'

Apparently ignoring him, Westbury assessed the significance of 'certain blonde' and 'certain box': and decided that they were intended to imply that she had been identified – which she couldn't have been.

'Tell us about her,' Cheadle suggested.

'Turns you on does it, the kiss and tell stuff?' Westbury sneered, relieved to be allowed at last to revert to his script. 'Get off on it, do you? Know what your trouble is, you've been reading too many books by ex-lovers of the likes of Joan Collins.'

'Funny you should mention her. Only the other night, at Elmsmere House, actually, the sergeant and I were discussing the possibility that Fred – you know who I mean by Fred, of course?'

'Astaire? Perry? Truman?'

'You didn't see me on TV when I said our name for the nutter who killed Mr Saxon and Sir Nicholas was Fred?' Cheadle seemed dismayed by the possibility that even a single British viewer had missed his moment of glory on the box.

'Riveting, were you?'

'Camera-man said I was a natural! Oh well' – setting disappointment aside – 'at least you *now* know who the sergeant and I were referring to. Anyway, the sergeant

171

here wondered whether Fred, as well as being stark, raving mad, mightn't also be a transvestite.'

'Does this interminable anecdote have a point?'

'Coming to that. I said no, a transvestite would've turned up as Joan Collins, not a punk.'

'Fascinating.'

'And now *you* mention her.'

'If that's typical of the way you conduct your enquiries, no wonder Fred's made such a fool of you. Transvestite indeed.'

'Now fair play, Chris. Everyone said he was pretty. Put him beside you in front of that mirror and ask who's the fairest of 'em all, it'd probably say him.'

'You seem obsessed by my mirror.'

'Just curious.'

'Well, if you must know, it was so grubby I couldn't stand it, so I covered it up: but when I spring cleaned the place it was too tall to reach without a ladder, and I don't have a ladder, so I left it covered up. Of course, if I'd known I was going to be inundated with querulous gate crashers, I'd have done something about it.'

'Did something about the walls, I see: and that wall's higher than the mirror.'

Westbury heaved a sigh, shook his head and seemed finally to decide that only the truth would exorcise Cheadle's absurd obsession.

'What a boring man you are,' he complained. 'Still, you've asked for it, so here you are. Everyone at the Opera House used to say the two best-looking guys in the place were Mike Saxon and myself. Course, everyone knew Mike was miles better looking than me – the most beautiful man in the world and all that – so when he collapsed' – tears began to fill his eyes – 'and there was a news flash, just after I got home – Dame Lyndsay, saying Mike . . . saying Mike was . . . dead,' he brushed away a tear, 'I couldn't believe it. I walked round and round the room, saying, "Why? Why, why, why?" And ended up screaming at that looking-glass, "Mirror, mirror, on the wall, he's still the fairest of them all." '

'And it said, "No, he's not, you are," did it?'

Just in time, Westbury refrained from nodding. 'Don't be daft,' he growled. 'We're talking about Mike and me, not Snow White and the Seven Dwarfs.'

'Snow White and the Wicked Queen, actually.'

Westbury flushed. 'Look,' he said, 'if you're mad enough to suspect *me* of being the elusive spiderman, that's your business; but when you start impugning my masculinity – '

'Impugning your masculinity, sir?' Cheadle looked aghast.

'Transvestite! Pretty! Queen!' Westbury recapitulated. 'Queen instead of Stepmother, as you very well know. Innuendo, innuendo, innuendo. I don't have to put up with that. Come to that, unless you've got a warrant, I don't have to put up with you.'

'Well, actually, sir, I do have a warrant.'

'For my *arrest*?' Westbury was incredulous and shocked – incredulous because he knew they hadn't any evidence on which to detain him: shocked because Atrax Four had convinced him that nothing could prevent Atrax Five from being equally successful.

'Good gracious me, no, Chris: a search warrant. To help us eliminate you from our enquiry. Unless you've been naughty.'

'I hate being patronized.'

'Had a bellyful of being patronized, have you? Your dad, your mum, Sir Leon?'

'Now you're talking nonsense.' The way Cheadle leapt from one subject to another, then to a third, then back to the first, irritated and disconcerted him. Wasn't how his interrogation should be proceeding. Made him sound petulant. Gave him no chance to shine. No one had ever allowed him to shine.

173

'I never met your parents, of course,' Cheadle was saying.

'Happily for them.'

'But I have met Sir Leon. And he seemed more concerned about you than patronizing.'

'Concerned?'

'Thought you weren't – how shall I put it – weren't always as *well* as you might be. That's why he didn't sack you.'

'Bollocks,' snarled Westbury, his face suddenly scarlet with rage: even his forehead scarlet with rage. 'He didn't sack me because he knows I know about the affair he was having with that blonde in the box you're always on about.'

Cheadle shrugged. 'That's as may be,' he argued, 'but the impression I got was he's concerned about your health.'

'Rubbish! I'm never ill. Never even catch a cold.'

'Not all ailments are physical. I mean, Sir Leon would hardly have debated keeping you on if all you'd been was a martyr to the common cold, would he?'

'He keeps me on because I'm a gifted violinist.'

'He had no complaints about your musicianship,' Cheadle conceded.

'So now you're saying that as well as being a pretty, transvestite queen, I'm a jibbering maniac? On the evidence of a singularly obtuse and philandering Director of Music! But you have to say that, don't you? You're on record as saying Fred's a nutter.'

Cheadle beamed. 'Ah,' he said, 'so you did see me on telly!' He glanced at the video under the TV. 'Taped it and watched it when you got home, did you?'

'My colleagues told me about it. Said you went right over the top.'

'Really? Which colleagues?'

'Kevin Maguire, for one. Really pissed off with you,

Kevin was. Everybody knew you'd interrogated him: now they call him the Demented Drummer.'

'And what do they call you: the Schizoid Soloist *Manqué*?'

'I'm going to bed.'

'Only joking, Chris. Anyway, there's nothing shameful about being schizophrenic.'

'I'm *not* schizophrenic.'

'Well, your doctor'd know: one word from him, you're in the clear.'

'The last time I saw a doctor,' Westbury hissed, 'was thirteen years ago, at boarding school.'

'What school was that?'

'Eton!' Westbury told him, rising to his feet. 'Or it may have been Harrow.' He walked to the hall doorway. 'Turn the lights out when you leave. After you've looked around. I've been very patient with you, Mr Cheadle, but my patience is exhausted.'

'Hitler said that in '39,' Cheadle mused. 'He was mad, too! Sweet dreams, young Christopher.'

For the next two and three quarter hours, Westbury lay in bed reviewing everything he had said, listening to every move the policemen made, straining to hear every word they uttered, becoming less anxious, more confident, by the second.

Granted Cheadle had rattled him with his sneaky questions: but he'd given nothing away. And Cheadle suspected no more than he was meant to, to keep the game alive, lend spice to the Series.

Nor had he found anything. Westbury had had to gag himself with his pillow to stifle his laughter when he heard them playing the cassette of his own rendition of the Haydn Sonata for Violin and Piano.

'Got him!' Cheadle had said when he found the cassette, labelled WESTBURY/HAYDN. And a minute later, 'The

175

little sod couldn't have used *this*: there's a piano on it. Look for another.'

'Loads of cassettes here,' Robinson had answered. 'None labelled Westbury, though.'

'Play 'em!'

'Take days.'

'Take 'em with us, then. *And* that mug on the table by the telly. Nothing else here, is there?'

'A few floppy disks: inscribed *Letters to mum*, *Letters to dad*. Terrible writing. No wonder he uses a processor.'

'Sitting-room now,' Cheadle had ordered.

Fat lot of good that had done them.

After that, they had gone through his kitchen, opening and shutting everything, clinking and rattling. And so on, right through the house – doubtless reading all of Aunty Deb's girlish love letters to Uncle Paul, and going through every pocket of Uncle's array of Savile Row suits. And finally they'd come into his bedroom, rummaging and pawing as if he weren't there. He had turned his back on them.

At one stage, Cheadle had shaken his shoulder. 'New gloves, Mr Westbury?'

'I'm allergic to detergents, and violinists have to protect their hands. But I've got a cleaner now, so take 'em if you want 'em.'

'Too small for me, laddie' – replacing all but the two soiled pairs in the drawer.

'Yeah, well you are a bit ham-fisted, aren't you?'

'We're leaving now.'

As soon as he heard their car depart, he went into his windowless music room, shut the door, turned on the light, sat in front of his word processor and inserted the disk inscribed *Letters to dad*.

27

Atrax Four (Cont'd) 3 a.m. June 24
Am sitting down to do this at 3 a.m. Wednesday because
you arrived here at 5.40 p.m. Tuesday and only left twenty
minutes ago. Enjoyed your visit. Hope you did too. And
hereunder as lucid an account as I can manage, at this
hour, of how I suckered you for the fourth time in eighteen days.

The last words I wrote yesterday were, 'To be completed tomorrow night: I hope!'

I lied.

I knew!

But the half of me I inherited from the God of Wrath
demands constant self-deprecation, while the half I inherited from the Whore of Wellington demands habitual mendacity: so I indulge indiscriminately in both.

Of the two, though, I prefer lying. Self-deprecation's so
insincere. Mendacity's so much less dishonest, so much
more fun.

People ask me the time, I look at my watch, it says five
to three, I tell them twenty past two, they stop running
for their train, and miss it!

Pollsters ask me my age, occupation, address and
income, I tell them twenty, bullion dealer, Belgravia and
two hundred thousand p.a.

The census form asked did anyone else live at this
address, and what age they were, I answered eight others,
all over sixty-five.

The guys in the orchestra asked where I'd been when
I went to New Zealand and Australia the winter before
last, I told them Klosters with Di and Sarah.

I mean, what right has anyone to ask all these questions? And what good does it do to answer truthfully?

I told Inland Revenue the truth about my increased

income last year, after Uncle died, and they whipped more than half of it off me.

I told Uncle's GP the truth about the God of Wrath, the Whore of Wellington, the judges at the Young Musician contest, and the Temptress who encouraged me to continue our correspondence, and what did the doctor do? Persuaded Uncle to section me! It was he who killed Uncle. And it's the Temptress who killed Mike, Nicky, Harvey and Bunty.

Naturally, I lied when I decided to go to Australia. Asked the God of Wrath to get me a hugely discounted return air ticket to Bangkok, and told Heathrow I was British. Once there, rang the God of Wrath for a discounted Bangkok-Auckland return ticket because, I said, I wanted to visit the Whore's grave in Wellington. Quite untrue, but it worked. From Auckland, I paid the full return fare to Sydney.

Nothing sinister about any of that: just didn't want anyone to know where I was. But it paid off, because when I got back to London I found I had a dilly-bag full of stowaways.

I realized straight away that I was meant to avenge the Temptress's treachery. God had persuaded two pregnant funnelwebs to take refuge from a Sydney cloudburst in my host's flight bag. God had persuaded my host to give me that bag. God gave each funnelweb lots of babies. And God gave me the New Zealand nationality that would make you think I'd never been to Australia.

In His great wisdom, however, He also gave me far more stowaways than I needed just to punish the Temptress.

His intentions were clear. I was to attempt a Series that would culminate in the punishment of the Temptress.

If you doubt any of this, consider the following:

No sooner had I accepted that the Temptress must be removed than Providence ordained a press announcement that she would be in London to attend a special function

178

on July 10 of this year: I had a date from which to schedule my Series backwards.

So I worked back from her to Atrax Four, by which time I knew I would be under surveillance: and there seemed no way I would be able to elude that surveillance. But at the very last moment a council official rang and asked was there a fire escape from the top floor of this house. I lied, of course, and said yes. Where? she asked. From the window at the top of the staircase, I said. Reaching ground level bang in front of your French windows, she sneered: and arrived on my doorstep the very next morning to check.

As a result, I had to have a cat-walk constructed from just below my dormer window to the penthouse patio of the house next door: and my neighbours had to put in a ladder from their patio down to the patio at the back of Simon's flat. The problem posed by probable surveillance had ceased to exist.

God moves in mysterious ways, does He not? Because, had He not, I can still think of no way I could have eluded the men in the scruffy blue van to keep my assignation with Bunty, and my return here, unobserved.

Finally, it was only a fortnight ago that Providence showed me how to contrive a meeting between Bunty and his hairy executioners. For months I'd wracked my brains, but no solution had come: and then, bored one night with all the other programmes on TV, I switched to Channel 4, which was showing a debate in the House of Lords. Was about to switch smartly back to ITV when the camera zoomed in on dear old Bunty, who was knitting.

I was fascinated. Could I put his executioners in a ball of wool? I wondered; but knew I couldn't. At which moment (and the commentator remarked upon it as another of Bunty's endearing eccentricities, one he shared with ex-President Reagan) he opened a jar of jellybeans, scooped out a handful and popped them into his noble

179

gob. Coincidence, you'll probably say; but I know it was yet another part of a divinely orchestrated plan.

Still, the Lord only helps those who help themselves, which meant that, before I made the first of today's two crossings to Simon's flat, I had to check that my neighbours were still away. They're Arabs, and when they're at home the pavement outside their house is littered with garbage, empty gin bottles, squashed Coca Cola cans and abandoned trolleys from the supermarket.

The pavement was pristine, so I crawled through the attic window, climbed down to the cat-walk, crossed to the Arabs' rear patio, climbed down to Simon's rear patio, let myself into Simon's flat through the glass door that won't lock, went downstairs, let myself out by the front door that's around the corner from the scruffy blue van, and toddled off for my weekly dose of sun-tan.

Returned by the same route in good time to admit my cleaner, an actor who was 'resting'. If he's an actor, I'm Lord Olivier; and if he's resting, Olivier never acted. Anton, he said his name was. Wore a purple velour hat with a wide drooping brim, a pink shirt knotted round his midriff and candy-striped cotton pants.

Seemed surprised I was wearing gloves, so I told him I was allergic to Pledge and detergents. Played some Haydn while he worked and got him to make us a pot of tea when he'd finished: but didn't let him wash the mugs, one of which now bears his fingerprints, as do various glasses, plates, door knobs and domestic appliances.

He said I was the nicest client he'd ever worked for, which I've no doubt I am, told me I was a terrific violinist, which is true, and grovelled when I saw him out, which is the least he could have done in return for being grossly overpaid to clean a spotless house and be genuinely enthralled, while he took tea, by my anecdotes.

These included my tearful account (I can be as lachrymose as Gielgud when it suits me) of Mike's death, my hilarious imitation of the Clanville colonel and his dotty memsahib and my hysterical telephone conversation with Mrs Green. If the Plodder questions Anton, and he's bound to when he searches this place and finds nothing (no stowaways, no Tuinals, no make-up, no nothing) he'll only get answers that prove all his suspicions groundless.

Anyway, as soon as Anton had left, I set all the time switches (for the benefit of the spies in the scruffy blue van) then nipped across to Simon's flat, where I changed into Gareth Williams' gear and packed my make-up, props and pocket mirror in a carrier bag.

Walked half a mile toward Shepherd's Bush before taking a cab to Harrods, which I left by the side entrance so that I could catch the tube from Knightsbridge to Green Park.

At Green Park station I locked myself inside a cubicle in the Gents, applied my scar, put on my gloves, neck brace and black glasses and extended my telescoped white cane.

Leaving the Gents, I scythed my way so convincingly across the ticket hall that people flattened themselves against the wall and an off-duty Italian waiter not only helped me up the staircase but even escorted me down Piccadilly to the Air Force Club. His hand on my forearm was firm and warm. No one else has ever touched me like that. He waited with me until Bunty's chauffeur picked me up and drove me down to Pall Mall.

By now you'll know everything that happened while I was in the club except how I managed to administer Bunty a heavy dose of Tuinal. Actually, I wasn't sure myself how I was going to do it; but I very much wanted to because I really hated the thought of him suffering.

In the event, it was easy. When he brought me my coffee, he said he'd brought me two lumps of sugar because he didn't know whether I took it. I told him I took sweeteners, pretended to be stirring them in, and popped a couple of Tuinals into his cup.

Later, he brought each of us a second cup, and I

repeated the operation: but only gave him one more pill because they're very strong and he was getting groggy.

In fact, I had only one nasty moment, and that was when he put my present aside and said it was doubly welcome because his jar at the House of Lords was almost empty. Having imagined he'd help himself then and there, I was confronted with the probability that he might not touch my jar for days: and, as you know, he had to die before midnight.

Problem: how to make him open the jar while I was there? Solution: pretend I was dying for something sweet because I'd just given up cigarettes. He responded exactly as I hoped by offering me my jar of jellybeans. I pretended to take some, returned the jar to him, he dug in for his whack, and that was that.

He escorted me out of the club and while we were saying goodbye I took advantage of the fact that there was no one around to whip off my neck brace, glasses and scar. He tapped his way back into the club and I sprinted along to St James's Street, through St James's Square into Green Park, where I ditched my neck brace and scar in a litter bin, and up the park to the Underground.

Just missed a train and while I was waiting for the next one felt my first moment of anxiety. Every minute was crucial if I was to get home before you rang my door bell. And it was as the next train was approaching that I realized that you had started to cheat.

'Jump in front of it!' I heard a voice tell me. But there was no one near me. Then I spotted the TV camera high up on the wall. It was pointing straight at me, and *your* voice was shouting, 'Go on, jump!'

'Almost did, too. Would have, in fact, as the train rushed toward me, if Solomon hadn't warned, 'It's a trick!' So I didn't. But I'm angry now. I challenged you to a duel of wits: but you're using electronics.

Granted it was shrewd of you (when I refused to let

182

you turn off my TV) to perceive that I'm vulnerable to sub-audible electronic transmissions, but *you're* vulnerable to a bullet between the eyes, and I haven't stooped to shooting you. So sometime in the next sixteen days, I don't know when, and I don't know how, but sometime, somehow, you'll pay for that, Detective Chief Superintendent Plodder.

Left the tube at Hammersmith, got a taxi to Simon's place, ditched my glasses and white stick (which I'd snapped into three pieces) *en route* (the peak-hour traffic will have ground them to bits by now) and changed into my own clothes. Returned by the fire escapes to my house, which was alive with the sound of music, *my* music, removed the tapes from the recorders, plugged the reset time switches into the lights and radio, burnt the tapes and the penultimate florist's plastic box in the incinerator, drank my penultimate toast to the success of the Series, repaired the telephone, and started playing my violin.

Five minutes later, the telephone rang. Telecom checking my line: they'd had a complaint. I said I was relieved to hear it, I'd had no calls for days. Didn't tell them I've had no calls for months.

Ten minutes later the door bell rang. Guess who?

Poor Plodder. The media are going to crucify you. Maybe I needn't bother punishing you,

Wouldn't bet on it, though.

28

It was daylight by the time Westbury had done with his word processor. Within minutes he was asleep. Only minutes later, however, his eyes opened wide and a chill crept from his ears down to his neck. 'The garden!' he whispered. Cheadle hadn't searched the garden. Couldn't in the dark. Would send his storm-troopers in at any moment.

Pausing only to drag on his track suit pants and jogging shoes, he ran across the parched lawn to the incinerator, knelt, retrieved the last plastic boxful of funnelwebs, and the tobacco tinful of meal worms, and returned to the open french windows.

There he removed his joggers and pulled off his pants before entering the house: grass blades on his legs, or dirt on the soles of his feet, would be a dead give-away.

Taking the steps two at a time, he ran naked to his uncle's desk and hid the box in one drawer, the tin in another. If the desk was searched again, the spiders and the meal worms would be an even deader give-away. But he didn't think they would. Careering downstairs, he flung himself on to his bed, to compose himself before they came.

His pants!

Leaping off his bed again, he darted to the french windows and snatched up his track suit pants. Life had become a minefield of dead give-aways. He slung the pants into his washing machine and darted back to bed, where he lay panting and sweating, his heart thudding.

He dried his face and chest with the top sheet and lay, eyes closed, waiting for his door bell to peal and the SS to start banging on his door. He had not the slightest doubt that both were imminent. Nor was he mistaken: which Cheadle would have described as yet another of those insights peculiar to the insane.

'Open up!' a voice bellowed as the bell shrilled and a fist pounded. 'Police! Open up!'

He resisted the impulse to run immediately to the door: he was supposed to be asleep. When he did at last open it, he peered around it, apparently to conceal his nakedness, and mumbled, 'What's up? What time is it?' He looked bemused and irritated: but despite the presence on his door step of two plain-clothes officers dressed as football hooligans, and four uniformed policemen armed with shovels, he exhibited no signs of guilt or fear.

Ignoring him, they pushed the door open, so that it forced him against the wall, marched down the hall, through the drawing-room and into the garden. Naked between the open french windows, he watched them begin digging and probing. 'If you want me, I'll be in bed,' he told the nearest of them; and seemingly more asleep than awake, stumbled off to his bed.

They left three hours later. It was only a few minutes after nine. They had not searched his house. Turning on to his side, smiling, he fell asleep until the late afternoon.

Cheadle's day was considerably less restful but scarcely more productive. He listened to his detectives' account of their failure to unearth funnelwebs from Westbury's garden. He perused a Photo-Fit of Gareth Williams. He interviewed both Anton de Vries and the taxi driver who had picked Westbury up at the Serpentine on June the ninth. He sent Westbury's two pairs of soiled gloves to Forensic, and read Forensic's report on each of the three beanies found at various times since June the ninth in various parts of Kensington. He was briefed about the dozens of sightings of Gleeson look-alikes and the dozens of futile follow-up operations they had inspired. And he was apprised of the great and growing concern of the Commissioner, who was partial to alliteration, about 'the predictable murder of a marquess' and 'the predicated plot against a Prince or Princess of the Realm.'

The Commissioner, he was advised, had reported the 'predicated plot' to the Prime Minister, whose response had been tart. How, the Prime Minister wanted to know, did the Commissioner suggest that this latest development in the Government's crusade against crime should most diplomatically be reported, at Tuesday's audience, to Her Majesty the Queen?

'Perhaps, Prime Minister,' the ever alliterative Commissioner suggested, 'plain speaking would be preferable.'

He had been dismissed with the promise that should the Spider Maniac touch so much as a hair on a royal head, even a Commissioner of the Metropolitan Police could be stripped of his knighthood.

Summoned to the Commissioner's presence, and asked what course of action he suggested to avert this impending catastrophe, Cheadle had quite seriously proposed that the entire Royal Family promptly succumb to diplomatic flu and cancel all its public engagements until July the eleventh.

'That proposal has already been put to the Palace, and was rejected as "inappropriate",' the Commissioner retorted. 'The implication was plain: the protection of Royalty is a police, not a Palace, problem: they intend getting on with their job, so why don't we get on with ours? Which prompts me to enquire, why haven't you detained your suspect?'

'Insufficient evidence. Plus he's got alibis supported by the statements of a load of reliable witnesses.'

'Such as?'

'His colleagues in the orchestra, who remember him being with them at the relevant time on the night of June the sixth: a taxi driver who's prepared to swear that Westbury's hair was still wet from swimming in the Serpentine at the relevant time on June the ninth: an estate agent in Andover, and the woman who lives in his basement flat, whose statements account for all his movements at the relevant times on June the fourteenth: and three members of my surveillance team, whose logged reports indicate that he was at home, playing his violin, before, during and after the relevant time on June the twenty-

186

third! And there are three other witnesses whose evidence, were the matter to go to court, would tend to corroborate his own account of his movements on June the twenty-third.'

'Names?'

'Anton de Vries, his cleaner; Derek Robinson, Detective Sergeant; Charles Cheadle, Detective Chief Superintendent.'

The Commissioner dropped his head and sighed. 'I hadn't realized,' he said. 'How long's he been planning this campaign, do you think?'

'We know he must have brought the spiders back from Australia eighteen months ago. We know he's since bought five or six lots of meal worms, to feed them, from a pet shop in Camden Town '

'Can't anyone in the pet shop identify him?'

'The proprietor gave us an excellent description of a Glaswegian punk who could have been the brother, he said, of the punk girl whose Photo-Fit he saw in the *Daily Mail*. That Photo-Fit bears no resemblance to Master Westbury.'

'But how many people in London buy meal worms to feed spiders?'

'The Glaswegian said he wanted them to feed his bushbaby.'

'What's your research team come up with?'

'Both parents born in England. Mother emigrated with her parents, as a child, to New Zealand, was naturalized, returned here, met the then Flight Lieutenant Westbury, married him, and after the birth of their son, Christopher, persuaded him to resign his commission and join what is now British Airways. He was subsequently grounded and given a desk job overseas. They divorced and Christopher, aged six, was taken to New Zealand by his mother. Aged ten, at his father's suggestion, because he hated Rugby and was being bullied by his Kiwi peers, he was sent to a boarding school in England.

'Couple of murky episodes there, as a result of which two older boys were expelled. Both now regarded as pillars of yuppie society, whereas the best anyone will say for Westbury, whose nickname was Poison Ivy, is that he was always too aware of his looks for his own good.

'Anyway, his headmaster persuaded his father that Christopher would be happier at a school for budding musicians rather than mediocre athletes, and he was sent to just such a school at the age of thirteen. When he left there, aged nineteen, he was said to be "an excellent violinist, but emotionally immature."

'Apart from his long school vacations, which he spent with his mother and stepfather in Wellington, and the one week a year he spent with his father in New York, he was looked after by his paternal uncle in London.

'His stepfather described him as "understandably jealous, but impossible to befriend". His father, according to the woman who cooked and cleaned for him, was into good works – mainly Rotary and Say No To Drugs – and threatened to hand him over to the police when he realized he was using LSD. And in his uncle's household – which included a wife and son – he was often insolent and always demanding: mainly of affection – which he seemed incapable of inspiring.'

'His defence counsel's going to love all that.'

'There's more, sir, and it gets worse. His mother died of asthma when he was eighteen. When he was nineteen, he was one of the six finalists in the Young Musician of the Year contest, and has never got over the fact that he lost. When he was twenty-two, his uncle gave his cousin a flat of his own, but Westbury's father refused to do the same for him. His cousin overdosed on heroin: his aunt was killed in a gliding accident: his uncle was told he had inoperable cancer: his father died: his first, and apparently last, love affair fell through: and his bed-ridden uncle asked him to make him a cup of tea, then used it to wash down the handful of pills the coroner said caused his "accidental death".

'Westbury thereupon inherited not only the estate his father had left in trust for him but everything of his uncle's as well. He's a wealthy young man.'

'But is there any evidence that he's mad?'

'No, sir. The New York cleaning lady says his LSD trip was "Real bad. Like he was out of his skull for almost three weeks", and his conductor thinks he's not always responsible for his actions: but there's no clinical evidence.'

'And even though you're convinced he's a multiple murderer, and you've had him under constant surveillance for twelve days' – the Commissioner's tone was derisive – 'you've no idea how he managed to play his violin throughout the afternoon of June the twenty-third and at the same time leave his home unobserved, murder Lord Uppingham and return?'

'With respect, sir, when finally we were granted a search warrant, we discovered exactly how he managed it. He used time switches to play tapes of himself practising: and he left his house via two fire escapes to his late cousin's flat on the top floor of the next house but one, the front door of which is around the corner from the street we had under surveillance.'

'You've found the tapes?'

'No, sir: only the time switches.'

'Attached to players of some kind?'

'No, sir.'

'Set for the afternoon?'

'For the evening.'

'Fingerprints on the fire escapes? In the cousin's flat?'

'No, sir.'

'What did he say when you confronted him with your discovery of his escape route?'

'I haven't confronted him with it.'

'Might one ask why?'

189

'The exit from the corner house is now also under surveillance. If we catch him emerging from it, we'll at last have evidence enough to arrest him and hold him at least until July the eleventh.'

'And if you don't catch him emerging from the house on the corner?'

'Every step he takes, and every move he makes on July the tenth, we'll be with him. And the second he gets within ten yards of a Royal, we'll nab him – *and* his bleeding spiders.'

'Always assuming', the Commissioner sighed, 'that the security bods haven't called in the SAS, and that one of *them* doesn't shoot him.'

'Can't pretend my heart'd bleed for him if one did, sir.'

'Well, the Home Secretary's would!' the Commissioner snapped. 'Mainly over me! So what I want to see is your suspect standing trial in the dock, not lying bullet-riddled on a slab. I want this case to culminate in a conviction, not a coronial enquiry. And so, coincidentally, does the Home Secretary.'

'Yes, sir.'

'Politicians!' muttered the Commissioner. 'Be that as it may, however – '

'They'll be told I've cocked things up!'

'No. Be that as it may, the rights of the individual and the laws of evidence being what they are, I don't see what more you could have done. And I've said so to the Home Secretary. So, should you succeed, all credit to you: should Westbury succeed, absolutely no blame will attach to you.'

'How'd it go, sir?' Robinson asked, as soon as Cheadle returned.

'He made it clear the Home Secretary had gone ape-shit on him, almost went ape-shit on me, resisted the temptation, and said he couldn't think what more we could've done.'

'Fantastic.'

'Have we done everything about Westbury we could've done, Derek?'

'Well, you could have used thumbscrews on him, stretched him a yard or two on the rack, held his head under water until he started drowning, connected his testicles up to a power point and switched on the juice, or promised to break his legs if he didn't submit to examination by a psychiatrist; but the Commissioner really would have gone ape-shit on you if you had.'

Cheadle laughed and relaxed. 'Found any loopholes in the plan for July the tenth?'

'None.'

'Have you put yourself in his position?'

'In his position, I'd change the date and the weapon. Have a Centre Court ticket for the Women's Final day at Wimbledon, for example, and shoot the Duchess of Kent when she came on court for the presentation of the trophy.'

Cheadle shook his head. 'He'd regard changing the date from Friday the tenth to Friday the third as definitely out of order. He's laid down the ground rules, and he's mad enough to stick to them. Royal Protection Squad couldn't agree less, of course, so they're stepping up precautions. Anything from Forensic?'

'Nothing on Westbury's gloves but household dirt and furniture polish. But do you remember the receptionist at the health club?'

'Cussed Cora?'

'Phoned to say she'd just remembered that Mark Gleeson had a chewed thumbnail. Always notices hands, she said.'

'And Westbury chews his thumbnail,' Cheadle gloated.

'His *left* thumbnail.'

'Don't tell me – '

191

'*She* insists it was his right.'

'Oh, well, roll on July the tenth,' said Cheadle, leaving Robinson with the impression that he would almost have been disappointed had he been denied his denouement.

'Did you see the film on the box last night?' Robinson asked.

'*Film*?' Cheadle was plainly in no mood for small talk.

'John Cleese's *A Fish Called Wanda*?' Robinson persisted, knowing perfectly well that Cheadle seldom watched films, and never watched them during the two weeks of Wimbledon. 'I'm not just prattling, sir.'

'All right, tell me.'

'Cleese had just pulled a girl. She was upstairs waiting for him. He poured himself a glass of wine and toasted her. And then he slung the glass into the fireplace.'

If Cheadle was slow to respond it was not because he begrudged Robinson his moment of inspired detection. 'Brilliant,' he said at last. 'I'm proud of you. The little bleeder's rehearsing in the Opera House: let's go over and confront him with it.'

29

Westbury had enjoyed the three days since Bunty's murder. The media had been full of him. The public had renewed its war against spiders with such indiscriminate frenzy that the Avon World Life Trust had published a letter of protest. A perverse Australian had launched a 'Save the Funnelweb' campaign. A stand-up television comic had had his contract cancelled for ad libbing that a funnelweb had bitten one of England's less popular princesses, and died five minutes later. And he himself had completely neutralized Cheadle's latest ploy of electronic subversion by hiding from the eye of every London Transport surveillance camera.

Everything was going to plan and the fact that his secret route to Simon's flat had probably been uncovered during Cheadle's search caused him no anxiety. It existed only because the officious bitch from the council had demanded it: and he wouldn't be using it again anyway. Wouldn't be doing anything to justify his arrest between now and July the tenth, in fact: by which time, from Cheadle's point of view, and hers, it would be too late.

To be honest, though, he was a bit bored. Another clash with Cheadle would help. Specially since the last one – with every detail of which he had regaled his delighted colleagues – had paid such dividends. For once in his life he was popular, one of the boys, an irrepressible victim of police harassment, the guy they'd unpardonably misunderstood. Kevin had even invited him to lunch on Sunday. Not that he was going: he hated children.

Then he saw Cheadle, with Robinson beside him, standing at the railing that separated the pit from the auditorium: standing immediately behind Bronowski. As their eyes met, Cheadle gave him a reproving nod. He raised his eyebrows in innocent response.

Noticing this, Bronowski glanced over his shoulder, saw Cheadle and angrily silenced his orchestra. 'What now, Chief Superintendent?'

'Just a few words with one of your musicians, Sir Leon: when you're ready.'

'Chris again?'

'Just a few words.'

An angry growl came from Westbury's new-found friends in the pit. Bronowski silenced it promptly. 'Take ten minutes,' he ordered them, waving them out.

'Want me to come with you, Chris?' Maguire shouted.

'We're not taking him anywhere, Mr Maguire,' Cheadle assured the indignant percussionist, at the same time beckoning Westbury out of the pit. 'All we want is a little chat in the stalls.'

'Don't worry, Kev,' Westbury called back. 'Give you a blow by blow description when it's over!'

His colleagues laughed and filed out. Sir Leon stood aside to allow him to mount the dais and vault the railing.

'Very athletic,' Cheadle congratulated him. 'You and Gleeson both!'

Shit, thought Westbury: but said, 'You're very cryptic today, Mr Cheadle.'

Not answering, Cheadle led the way a dozen rows up the aisle. 'Sit!' he ordered, pointing at a seat on the aisle.

Westbury sat. Robinson stood in the aisle behind him. Cheadle rested his rump on the back of a seat two rows down and stared at him reproachfully.

'Well?' he accused.

'Very, thank you.'

'Enjoying your telly?'

'Bit sick of tennis' – Solomon urging him to attack, reminding him that Cheadle's eyes, during their second interview, had constantly strayed to the TV and its coverage of Wimbledon. 'Row upon row of doddering wrinklies watching lithe youngsters doing superbly what they always did badly. You were never any good at it, were you?'

'No, but watching it reminds me of my misspent youth.'

'Well, they do say that all most ancients can recall is their childhood.'

'Happy days,' sighed Cheadle. 'Hop picking in Kent, sixpences in the Christmas pud, cinema on Saturday, bush rambles, poison ivy – '

'Jerking one another off in the bog!'

'Boys will be boys, Chris.'

'Not all boys, Charlie.'

'More sophisticated stuff in your day, was it?'

'You're obsessed with it, aren't you?'

'Just with you, laddie.'

'Fascinate you, do I?'

'In a macabre sort of way.'

'Ooh, we are getting literate, aren't we? *Double entendres*, macabre, who'd you learn them from? Your boyfriend?' – jerking his head back toward Robinson.

'Well, he does have a couple of degrees, so some of it may have rubbed off. Tell you what, though: the only other people I've met with a tongue as vicious as yours were all nutters. And while I'm at it, I'll tell you something else: they all thought their enemies got at 'em via the telly. Some wouldn't go within miles of it: the others only felt safe when it was on. Talking of which, what'd you think of *A Fish Called Wanda*?'

'Didn't watch it,' Westbury lied sullenly. 'I hate Cleese.'

'Pity,' said Cheadle. 'My sergeant tells me it was brilliant. By the way, those fragments of glass in your fireplace: why are they there?'

'Designer debris,' Westbury quoted from his script. 'Probably won't reach Balham for another five years. You, I imagine, are still into a coach lamp outside your front door, an artificial log fire in your "lounge" and a teak veneer in your fitted kitchen?'

'Piercing insight,' thought Robinson.

'Tell him about Mr Cleese in *A Fish Called Wanda*,' Cheadle instructed him.

Robinson moved down the aisle so that he could face Westbury. 'Cleese had just pulled this girl,' he recounted, 'and when she went up to his bedroom, he poured himself a glass of wine, toasted his success and threw the glass into the fireplace.'

'So?'

'Three murders the first time we saw you,' Cheadle explained: 'three shattered glasses. Four murders the last time we saw you: four shattered glasses.'

'Must've pulled another girl, then, mustn't I?'

The time had come, Cheadle decided, to fight insight with insight. 'I don't think you've pulled a girl in all your life,' he said. 'But that's beside the point. The point, young Christopher, is this: we're on to you. And one day, very soon, we're going to take you in, a judge is going to send you down and a warder's going to bang you up.'

30

'Good line that: take you in, send you down, bang you up,' Robinson congratulated Cheadle as they left the Opera House.

'Pinched it from a play on telly. Give him something to think about over the weekend.' Obviously preoccupied, Cheadle came to a halt. 'What about Swansea, the council and the keys?'

'Swansea says the car's still registered in the name of Westbury; the council says the fire escapes were installed last April at their insistence; and we found Simon's keys on a table in his flat.'

'Any prints?'

'None. Not Simon's, not Christopher's, not anyone's; not on the keys, not anywhere in the flat, not on either of the fire escapes.'

Cheadle nodded his satisfaction. 'So we're getting to him at last. Been a silly boy, hasn't he? Murders Lord Uppingham, returns via Simon's flat and the fire escapes, but forgets to bring the keys with him.'

'Maybe there's another set somewhere?'

'Just the one, according to his uncle's executor: in the old boy's desk. Except, when we searched the desk, it wasn't. So if you were Christopher Westbury, how'd you explain the absence of prints and keys?'

'I'd say,' Robinson replied, after only the slightest of pauses, 'that I'd decided to spring clean my late cousin's flat as well as my late uncle's house, so I took the keys from my uncle's desk and let myself into my cousin's flat; but forgot to take the keys with me when I left.'

'Why'd you clean so fanatically that there isn't a fingerprint to be found anywhere in the flat?'

'It'd been empty for three years and had got filthy. I've decided to sell it. Easier if it's pristine.'

'If you can't let them in, prospective buyers can't see whether it's pristine or filthy.'

'I'm getting a locksmith to open the door so I can collect the keys.'

'Why not go back for them via the fire escape?'

'The Arabs next door are paranoid about burglars.'

'You could ask their permission.'

'They're Shi-ites, hate infidels, wouldn't give it.'

'Well, how come my surveillance team never saw you walking to Simon's flat and back the day you cleaned it?'

'How come your surveillance team never saw me leaving Notting Hill station?'

'But you don't even *know* you're under surveillance! Anyway, if it comes to your word against my officers', the jury'll believe theirs.'

'And my counsel will ask them where they told you I was the afternoon Lord Uppingham was murdered: and they'll have to admit they told you I was at home playing my violin.'

'What an accomplished little liar you are.'

'Me, sir, or Westbury?'

'Both of you. Which is why we'll never get a conviction until we catch him red-handed.'

'And in the mean time?'

'We interview Whosit, the boozy cellist, again – '

'Gavin Wilson.'

'That's right – and persuade him we've established *he* couldn't have murdered Corder, Allison or Uppingham, because he was otherwise engaged at his local on each occasion, so there's no need for him to go on corroborating Westbury's statement that they were together in the wings

197

all through the disco scene. And then, having established that Westbury could've slipped away to Saxon's dressing-room during the disco scene, we're going to interview Sir Leon again and make him tell us the name of his blonde mistress. And who was with her in the Royal Box.'

'Why?'

'Because if it wasn't Sir Leon's mistress Westbury was eyeing up, it was someone beside or behind her: someone whose identity he's gone to great pains to conceal.'

'Has he?'

'He deliberately misdirected us into thinking it was the blonde – until I provoked him, and *he* couldn't resist pointing out how gullible I'd been. But why would he have bothered misdirecting us unless there was someone in the blonde's party whose identification would be dangerous to him? About everything else he's actually volunteered details – '

'All misleading.'

'So why nothing about his rumoured affair with who-ever it was he picked out in the box the night Sir Leon thought it was his mistress who was being pulled?'

'You think that affair prompted all these murders?'

'Hoping it did. Helps get a conviction if you can estab-lish a motive.'

'Provided you can also break his alibis. Like his wet hair the day Corder was killed – '

'There's a drinking fountain a hundred yards from where he caught his cab.'

'And his house-hunting in Hampshire?'

'Three of the houses, and the clock tower, he could've photographed on a previous visit.'

'And his practice sessions were taped,' Robinson reflected.

'And he got to Uppingham and back unobserved via Simon's flat.'

'So how'll he get out of the house unobserved on July the tenth?'

'Buggered if I know. Bet he does, though. So what we've got to do is pinpoint his destination, identify his prospective royal victim and lie in wait for him armed with a dozen cans of insecticide to kill his bloody spiders.'

'Not insecticide, sir,' Robinson demurred.

'Why?'

'Before it kills them it drives them into a frenzy.'

'Does it now?' said Cheadle thoughtfully. 'Thank you, Derek: I'm glad you told me that.'

Gavin Wilson's resistance was short-lived, and his capitulation shame-faced. He refused, however, to incriminate Westbury.

'He was right where I left him when I got back and I didn't ask him to cover up for me.'

'Ever think he could've been covering up for himself?'

'If I hadn't gone for a drink, he wouldn't be a suspect.'

'If you hadn't gone for a drink, he *couldn't* be a suspect.'

'He liked Mike.'

'Everyone liked Mike. But someone killed him.'

'Well, it wasn't Chris. When I got back to the wings, he was so wrapped up in the disco bit he didn't even notice me. Probably hadn't even noticed when I left.'

'We'd rather you didn't tell him that, sir.'

'Tough!' retorted Wilson. 'Cos I'm going to.'

As they waited for someone to open Sir Leon's front door, Robinson said, 'You *want* Wilson to tell Westbury, don't you?'

'That's a most improper suggestion,' Cheadle rebuked.

Lady Bronowski opened the door. 'You're early again,' she said.

'But this time we're not prepared to await your husband's convenience,' Cheadle told her. 'I must ask you to inform Sir Leon that he must see us immediately.'

Whereupon he walked purposefully into her drawing-room, sat down uninvited and, when Bronowski entered the room, which he did promptly and angrily, remained seated. So did Robinson.

'How dare you threaten my wife?' Bronowski rasped.

'How dare you obstruct a police enquiry?' Cheadle rasped back. 'We know about your mistress.'

Bronowski glanced toward the doorway, fearful lest his wife might still be standing there: then walked swiftly to the door, closed it, returned to an armchair, sank heavily into it and said, 'It's over. My wife mustn't know.'

'We must.'

'I met her in Helsinki – '

'Name?'

'Svetlana Naroyan. The pianist. She'd just defected.'

'When?'

'Three years ago. I was conducting a performance of – '

'No concern of ours what you were conducting in Helsinki when you met her, Sir Leon: what we need to know is what you were conducting at Covent Garden the night you thought she'd clicked with Westbury.'

'*Die Freischutz.*'

'Date?'

'Can't remember. The first performance. You could easily check.'

'We will. Did you get that box for her?'

'And three of her friends. I had to be discreet.'

'Names?'

'Her agent, Isaac Feldmann, and another couple. No idea who they were. Wasn't interested.'

'And you reprimanded Westbury – '

'Visually, not verbally.'

'For being too attentive to Miss Naroyan, not for being insufficiently attentive to you?'

'And he made it plain he knew it!'

'He was habitually inattentive: why didn't you just sack him?'

'I wasn't only afraid of him, I was concerned for him. It was he who told you about my affair with Svetlana, no doubt?'

'We don't reveal our sources, Sir Leon.'

As if Cheadle had not left his question unanswered, Bronowski muttered, 'How'd he know?'

'Insight, I suppose: assuming he did know.'

'Need any of this come out?'

Cheadle pondered the question, then said, 'It'd serve you right if we dropped you in it. Not because you had an affair: because you didn't trust us to treat the truth as confidential. Thing is, would the truth have enabled us to make an arrest or did your lies cost anyone his life? Answer: no. So, much as I dislike you and Lady Bronowski, because basically you're a pair of jumped-up, posturing prats, I see no reason why any of this, as you put it, need come out.'

'Chief Superintendent, how can I thank you?'

'Sir Leon, you even try to "thank" me and I'll arrest you for attempting to pervert the course of justice!'

'Quite a morning,' Robinson congratulated him as they headed away from the Bronowski home.

'Gonna be quite an afternoon and evening as well. Mrs Green about that car, Isaac Feldmann about the other couple in Miss Naroyan's box, You Know Who about July the tenth, then the Wimbledon Women's Semi-Finals, which Mrs Cheadle is taping for me.'

'I'll try not to disturb you,' Robinson promised.

31

On Friday and Saturday, July the third and fourth, the three royal ladies most obviously at risk from the Spider Maniac appeared either to share Cheadle's view that they were safe until July the tenth, or to subscribe to the Palace view that danger was an occupational hazard from which others would presumably protect them.

As she presented the women's trophy on the Centre Court, HRH The Duchess of Kent, a Worsley before her marriage, refused to be hurried – and positively dallied the following afternoon after her husband had presented the men's trophy.

As she opened a refuge for battered mothers and children on Saturday, HRH Princess Margaret, a Windsor until her marriage to the Earl of Snowdon, declined absolutely to be hidden from sight amid the scrum of minders.

And after she had come a good second in the third race at Cheltenham, the Princess Royal, a Windsor until marriage made her a Phillips, instructed an over-zealous Special Branch officer to naff off.

Others in high places were less philosophic. On Monday, the Home Secretary was summoned to No. 10. 'I have not become the Queen's first minister,' the Prime Minister told him, brazenly plagiarizing, 'to preside over the decimation of her family.'

The Commissioner was summoned to the Home Office. How *exactly*, the Home Secretary demanded, did Scotland Yard propose protecting Her Majesty's sister, daughter and cousin-in-law throughout the twenty-four hours of July the tenth?

Cheadle was summoned to Scotland Yard. 'How precisely,' the Commissioner enquired, 'do you plan to prevent your psychotic suspect from planting poisonous spiders on the person of one of the three possible princesses?'

'Westbury will lead us to his intended victim, sir; and when he does, we'll keep him from her even if we have to interpose ourselves. We'll be carrying anti-venene from Australia, and crêpe bandages, so we'll survive if we're bitten.'

'And despite the DPP's decision that there's so little hard evidence against him that a prosecution would fail, you're still certain Westbury's your man?'

'Of all those employed at the Opera House, *one* of whom must have murdered Michael Saxon, only Westbury could also have murdered Corder, Allison and Uppingham.'

'Why?'

'Only he had the opportunity. The time, that is. And the cash.'

'Cash?'

'It's been costly: and he's loaded.'

'Weapon?'

'Only he visited Sydney, domicile of *Atrax robustus*. And only he led us to believe he'd never even been to Australia, let alone to Sydney.'

'Motive?'

'A madman scorned.'

'Which you can't prove!'

'He'll prove it, sir. On July the tenth.'

For Westbury, waiting was not easy. He had too little to do, was assailed by conflicting advice from Solomon, the Advocate and the Provocateur, received subliminal messages flashed like subtitles on the TV screen, and had no idea what the Plodder was up to. Time was his enemy. There was too much of it. But he could do nothing yet.

Ironic that it was she who had appointed the date and place of her execution. Wholly fitting that he should be her executioner. Intolerable that time and the Plodder might reprieve her.

Since Bunty, he'd done everything possible to allay suspicion. Not provoked the watch dogs. Refrained from gloating at Sir Leon. Been a sociable employer for Anton. Stopped hitting the bottle. Begun to eat. Everything, in fact, except take the quite unnecessary medication about which the Advocate never ceased to nag him.

'Mirror, mirror on the wall?' he'd wheedled archly: but shockingly, the looking-glass had cut him short. 'Not you, arsehole,' it had interrupted. 'You look more like your dying Uncle Paul.'

Then Anton had scolded, 'You look tired, sir. You really *shouldn't* practise so much. Let me make you a nice, light lunch.' That was the Friday after Bunty. So he was getting used to nice, light lunches. What would he do without his lissom Anton de Vries of the Cecil Beaton hat and the candy-striped pants? Mirror, mirror on the wall? You are Baron Kristov Paul: Baron Kristov Paul: trend-setting, jet-setting virtuoso: killer diller amoroso: the serious killer's serial killer: five for the price of one.

Atrax Five: Thursday, July 9

Tomorrow, the dénouement. Twenty-four hours from now, I'll have pulled it off. The Temptress will never betray again. Her ambition has cost me my career, and four other men their lives. They will not have died in vain. I must now tell you about her.

Emma Waterhouse is three years my senior. Old money on her father's side: new on her mother's. Won the Young Musician contest two years before I was robbed of the title. But made no effort to cash in on her success. A dilettante.

I'd only ever seen her on TV (during the heats and final of the contest she won) until I spotted her in the Royal Box sitting behind the much publicized Svetlana Naroyan – who subsequently ditched Sir Leon for a younger, more influential conductor from America. That night, though,

Naroyan was so obviously giving Sir Leon the come-hither look that I knew they were having it off. I would have cut him out if Emma hadn't been just as obviously come-hithering me!

When she wasn't waiting for me at the stage door, I realized she expected me to make the running and wrote to her that night (care of her daddy's ancestral pile) about how we were fellow virtuosi, how I'd like to play for her, how we were both good-lookers, how her wealth was no problem 'cos I'd soon have a fortune too, stuff like that.

She replied promptly. *Dear Mr Westbury, thank you for so flattering a letter, specially since it's neither my money you're after, because you have expectations, nor my body, because you too are beautiful. Sadly, a prior engagement makes it impossible for me to accept your invitation to a candle-lit dinner à deux: we heiresses are much in demand. Better luck next time. Emma Waterhouse.*

Reading between the lines, she plainly had the hots for me. Uncle Paul, of course, said she'd only replied out of common courtesy; but he hadn't read her letter. That reference to my beauty: the gratuitous suggestion of sexual congress: the overt promise, if I wrote again, that I'd have better luck.

So I wrote again. Wrote every day, in fact, usually twice a day, and sent flowers. For a month she didn't write back, but I understood. Heiresses have to be careful about what they put on paper, can't just come straight out with it and say, 'I've got the hots for you', need to know more about the guy they fancy than his chemistry.

Anyway, the second letter duly arrived, and confirmed all my suspicions. *Dear Mr Westbury, how flattering that you, a cross between Adonis and Menuhin, have chosen me to be your paramour and patron. But I know nothing about you or your allegedly massive talent, so I remain Yours, unconvinced, Emma Waterhouse.*

Well, you can hardly be more explicit than that, can you? Not on paper. Not if you're Emma Waterhouse. And even if I did find her erotic innuendoes a bit off-putting (rather too reminiscent of the Whore of Wellington, whose younger self she very much resembled), I obliged with a Polaroid photograph of my massive talent and a daily quota of searing sonnets that made Shakespeare's to his Dark Lady seem tepid.

At the more spiritual level, I also made a very expensive recording of my rendition of the Haydn Sonata for Violin and Piano (the pianist alone set me back two hundred quid) and sent it to her as evidence of my *artistic* talent.

Though we now understood one another perfectly, she was plainly having problems replying in suitably ambiguous terms: I heard nothing from her for another month. Understanding as ever, I wrote it all for her, three letters a day, in the last of which I told her I'd booked us a suite at the Savoy for the following Saturday night through to Monday. Told her the room number, said I'd be there by eleven and asked her to arrive at eleven thirty, to give me time to freshen up.

By eleven fifteen that Saturday night all was ready. Enough flowers for a Mafia funeral, champagne, caviare, supper ordered for midnight and me in a new silk dressing-gown with nothing underneath but Pierre Cardin perfume and my massive talent.

She was late.

The supper was wheeled in by a flunkey.

The poached salmon went cold and the sorbets melted.

At last she knocked on the door.

I opened it.

It was a page boy, offering me a letter.

Mr Westbury, you presume too much. I don't know you, I never wanted to meet you, I have done my best to discourage you from inundating me with your literary effusions and floral tributes, I have no intention of financing your debut at the Wigmore Hall, nor of attending upon you this evening, and if you send me even one more pornographic letter or pseudo Shakespearian sonnet I will instruct my lawyers to take the appropriate action. This I would have done long since had you not so obviously been emotionally unstable and artistically frustrated.

As to your self-proclaimed virtuosity, I must advise you that your Haydn, though technically impeccable, lacks all the composer's warmth and, as one critic recently put it, pawky humour. Your sound is too lean. In my opinion, you will never become a soloist, any more than I would have. You should reconcile yourself to an honourable career as an orchestral performer, preferably in Prague where the lean sound is fashionable. Emma Waterhouse.

I had been conned by a prick teaser.

Three weeks later her engagement was announced. To an Arab prince. A title and even more money, that's all she'd ever been after. And for them she'd betrayed me.

Uncle Paul and Aunty Deb made all the right noises, but the very next morning Uncle called the doctor in to see me, which was when the plot to section me was conceived, and Aunty Deb was so genuinely concerned about me that she went gliding and killed herself. All because little Miss Emma, the temptress and traitress, was determined to be a princess.

Princess Farida she became, which should have been a warning to her (the last Princess Farida being the late divorced wife of King Farouk). Anyway, having presented her royal, black-haired, tawny-eyed husband with twin flaxen-haired, blue-eyed daughters, Emma too was divorced. But clung to her courtesy title. And sought to ingratiate herself with her ex by lending her name to the charity (now very trendy) that supports a number of ludicrously indulgent orphanages for the children of gassed Kurds, pogromed Armenians and terrorist Palestinians.

Her next, and last, appearance in that role will be on Friday. There is no need for me to describe what will happen. Events will speak for themselves. Suffice to say that money, which I have spent like water, has been no object; and that I am proud of the Atrax Series which (with the help of two call girls, a gigolo and my devoted handmaid, Anton) I will shortly bring to a triumphant conclusion.

32

Anton arrived early for work on Friday. He was supposed to work from twelve until one; but lately, since they had got friendlier, had been arriving at about a quarter to twelve and leaving at about a quarter past one.

Time for a cuppa and a chat (or tea and sympathy as Chris called it) before he started working – not that there was ever much to do – and then drinkies together while Chris ate the snack he'd prepared for him.

Actually, it was these snacks that had changed their relationship. Before them it had been very much a case of yes Mr Westbury, no Mr Westbury and whatever you wish Mr Westbury, with Mr Westbury himself hardly uttering, and only in the form of soliloquies (like Hamlet) or *non sequiturs* (which is Latin) when he did; but during their second snack, he'd quite suddenly tapped the table and said, 'Join me. Have a drink.' And later, 'Cut the Mister crap, Anton. Call me Chris.' And last Wednesday had gone so far as to remark, 'That hat suits you. But I much prefer your striped pants to those jeans.'

So Anton arrived early on Friday wearing the hat Chris said suited him and the pants Chris preferred to jeans; and Chris opened the door to him wearing only a suntan, a hint of perfume and a silk dressing-gown.

As they drank their coffees – which Chris had ready, awaiting his arrival – Anton envisaged himself moving in as Chris's companion. Together they'd give dinner parties, attend first nights, go on luxury cruises.

arm:
Task

s he
ir of
ther

oved
shirt
nder

did
vhat
adi-
nity

his
an
who
trax
be
ive.
was
ed,
om
tall,
dly
pro-
sn't
as

an,
the
der
the
en
ief

the housework,' Chris interrupted this
neeled domestic bliss as Anton stood to
mpty cups. 'Just whip me up a bite of
istibly edible and then we'll share a bottle
ou can tell me all about *you* for a change.'

eaving,' surveillance radioed the Incident
ere two of them in the grey Ford that had
aroon Vauxhall that had replaced the blue
, which had stared unmoved at the worst
vities, narrowed as they followed Anton's
buttocks, skittishly knotted pink shirt and
at. But they said nothing. Having watched
d go three times a week, they had run out
y, couldn't even be bothered speculating
vas leaving at one thirty-five instead of one
become his custom since Wednesday, July

of their disapproval, he waved gaily at
m window and flounced down the pave-
orner; around which, with a final defiant
, he vanished leftwards. Then crossed the
past three more houses and, retrieving the
l switch from the trunk of the flowering
h he had taped it seven weeks previously,
the garage of the fourth.
was hot and humid, the BMW it housed
k, despite its film of dust. Tugging off
Westbury patted the warm coachwork.
ught of this, Mr Plodder. I mean, everyone
's position has a car, and I told you I'd
rything of his, so you really should've

d off the central heating panel that had kept
t, and turned off the tap that dripped on to
and kept the atmosphere humid. Until June

the second, he had used Simon's flat as his spider
since then, this garage had been it, except for the
Force he had kept at home.

'This was your big mistake,' he told Cheadle
unlocked the BMW's door. A clean shirt and a p
expensive Italian slacks lay on the front seat; a le
suitcase on the back.

He untied the knotted tails of Anton's shirt, rem
Anton's candy-striped pants, changed into the clean
and Italian slacks and stuffed the discarded clothing u
the damp sacks.

Clever the way he'd made use of Anton, even if h
say so himself. He hadn't planned to, but that was
made him exceptional: his ability to improvise, his r
ness to vary the plan, to improve it if the opport
arose.

And nothing could have been more opportune tha
decision to hire a cleaner who had turned out to b
effeminate, gullible male of his own age and height
dressed with eccentric flamboyance. By the time A
Four had proved successful, he'd realized it woul
idiotic not to incorporate Anton into the cast of Atrax I

So now, despite Solomon's furious protests, it
Anton (not, as planned, Uncle's gardener) who lay na
unconscious and securely bound on the drawing-r
floor. Just as well, too. Uncle's gardener was a bit too
a few years too old and much too muscular. Admitt
the jungle combat gear he always wore would have
vided a reasonable disguise, but his military stride w
easy to emulate, and he certainly wouldn't have bee
susceptible as Anton.

But what would have wrecked the whole p
Westbury reflected as he drove out of the garage, and
door closed automatically behind him, was the Ploc
checking on the BMW. It hadn't been anywhere in
short street outside Uncle's house, and it hadn't b
sold: it must still be the property of the Plodder's c

suspect. A worthy adversary would weeks ago have tracked it down to the garage Uncle had rented from the TV star who'd been banned from driving for life two years ago.

'And that', Westbury freely confessed, 'really would've put the cat among the pigeons.'

As he approached Marble Arch, the traffic on the Bayswater Road slowed to a crawl. Westbury was unconcerned. It was only a few minutes after two and he didn't have to meet the three escorts he'd hired for the night until six forty-five.

Meantime, Solomon suggested – or was it the Provocateur? They were beginning to sound the same nowadays – anyway, someone suggested, 'Why not make that call now? While you're inching your way toward Park Lane. Use the car-phone.'

'It's too early,' the Advocate admonished.

'*DO IT*,' flashed a neon sign in Oxford Street.

'Mrs Cheadle?' he asked when she answered.

'Yes.'

'This is Fred.'

'Fred who, dear?'

'Ask your husband.'

There was a moment's silence: then she said, 'For everyone's sake, including yours, I hope they shoot you.'

It was not the reaction he had expected. 'Frightened?' he taunted.

'You're the one who's frightened, dear.'

'Of *you*?'

'I'm a woman, aren't I?'

He hung up, swung right into Park Lane and drove with controlled fury to the car-park behind the Hilton.

Removing a wallet from the glove box, and his suitcase from the rear seat, he locked the car and made his way to the Hilton's reception desk, where he presented his New Zealand passport.

'A room was booked for me in April,' he said: and five

211

minutes later was alone in a room on the sixteenth floor, overlooking traffic-clogged Hyde Park Corner and the empty gardens of Buckingham Palace.

33

It was six forty and Westbury sat in the BMW where he had parked it. He had spent the entire afternoon grooming himself and dressing, and now, as he inspected himself in the rear vision mirror, he knew it had been well worth while.

'Shan't even bother to ask,' he told the mirror, peering into the clear, long-lashed eyes of the beautiful man with the blond hair, jet black eyebrows and stunning make-up.

Opening the glove box, he took out a box of chocolates.

Kissing the box's lid, he murmured, 'My gallant commandos': then, as he patted each of the three shoe boxes laid out along the top of the dashboard, 'And my devoted bodyguards.'

He got out of the car, locked it and strolled the fifty or so yards to the Opera House. He could see his three hired companions waiting outside the portico: a voluptuous redhead, a raven-haired clothes horse and a white-toothed Californian. Each formally and beautifully attired. None obviously from an agency. All exactly as ordered: perfect foils for his superbly tailored, devastating self.

He halted in front of them, clicked his heels and bowed slightly.

'Baron?' queried the beach boy.

'Of course.' He took the clothes horse's hand and kissed the air above it.

'Lucinda,' she introduced herself.

'Von Paulus,' he told her. 'You may call me Kristov.'

He took the redhead's hand and bent his head gallantly toward it.

'Vicci,' she said. 'With two c's and an i.'

'Naturally,' he acknowledged. 'With a c-k-y it would be quite vulgar.' He turned to the beach boy. 'And you?'

'Kenneth, sir.'

'Thank God. I was afraid it would be Dwight. Well, a drink, I think' – and extracting their four tickets from his wallet, which he opened on top of the box of chocolates, he led Lucinda firmly through the foyer, up the staircase and into the Crush Bar.

Kenneth and Vicci followed them closely: at Westbury's heels, in fact, like part of his entourage – as they had been instructed. Nevertheless, they made a striking quartet. Heads turned, conversations faltered, questions were whispered.

'Who is he?' girls asked their escorts. 'My dear,' women asked their husbands' colleagues' wives, 'who is that gorgeous man?' Young men said he must be a German actor, or yet another Australian pop star, or a Danish dancer, or a European princeling. Older men said he must be a poof. And they all meant Westbury, not the beach boy. His combination of exotic looks, hermaphroditic make-up, sartorial elegance and male arrogance was creating exactly the illusion he desired – that whoever else they might think he was, it wouldn't be Christopher Westbury, the failed finalist of the Young Musician of the Year contest.

Actually, he was giving the performance of his life, and was revelling in it. For the first time in his life he was in command of an audience, and loved the power of it. He forgot that he was a violinist: he forgot Atrax Five: he forgot Solomon, the Provocateur and the Advocate: he became the exotically beautiful Baron Kristov Paulus. And when the bell rang for the audience to take its seats, he almost floated toward the Grand Tier, quite forgetting the lethal box of chocolates sitting incongruously among empty champagne glasses on a Crush Bar table.

The penetrating accents of two Sloane Rangers reminded him. 'Poor Emma,' sighed the first, without a trace of sympathy. 'What a cock-up.'

'Surprised she wasn't stoned to death,' snapped the second.

He rushed back to the Crush Bar, collected the chocolates and led the way into the second row in the centre of the Grand Tier.

Having been one of the first of the few prepared to pay an exorbitant price for a few hours' proximity to ex-Middle Eastern royalty, he had obtained the four seats immediately behind the right flank of Farida's party. Farida herself, when she made her grand entrance, would sit in the centre of the front row, below him and four seats to his left. To kill her, he would edge past those sitting on his left, removing the lid of his chocolate box as he went, and as he passed, shower her with funnelwebs – six of them, the last two from his Task Force at home and four from his reserve in the garage – as he passed.

He'd make his move, he had decided, the instant Ouspenskaya shrieked her last sour high E flat: while the audience was reluctantly applauding and she was embarrassing it by demanding more.

No one would resent his departure. Others would be doing the same.

All he had to do was hold the box upside down over her shoulders, shake it, and get to the centre aisle before the disco scene began.

At that moment the audience would become tense with anticipation, hoping for a successful finale to a disappointing programme, disappointed by the prospect of a disco finale without Michael Saxon. No one would notice that he had left the auditorium. No one would notice that the royal guest of honour was strewn with spiders.

And she'd feel nothing – till they bit her. And even

then no one behind or beside her would notice anything
– till she began to thresh.

By which time he'd be miles away, in the BMW, leaving
Kenneth, Lucinda and Vicci to enjoy what little was left
of the Gala, and the Temptress to enjoy what little was
left of her life.

34

Constantly aware that he was the cynosure of many eyes
during the first half of the programme and that part of
the second half that preceded Ouspenskaya's keenly
unanticipated appearance, Westbury sat aloof and almost
contemptuous.

His seat in the pit, he noted with sardonic pleasure,
was unoccupied: and Sir Leon was *distrait* and anxious:
and the programme was under-rehearsed, ill lit and
poorly staged: and the house was only eighty per cent
full. A gala to raise funds for the orphaned children of
the PLO, among others, was clearly not to the taste of
London's philanthropic Jewry: and Michael Saxon's
unavoidable absence from the programme as it had originally been conceived was the kiss of death.

Princess Farida looked ill at ease: as well she might,
thought Westbury. Beside her, Dame Lyndsay was professionally animated. The young man who sat on
Westbury's left looked grim; and his partner, a strapping
girl in the only evening dress in the Grand Tier that could
by no stretch of the imagination be described as a gown,
seemed more interested in the Princess than the stage.

She was also, Westbury observed with irritation, the
only woman in his vicinity who had declined to spare him
so much as a glance. He was doubly irritated when he
realized that she was equally uninterested in her escort.

Frigid, he decided: and made himself briefly attentive to the raven-haired Lucinda, who responded with affectionate vivacity, prompting Vicci to lean flatteringly toward him whilst clasping Kenneth's forearm.

At least, Westbury thought, *they* were giving a good performance.

The orchestra played the opening chords of Ouspenskaya's aria, and the diva made her appearance.

She was in poor voice and Sir Leon had even more trouble than usual with her erratic tempi. As she visibly prepared for her onslaught on the final note, Westbury turned to Lucinda. 'This is too atrocious,' he murmured. 'I must ask *you* to excuse me a moment.'

'Shall I – ?' she began.

'No, no. Stay where you are. I shall return.' And, chocolate box in his right hand, he rose to his feet as the audience began grudgingly to applaud.

'If you would be so kind,' he requested the grim young man on his left, who had made no effort to let him pass and whose long legs blocked his progress.

The young man rose, faced him, put a large hand on his elbow and, leaning toward him, said quietly, 'Police, Mr Westbury. May we see you outside? Don't want to spoil things for all these charitable people, do we? That way' – pushing him rightwards – 'if you'd be so kind.'

By now the strapping girl was also standing. Westbury made his way numbly past Lucinda, Vicci and Kenneth, who stared anxiously up at him.

Struggling past the two couples who sat on their right, Westbury reached the aisle. The two police officers followed unhurriedly. Madame Ouspenskaya demanded yet another curtain. Westbury, resentful now of all the eyes that followed him, climbed like an automaton toward the exit.

'You *would* vary the plan,' Solomon berated him.

'Run!' shrieked the Provocateur.

'Poor Chris,' the Advocate consoled.

216

The two police officers, deliberate, unhurried, ten feet behind him, followed him out of the auditorium.

'Evening, Mr Westbury,' Cheadle greeted him, stolid in his ill-fitting navy blue suit and gleaming brown shoes. He gestured toward the foyer. 'After you.'

Between a wide gauntlet of enigmatic plain-clothes officers, Westbury descended fatalistically into the foyer. For a moment he contemplated hurling his commandos at them, but they outnumbered him twenty to one: and anyway were watching the box in his hand as if it were a grenade from which the pin had been pulled.

Cheadle, accompanied now by Robinson, followed him at a safe distance, motioning him forward whenever – as, in his uncomprehending terror, he did constantly – he looked over his shoulder.

In implacable silence, the gauntlet herded him through the foyer, across the portico and on to the pavement.

An arc of mounted policemen blocked Bow Street to the left.

Television lights came on. Three cameras focused on him. Dozens of press photographers took hundred of shots of him. The police horses, solid and remorseless as tanks, hoofs clopping almost absent-mindedly, shepherded him downhill.

Abandoning his air of patrician hauteur, Westbury fled toward his BMW.

The TV crews sprinted after him.

The mounted police followed at a stately trot.

Cheadle and Robinson strolled in their wake.

Westbury slithered to a halt, thrust the key into the door, opened it, hurled the chocolate box on to the front passenger seat, slid in behind the driver's wheel, locked all the doors and windows and inserted his ignition key. Irrationally, he felt safe again, even though press and TV cameras were peering at him through the windscreen and front window and the phalanx of mounted policemen, reflected in his rear vision mirror, was only twenty yards away.

He patted each of the three shoe boxes on top of the dashboard, said, 'Now we must fight,' and turned the ignition key. The engine started promptly.

The car-phone chirruped. Frowning, he picked it up. 'Yes?'

'It's no use, Chris.' Cheadle's voice. 'Be a good lad. Give yourself up.'

'You think I haven't prepared for this?' he lied.

'You think *we* haven't?'

Westbury slammed down the car-phone, released the hand brake, engaged first gear and accelerated hard.

The BMW bucked and convulsed, the three shoe boxes flew backwards off their perch, a dreadful metallic thump reverberated through the car, and the engine died.

The car-phone chirruped afresh.

Westbury, wide-eyed and breathing hard, picked it up and listened.

'We wheel-clamped you,' Cheadle explained. 'Now you've buggered your whatsit.'

Where was the bastard? Westbury peered frantically in every direction. Cheadle, cordless phone in hand, saluted him gravely from behind the TV crew.

'*How?*' Westbury snarled.

'You told me. "I inherited everything of my uncle's," you told me. "His money, his house, his car, everything." So I checked that you hadn't sold the car, and when we couldn't find it, I asked Mrs Green where your uncle kept it. The garage has been under surveillance ever since. Nice try, the Anton bit, though. And the disguise. Dressed to kill as usual, weren't you?'

'Prove it!'

'We found Anton, had him stomach-pumped. He's made a statement. That plus the Hilton reservation in your own name, plus the disguise, plus two thousand pounds' worth of seats in the row behind the Princess, plus the statements your charming companions are making at this very moment, plus the box of chocolates, plus your attempted escape – that's all we need to get a conviction.'

'Bullshit.'

'You know better than that, Chris. And even if we had only half that evidence, we could still nail you on the strength of your letters to the Princess.'

'She's given *them* to you?' Westbury couldn't believe it: not even of her.

'She's prepared to instruct her solicitor to hand 'em over.'

'Letters won't prove I was going to kill her. And *you* can't prove that I killed Mike Saxon.'

'Wilson the cellist has admitted you lied to us. And none of your other alibis will stand up to cross-examination. The taxi driver at the Serpentine, the occupants you *didn't* see when you allegedly inspected their three houses in Hampshire, my surveillance officers who *thought* they heard you practising – they'll all be cross-examined.'

'I'm not getting out.'

'Makes great television. Justice being seen to be done.'

Floodlit, blinded by flashlights, and trapped, Westbury apathetically capitulated. It didn't matter anyway.

'What about my side of the story?' he asked nevertheless.

'Accompany us to the station, we'll be all ears.'

'Don't trust verbals. There's a floppy disk at home labelled *Letters to dad*. Access it with the code Atrax Series. It's all there.'

He hung up, wondering why, in all the long months of elaborate preparation, he had never given a second's thought to a line of retreat should this, the last of his murders, be thwarted.

'Should've brought a handful of Tuinals,' he muttered ruefully.

Leaning back, his head against the headrest, he closed

his eyes. He longed to sleep, to feel his mother tucking him in, stroking his head. He hadn't really meant to kill her when he emptied all the huffer-puffers she kept in her bedside drawer in case she had an attack of asthma. But she shouldn't have rejected him in favour of a toy boy.

'Why?' he asked her.

He didn't see one of the camera-men motioning urgently to Cheadle: didn't see Cheadle come and peer through the camera's eyepiece: didn't hear Cheadle utter a laconic 'Oh dear, oh dear' as he looked at three shoe boxes and a chocolate box which had fallen from the dashboard, their lids dislodged, when the BMW bucked and convulsed.

'Oh deary me,' sighed Cheadle as the camera tracked up Westbury's black-trousered legs and white dress shirt and superbly tailored dinner jacket – all of which were being explored by a posse of spiders.

Cheadle stepped quickly to the driver's door and rapped the window with an urgent knuckle. Westbury opened his eyes, stared blankly at the window, and closed them again.

Cheadle tapped out the car-phone number. Twenty seconds later it chirruped. Westbury picked it up with awful weariness.

'What now?' he demanded.

'Open your window, Chris.'

'So you can shoot me?'

'Have I ever broken our rules?'

Westbury thought about that. 'No.'

'Ruin everything, wouldn't it? I want to give you something.'

'Through the window?'

'Just a couple of inches.'

It would look good on TV, Westbury decided: the Atrax man having the bottle to chat to his persecutor. He stared into one of the cameras and favoured it with a long, devil-may-care close-up. As he turned away, he noticed for the first time that the car was encircled by uniformed policemen, arms linked: and that behind them was a crowd, ten deep, of enthralled patrons from the Opera House. Once again, he had an audience.

He opened the narrow ventilating window.

Cheadle closed down his cordless phone, stepped forward, reached into his inside jacket pocket and brought out an aerosol can. 'Use this,' he whispered, thrusting it through the aperture.

'What is it? Nerve gas?'

'Something to kill the spiders that're crawling all over you,' Cheadle murmured.

Westbury glanced quickly down: and snatched the can.

Cheadle stepped back from the car. Westbury jerked the window shut and locked it. Then frantically sprayed his chest, legs, arms, neck, throat and head with insecticide.

As if perplexed, a dozen funnelwebs at once ceased their aimless meandering. But seconds later, like sharks in a frenzy, headed voraciously for the scent of flesh. Rearing up, tracked by three cameras, they struck at wrists, thighs and groin.

Cheadle tapped out the car-phone number for a fourth time. He seemed unsurprised that the chirruping phone meant nothing to Westbury who, still desperately spraying his assailants, did not answer.

'Answer!' Cheadle shouted. 'We've got some anti-venene.'

Westbury heard nothing: not even when the television crews and journalists and press photographers and hundreds of onlookers added their voices to Cheadle's.

Westbury's face was sweat-drenched. Tears had begun to gush from his eyes. His arms flailed and his legs thrashed. Uniformed policemen battered in vain against the BMW's windows with their truncheons, armed CID officers used the unavailing butt of their revolvers.

221

'It's not fair,' Westbury grumbled. *Every*one had betrayed him: his mother, the panel of judges, his father, his uncle, Emma, Gavin Wilson, Anton, Ma Green. All traitors. No gratitude.

He took refuge in hatred.

'Hate traitors,' he mumbled. 'And ingrates . And . . . digital watches. And health foods . . .' He knew he was dying. 'And air hostesses who hope you enjoyed your flight. And green ink. And yellow jam . . .' He hadn't the breath to continue much longer. 'And stepfathers' – almost managing to giggle at the absurdity of it all. 'And vending machines. And' – wryly, because it was his epitaph – 'bad losers.'

At which his head snapped backwards, his eyes rolled upwards and he became preternaturally still. The TV cameras closed in on his contorted, floodlit face. Satellite television transmitted the picture all round the civilized world.

'Oh, *sir*,' Robinson rebuked his superior.

'He threatened my wife!' Cheadle hissed. 'Ten years from now, they'd probably have released him, he'd have been hell-bent on revenge, and I'd have been too gaga to protect her.'

A TV reporter confronted him. 'Any comment, Chief Superintendent?'

'We did everything we could to save him,' Cheadle responded soberly. 'There will, of course, be a coronial enquiry; but as far as the Metropolitan Police Force is concerned, this enquiry is now closed.'

Later that night, Derek Robinson and Diana Radford had their first row.

'He stage-managed the whole thing,' he raged.' Television crews, the press, Westbury's death, the lot. All in the name of Justice.'

'It *was* just,' she said coldly.

'To bring the Tyburn Tree to Bow Street and contrive a public execution?'

'Yes!'

'I've been living with a monster,' he told her.

'And I've been living with a wimp.'

For the first time in almost four years, they slept apart.

Cheadle and his wife lay side by side. He pulled her to him. 'Way you handled that phone call, I'm proud of you.'

'I'm proud of you, Charlie.'

He wanted to make love to her, but first he had to make a confession. He knew she was fond of Robinson.

'Derek's pissed off with me,' he confessed.

'He'll get over it. He's too soft to be a copper, really.'

Soundly asleep, Cheadle did not reply.

'Poor thing,' she murmured. 'You work too hard.'